COO … LE

Fat…

Parishioners at the Church of the Good Shepherd may find it hard to believe that Father Tom Christen has been ministering to their souls for an entire year. There were tears when his predecessor, Father Ude, retired from Cooper's Corner's Episcopal church, but since he is now ninety-six, no one could argue that he deserved a little time off! It took the church a while to adjust to our handsome young rector when he arrived here last spring from his former parish in Boston. But no one was really surprised by the sudden increase in young female worshippers filling the pews each week.

In just a short time, Tom Christen has become a valued member of our community. Besides the recent spate of weddings he's had to perform, Tom has expanded his ministry to include a children's choir, educational classes for our teenagers and Sunday visits to the local seniors centre. (Word is out that our new minister is quite an accomplished arm wrestler!)

Tom's latest responsibility involves the little boy who was abandoned on the church doorstep. The women of the community have rallied to help, but after seeing Tom in action this past year, his parishioners know he'll bring the same commitment to this new task that he brings to all the others. Happy first anniversary, Tom!

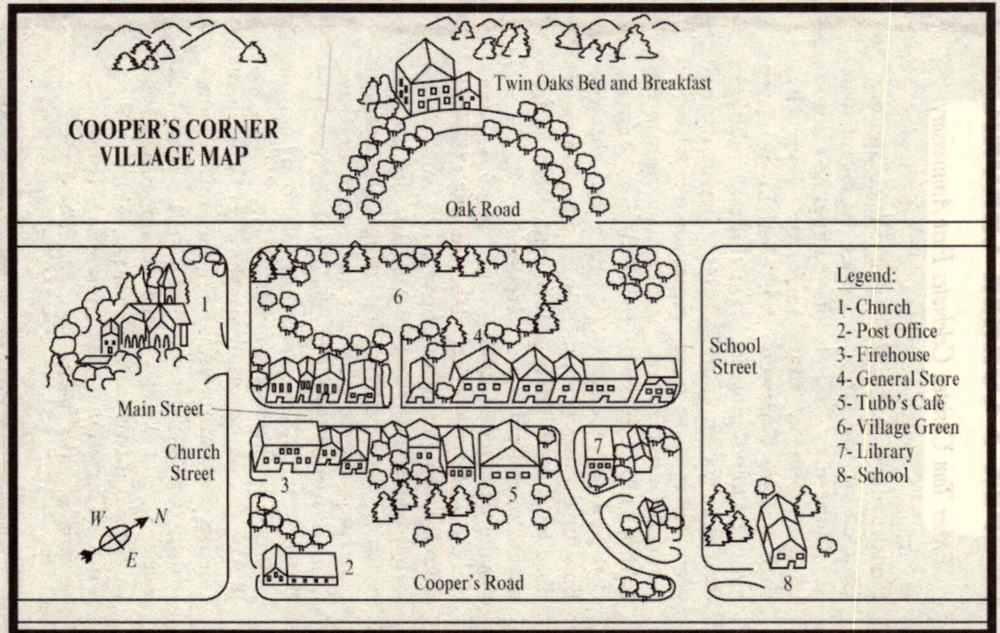
COOPER'S CORNER
VILLAGE MAP
Twin Oaks Bed and Breakfast
Oak Road
1
6
4
Main Street
Church
Street
3
5
7
2
Cooper's Road
School
Street
8
W
N
E
Legend:
1- Church
2- Post Office
3- Firehouse
4- General Store
5- Tubb's Café
6- Village Green
7- Library
8- School

COOPER'S CORNER

MJ RODGERS

Cradle and All

MILLS & BOON®

All the characters in this book have no existence outside the imagination of the author, and have no relation whatsoever to anyone bearing the same name or names. They are not even distantly inspired by any individual known or unknown to the author, and all the incidents are pure invention.

First published in Great Britain 2005
by Harlequin Mills & Boon Limited,
Eton House, 18-24 Paradise Road, Richmond, Surrey TW9 1SR

MJ Rodgers is acknowledged as the author of this work.

ISBN 0 263 84695 4

142-0805

Printed and bound in Spain
by Litografia Rosés S.A., Barcelona

Dear Reader,

Like many of you, I was brought up in the bustle of big cities. It was often exciting. But there came a time when I realised that the constant demands and commitments of city life distracted me from what were my true joys—the beauty of nature and being with the ones I love. So today I live in a rural community where the biggest demands are to watch eagles soaring over deep green forests and count the thousands of stars spilling into diamond-black nights.

Cooper's Corner reminds me of my own rural community. I can't help but be drawn to the bold beauty of the Berkshires with its deep woods and bouncy brooks, its meadows frantic with wild flowers, the charm of the quaint shops and storefronts, and the plain and simple decency of its people.

And decency could be Reverend Tom Christen's trademark. He is an independent spirit with a dark past and a deep love of the land. He's a perfect example of what makes this small community in the Berkshires so wonderful and so real. I hope you enjoy reading about Tom and the very special woman who is about to enter his life—and change it forever.

Warmly,

mj

MJ Rodgers
PO 284
Seabeck, WA 98380, USA

THE COOPERS OF COOPER'S CORNER

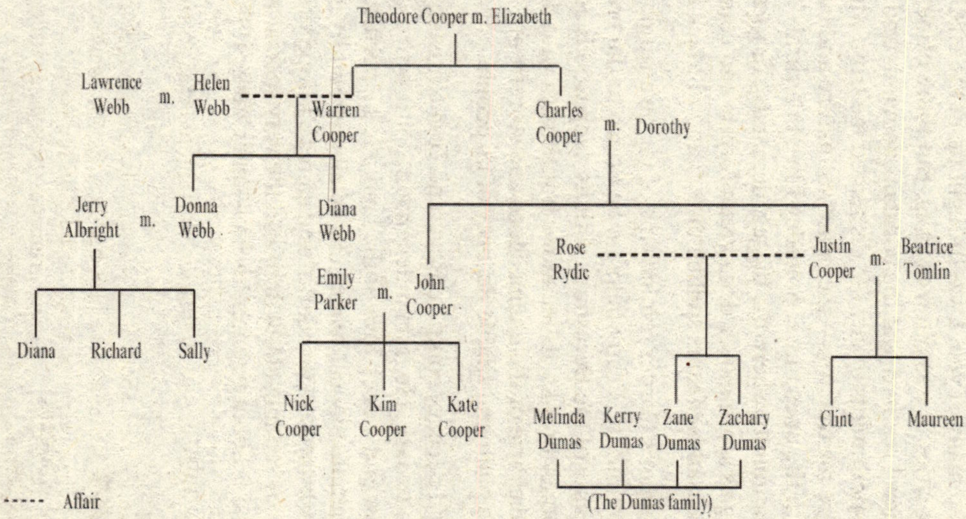

CHAPTER ONE

"TONIGHT, GENTLEMEN, we talk about sex."

Episcopal priest Tom Christen wasn't surprised when his opening statement brought immediate smiles to the faces of the adolescent males sitting before him.

Keegan Cooper's long legs stretched out from beneath the table as he crossed his arms over his chest. "So, Father Tom, what was it you wanted to know?"

The resulting guffaws from Keegan's adolescent peers filled the corners of the meeting room in the old stone parish house of Cooper's Corner's historic church.

Tom had been waiting for just such a remark to this night's topic. A lot of inaccurate assumptions were made about a man who wore a white collar. And naiveté about sex ranked right up at the top of the list.

Nor was he surprised that Keegan had been the one to express what all these boys were thinking. Keegan had lived in New York City before coming to this quiet village in the Berkshires, which was why he displayed a little more bravado than the rest. But Keegan was a good kid—they all were. Tom knew he was lucky to be working with them.

"So, Keegan, got all that sex stuff figured out, do you?" Tom said baiting him.

"We learned about it in school," Bryan Penrose called out. Bryan and Keegan were best buddies. If you challenged one of them, you'd better be ready to take on the other.

"Go on, Father." Bryan grinned. "Ask us anything."

"Okay," Tom said. "When is it *right* to have sex?"

The room suddenly became very quiet as the boys looked

everywhere but at Tom. He hid his smile. ''Looks like one or two things got left out of your sex education classes.''

''We know all about the biological part,'' Keegan said.

''Which is critical stuff,'' Tom admitted. ''But the emotional and social impact of sex is just as important.''

''That's because sex is a rite of passage,'' an older youth asserted. ''It's what separates the men from the boys.''

''I'd have to disagree with you there,'' Tom said. ''I've found that it's *sense,* not sex, that separates the men from the boys.''

''So what's the answer, Father?'' Bryan asked. ''When is it right to have sex?''

''That's what we're going to talk about tonight. How you make the right choice.''

''We get to decide?'' Keegan asked.

''You're the only one who can,'' Tom said. ''Your right to choose is the most powerful right you possess. And with every choice you make, you create who you are.''

''How do we know we're making the right choice?'' Keegan asked.

''Always ask yourself two questions. First, what is the consequence of your choice? And, second, what emotion is prompting you to select one choice over another?''

''But wanting sex is the emotion, right?'' another boy asked.

''Wanting sex is a natural urge, but *choosing* to have sex could be motivated by anything from selfishness to love,'' Tom replied. ''Be clear about which emotion is driving your choice. Which means, gentlemen, listen to your head, not those urges coming from between your legs.''

''Those urges can get pretty strong,'' one of the older boys in the back said.

''Yes, they can,'' Tom agreed. ''But choose to be stronger and you will be stronger.''

The back door buzzer echoed through the parish house. Tom wasn't expecting anyone. Still, the people in the village and surrounding farms knew he was always available to them. They often stopped by unannounced.

"You make it sound easy," the older boy commented, a clear note of complaint in his voice.

Tom made his way toward the door. Before opening it, he turned to face the boys.

"It's far from easy. None of the really valuable things in life come easy. But I believe you'll find they're worth your time and effort. Just remember. You can become men who control their urges or men whose urges control them. The choice is up to you."

Letting his words hang in the air, Tom turned toward the back door and pulled it open, ready to greet the caller. But no one was there.

He peered into the pitch darkness outside. A car's headlights suddenly blinded him as it sped out of the parking lot, tires spewing gravel in its wake.

Tom sensed a sudden movement near his feet. He quickly stepped back and stared down at what lay on the doorstep.

"So, Father," Keegan began, "sounds to me like a guy who chooses sex better be prepared for—"

"—a baby," Tom finished, with a long exhalation.

And the bundle at his feet began to cry.

ANNE VANDREE SIGHED in satisfaction as she sat back in the comfortable chintz-covered chair pulled close to the mahogany table at the Twin Oaks Bed and Breakfast. Not a scrap of sweet fresh fruit or fluffy scrambled eggs was left on her plate.

It had been two long years since she'd taken vacation from her job as an associate justice of the Berkshire Probate and Family Court. She really needed these next couple of weeks away from the emotional drain of divorces and deadbeat dads.

It felt great to know that she didn't have a long list of things waiting for her to do. She could just relax and let this peaceful Saturday unfold in the quiet, quaint village.

Tall and graceful, Maureen Cooper glided out of the kitchen carrying a fresh, steaming pot of coffee. She filled Anne's cup.

Anne frowned at the large blue-and-purple bruise on Maureen's exposed arm. ''Hey, what happened?'' she asked, pointing to the marks.

''Fell into an old well I was trying to board up,'' Maureen said. ''The bruise still hasn't faded.''

Anne shook her head. ''First you get buried beneath a bunch of logs. Now you're falling into old wells. And I thought you B and B owners lived such sedate lives.''

''Ah, the stories I could tell,'' Maureen said lightheartedly as she glanced around. ''Where's that nice couple from Canada?''

''They just left to explore the village,'' Anne said.

''Our only other guests this morning are on their honeymoon,'' Maureen told her. ''I served them breakfast in bed about thirty minutes ago.'' She paused to send Anne a wink. ''Doubt they'll be down anytime soon.''

Maureen slipped onto the chair across from Anne and poured herself a cup of coffee. Anne loved the informality of a B and B. It always felt more like staying at a friend's place than renting a room.

When Warren Cooper, Maureen's great uncle, died and left his 1875 farmhouse to Maureen and her brother, Clint, Anne had handled the probate. The lovely bed-and-breakfast the brother and sister team had created had fast become Anne's favorite. And the warmhearted Maureen had fast become a friend.

Anne raised her coffee cup to her lips, savoring the rich aroma of the homemade brew before taking a sip. It was superb, as always.

''Since Clint's in the kitchen watching the twins, we have time for some girl talk,'' Maureen said, a conspiratorial smile on her lips. ''Tell me, how are things going with that tax attorney?''

''Turns out he was sleeping with one of his married clients at the same time he was trying to get me into the sack.''

''Oh, Anne. I'm so sorry.''

''Don't be. We only dated a couple of times. And I have a firm rule. No emotional involvement or sex until I'm sure a guy meets my criteria.''

''What criteria?'' Maureen asked curiously.

Anne ticked them off on her fingers. ''He has to be honest, open, have no other women in his life, no desire to get serious, some brains in his head and something that resembles a heart in his chest.''

''I think most women would agree with what you're looking for in a man,'' Maureen said, ''except that they'd want a serious relationship that included love.''

Anne shook her head as she set down her coffee cup. ''That love stuff and happily ever after nonsense is nothing but a fairy tale—as the constant stream of divorces passing through my court proves to me every day.''

''You never think of getting married again?'' Maureen asked.

''Absolutely not,'' Anne assured her. ''The only place a woman can find a committed man these days is in a mental hospital.''

Maureen chuckled. ''So, how did you find out about the other woman in the tax attorney's life?''

''Her husband suspected something and hired a private investigator. The P.I. surreptitiously took pictures of the wife and tax attorney together. I got to see the eight-by-ten color photos when the divorce case came to my court.''

''Must've been a shock,'' Maureen said.

''I'll say,'' Anne agreed. ''When that tax attorney got naked, I found out he was short on a lot more than just ethics.''

Anne winked and Maureen burst out laughing.

Keegan Cooper charged into the dining room and made a beeline for the buffet. He sent a wave in Anne's direction. ''Hey, what's so funny?''

Maureen got herself under control as Anne answered, ''Oh, I was just sharing a *teeny tiny tidbit* from court life with your aunt.''

The ''teeny tiny tidbit'' remark had Maureen doubling over again.

Keegan looked questioningly at Anne.

''Sorry, this story's rated F, for female funny bone only,'' she explained.

Keegan grinned good-naturedly, turned back to the buffet and packed his plate. He was a handsome young man with the Cooper family's tallness genes.

At a petite five foot two, Anne was quite envious. Her short stature had been a sore point with her all her life. So many people associated being small with being childlike, and made the mistake of not taking her seriously.

It was a mistake she quickly corrected.

Anne had worked hard to earn her reputation for being tough. She was well aware that the Berkshire court clerks and bailiffs called her the "bad-ass munchkin" behind her back. As far as she was concerned, it was a compliment.

Maureen got her laughter under control and wiped her eyes with a tissue. "And I thought you judges lived such sedate lives."

"Ah, the stories I could tell," Anne said, repeating Maureen's earlier comment with a grin.

"If you guys want a good story, you should hear what happened last night at Father Tom's class," Keegan said as he hunkered down on the chair next to his aunt, his plate piled high with his dad's specialty—walnut griddle cakes.

"Well, why don't you tell us *guys,*" Maureen said with an affectionate bump against her nephew's shoulder.

Keegan drenched his griddle cakes in maple syrup. "Father Tom was talking to us about sex and stuff, and suddenly there it was. Just like that."

"There was what?" his aunt asked.

"A baby," Keegan said after he wolfed down a syrup-laden mouthful in one enormous gulp. "Somebody dumped it on the doorstep."

Anne's relaxed attitude vanished. She came forward in her chair. "Who?"

Keegan shrugged. "Whoever went squealing their tires out in the parking lot, I guess. The baby started screaming its head off, so Father Tom picked it up. That's when he found a note pinned to its blanket."

"What did the note say?" Anne asked.

"Father Tom didn't tell us."

Anne reached into the shoulder bag hanging over the back of her chair and rooted around for her cell phone. "I'd best call in to the trooper's station to find out what was in the note."

"Hey, you're on vacation, remember?" Maureen said from across the table.

"In my job there are no vacations from abandoned babies," Anne replied as she pulled the phone out of her bag.

"I doubt Father Tom called the state police," Keegan said, before Anne had a chance to punch in the number.

"Who else would he get to pick up the baby on a Friday night?" Anne asked.

Keegan forked up more griddle cake. "Don't think he got anybody. He's the kind of guy who likes to handle things himself."

"Are you saying he still has the baby?" Anne asked.

"He was trying to figure out how to change its diaper when we left," Keegan said, before shoveling the food into his mouth.

Anne stood up, swung the strap of her bag over her shoulder and headed for the door.

"Where are you going?" Maureen asked.

"To see Father Tom Christen, of course," Anne called over her shoulder. She paused at the door, turned around and faced Maureen and Keegan. "I've no doubt he means well, but the law is the law. I'd best remind him of that unofficially before he gets officially into trouble."

Anne waved, turned and walked out.

Maureen stared at the empty doorway, her fingers tapping on her coffee cup. "Maybe you shouldn't have said anything, Keegan."

"I'm sure Father Tom is doing what's right," Keegan said as he picked up a big glass of fresh-squeezed orange juice. "He always does."

"Oh, I'm not worried about Father Tom."

"You're worried about Anne?" Keegan asked, his voice rising in surprise.

Maureen smiled. "Last fall I made a passing remark to Tom Christen that a couple of the cushions on the church pews were frayed. Before I knew what hit me, he had me recovering all of them. And I still don't know how he did it. The man's not a force to be taken lightly."

"But Anne's a judge. He's not going to have her sewing cushions."

"Maybe not," Maureen said. "But if she's not careful around our Father Tom, she might just discover that her vacation has come to an abrupt end."

ANNE PULLED HER SILVER Camry into the parking lot of the Church of the Good Shepherd. It was a beautiful April morning, sunny and unseasonably warm. She could have walked the relatively short distance from the B and B, but accustomed to taking care of business in the most expeditious manner as she was, it just hadn't occurred to her.

The historic Episcopal church was constructed of white clapboard and featured a tall steeple with a graceful spire. The original building had been erected in the 1880s and a rectory and parish house were added a few decades later. Altogether, the weather-worn structures emitted a serenity perfectly in keeping with the sleepy village.

A woodchuck scampered into a hidden burrow under the old stone wall as Anne approached the church's thick, carved wooden door. She tried the bell.

A couple of minutes passed, but there was no answer. Someone had to be around. She could swear the sound of drumbeats was coming from nearby. She decided to check the back.

With every step Anne took, the drumbeats grew louder. By the time she rounded the far corner of the church, it wasn't hard to locate the boom box perched on the rectory porch. Or the man marching in time to the drumbeats as he pushed a lime spreader over the newly turned, acidic New England soil.

Anne had first seen Father Thomas Christen one Sunday a few weeks back, when she'd attended service at the church with Maureen. She'd heard that the priest who'd come to Cooper's Corner the year before was a man of unusual contrasts, but nothing had prepared her for meeting him.

Tom Christen had a strong chin and cheekbones, ready complements to his light-bronze skin. But he had hair like thick, warm sunshine and eyes as blue as a summer sky. And when he talked about living a good life, he had quoted not just the Bible, but Mark Twain and Henry David Thoreau.

Anne would never forget how the deep richness of his voice carried to every corner of the old church. Or how he had smiled when his eyes had looked into hers. Or how that smile had made her acutely aware of every red-blooded corpuscle beating through her body.

Tom Christen was definitely not your average Episcopal priest.

Anne had left before the services were over, despite Maureen's urging that she stay and meet the eligible Father Tom. Anne knew better than to shake hands with that much temptation.

Episcopal priests only had serious relationships, and that was the last thing she wanted.

She didn't think Tom could possibly look any sexier than he had that Sunday in his formal black suit with white collar. But now, as she looked at his bare back retreating from her, she knew she had been wrong.

Tom Christen was wearing nothing but shorts.

He was just under six feet, and slender. The beautifully contoured muscles of his shoulders and back bunched with sinewy strength as he guided the large tires of the spreader over the hilly terrain in rhythm to the bouncing beat. Power pumped through his long legs, his calf and thigh muscles flexing in convex bulges as they propelled him forward.

The sun caught the light bronze of his skin, set fire to the pale gold of his hair. Anne had never stared at a man before in her life, but she was staring now. And her thoughts of the Reverend Tom Christen were anything but reverent.

Tom reached the end of the row of soil he had been sweetening with the lime mixture and turned around. He must have sensed her presence, for he suddenly stopped, turned and looked directly at her. And smiled.

Anne had the exact same sensation of blood beating through her body that she had experienced when he'd smiled at her that Sunday in church.

And then she saw the baby. It was securely wrapped in a large beige bath towel. The ends of the towel were tied around Tom's neck—what she had originally thought to be a handkerchief—supporting the baby's weight against his chest.

Tom set the lime spreader aside and walked over to the porch to switch off the boom box. He moved with that unconscious, sinuous grace of a man in prime physical condition.

Anne's pulse started to skip. She quickly summoned the cool, dispassionate demeanor for which she was renowned.

Get a grip. He's gorgeous, thirty-three and still single. The guy's got to be gay.

The drumbeat ceased abruptly. Tom quickly closed the distance between them. "It's nice to see you again, Anne."

"You know who I am," Anne said, thoroughly surprised.

Before Tom could answer, the baby against his chest stirred and let out a wail. Tom wrapped his arms around the tiny bundle and rocked it gently.

It was a red-faced, towheaded elf, emitting enough decibels to shatter steel. Anne's eardrums started to ache.

"Only thing that seems to get him to sleep is a loud beat." Tom yelled to be heard over the baby. "Which is why he and I have been gardening to African music this morning. Tiny little guy for such powerful lungs, isn't he?"

Tom was standing close to Anne, nearly naked and smelling of warm, enticing male. Every female cell in her body was standing up and cheering. She had barely noticed the baby, outside of the noise it was making.

Anne forcibly reminded herself that she was a sober, sedate judge who was here on serious business.

"Where's the baby's mother?" she asked, determined to project her most solemn judge's tone, even at four times its normal volume.

"Not here at the present," Tom said smoothly.

"When will she be back?" Anne asked.

''Hard to say,'' Tom answered as he continued to rock the little boy in his arms.

''She's one of your parishioners?''

''Everyone who visits the Good Shepherd is part of the flock.''

''What's the mother's name?''

''Why so curious, Anne?''

Anne figured she'd given Tom enough time to open up and tell her the truth. Now it was time to tell him.

''Look, I know this baby was left on your doorstep last night.''

He had the nerve to smile. ''Nothing like the grapevine of a small village, is there?''

She was not going to be sidetracked. ''You should have called the state police the moment you found him.''

Tom gestured toward the rectory. ''Come on inside. I can offer you stale crumb cake and the worst coffee in Cooper's Corner.''

''As hard as it is to refuse such a tempting menu, I've had breakfast, thank you. Now, about—''

''Good,'' Tom interrupted. ''Then you can keep us company while I give the baby his. Poor little tyke had a hard night.''

Without waiting for a response, Tom bounded up the porch stairs, swung open the door and disappeared into the rectory.

Anne stared after him for several long moments without moving. Her statements about the baby had been direct, clear, unequivocal. And he had ignored them. Irritation licked along her nerves.

They were going to settle this. Right now.

She charged up the stairs, ready to do battle. But when she opened the back door and entered the kitchen, she found herself already in the aftermath of a war zone.

Dishes littered the surfaces and sink. Banana skins turned brown on the counter. The blender spilled over with mushy gray liquid. Empty cereal boxes lay scattered everywhere. Cans of beef and chicken broth and several bottles of juice stood open, most of their contents congealing inside them. Dishcloths and paper towels soaked in messes on the table and floor.

And Tom was calmly standing over the stove, bouncing the wailing baby as he warmed a bottle that sat in a pot of water.

"What happened here?" Anne asked.

"He refused to eat his formula," Tom called over his shoulder. "Took me a while to come up with the winning additives of a teaspoon of chicken broth and one of cranberry juice."

Anne shook her head. "That can't be good for him."

"He's getting it down," Tom said amicably. "Some of it, anyway. The general store should be opening in about thirty minutes. I'll try him on some different stuff then. Would you mind pouring me a cup of coffee?"

It was clear to Anne that Tom had been up most of the night trying to take care of the baby that had been dropped so abruptly on him. She didn't know of many men who would have made the effort. Hell, she didn't know of any men who would have done that.

"Where's the coffee?" she asked.

She followed Tom's pointing hand to the coffeepot, drew a cup out of the cupboard and filled it to the brim. She had seen sludge that looked and smelled better.

"How do you drink this stuff?" she asked.

"By the gallon," Tom said cheerfully.

"You realize that baby has to be handed over to the authorities so that he can be properly cared for?" Anne said.

Tom turned off the burner and picked up the bottle. He dripped its contents on his forearm, seemed satisfied with the temperature and eased onto the nearest chair.

"I'll be ready for that coffee in just a minute," he said.

He had ignored her question again. Anne was not pleased. Good intentions aside, the guy obviously didn't have a clue what he was doing.

It was time for her to lay down the law.

But before she could, Tom stripped off the towel from around both the baby and his chest, and tossed it onto the table.

His exposed bare chest was magnificent—two mounds of

smooth muscular pecs over a six-pack of rock-hard abs. Anne forgot whatever it was she had been about to say.

Damn. It had to be a sin for a man of God to be this sexy.

Tom rewrapped the towel around the baby before cradling him in the crook of one muscular arm. He held the bottle up to the infant's mouth, but the baby fought taking it. It took some gentle nudging before the little boy finally accepted the bottle and settled down.

A blessed quiet descended on the kitchen.

When Tom's eyes rose from the baby's to Anne's, she knew she had been caught staring, and quickly held out the cup in her hand.

As Tom freed one hand and took it from her, he flashed her a knowing smile that made her short of breath. Anne had never seen a man who exuded such a relaxed air of self-awareness. Tom Christen knew exactly who he was, and was comfortable with that knowledge. His eyes never left hers as he drank the coffee.

"Are you passing through the village today?" Tom asked when he was finished drinking and had set down the cup.

"I'm staying at the Twin Oaks B and B this weekend," she said.

"You've picked the right time. April has never begun better here in the Berkshires, so I'm told. Why don't you sit down, Anne?"

Anne wished she could make herself comfortable, eat his stale cake, drink his terrible coffee—and drink in this mouthwatering man who was muscle everywhere she looked. His self-knowledge and scintillating sex appeal were such a compelling combination.

"This isn't a social call," Anne said, ignoring the offered chair. "I'm here to talk about this baby. Father Christen—"

"Call me Tom."

Oh, no. Appreciating this good-looking man was one thing. Getting personal with him was quite another. She was here on business and she was sticking to it. "That baby must be placed in the hands of the proper authorities right now."

"And what proper authorities would that be?" Tom asked.

The deep timbre of his voice hadn't changed. But something about his eyes belied his easy conversational tone.

"I'll call Child Care Services," Anne said. "They'll put him in a foster home until his mother can be located."

"Child Care Services will not return this baby to his mother even if they're able to find her."

Anne didn't know how he'd done it, but she suddenly felt herself on the defensive. "She'd have to face charges for abandoning him. But it's possible—depending on the circumstances and her willingness to get her act together and provide a safe and healthy environment for her baby—that they would eventually be reunited."

"And how many times have you seen that happen?" he asked.

"It's not always in the best interest of a baby to be reunited with its birth mother," Anne said.

"So instead he gets dumped in some foster home."

Anne didn't miss the sudden, albeit subtle change from his conversational tone. "What do you have against the foster care system?" she asked.

The baby stopped feeding and began to fuss. Tom put the bottle aside, held the baby up and gently rubbed its back. It burped, spitting up all over Tom's shoulder.

He looked around, probably for something to wipe up the spit. But all the available dishcloths had already found similar use, and the paper towel roll was empty. Spying a box of tissues, he pulled one out and swiped at his shoulder.

The baby's fussing escalated into a cry. Tom spread the blanket across the kitchen table and laid the baby on top of it. He set about removing the wet diaper, which turned out to be several sheets of paper towels secured around the baby's bottom with duct tape.

"You didn't answer my question, Father Christen," Anne yelled, trying to be heard over the wailing baby.

"A baby belongs with his mother," Tom yelled back.

"Not with a mother who abandons him."

"This baby wasn't abandoned. He was left with me so that I could care for him."

"Without enough diapers or the right formula? What kind of a mother would do that?"

"You don't know the circumstances, Anne."

"Tell me about them."

"It's a confidential matter," Tom said.

"You're refusing to tell me?"

"Would you tell me about confidential courtroom matters?" Tom asked.

Anne didn't know which urge was stronger—the one to strangle him or the one to run her hands across his smooth, muscled chest and see if it could possibly be as warm and hard as she imagined.

Out of the corner of his eye Tom saw Anne shake her head in frustration. He wished he could explain so that she would understand.

The crying baby kicked his feet, impeding Tom's progress as he removed the damp paper towels and threw them into the wastebasket. There was a flat, pink rash on the baby's tiny chest and tummy. Was that rash hurting him? Tom wondered. Was that why he cried so much?

"There's a fresh roll of paper towels in that drawer over there," he said, gesturing to an end cabinet. "Would you hand it to me?"

He heard Anne moving behind him, opening the drawer. A moment later she was standing close beside him.

"Well, I can give you points for creativity when it comes to diapers, if nothing else," she said as she held out the paper towels.

Tom recognized Anne's tough, by-the-book judge's tone. She had been using it on him ever since she arrived. But he'd also caught her looking at him while he fed the baby, and that look had been anything but judicial.

He could feel the warmth of her now, smell the subtle, sweet scent of her freshly shampooed hair. From the first moment he saw her this morning, every nerve ending in his body had come alive.

"Thanks," he said, turning to take the paper towels she held out.

She looked even lovelier than he remembered. As he constructed a new makeshift diaper out of the paper towels, Tom's mind replayed the first time he'd seen Anne Vandree.

She was sitting in the first pew of the church, her white skin glistening like February sun on fresh snow. Her light copper hair shone like a fiery halo around her head and her large, silvery eyes glowed up at him—lit with intelligence and a touch of wonder.

Tom had been filled with quite a bit of wonder himself. When he smiled at her and she'd smiled back, his heart started to race with an unexplainable and yet undeniable sense of recognition.

Then, to his deep disappointment, he'd watched her whisper in Maureen Cooper's ear, get up and leave the church.

After the service was over, Tom had made it a point to find out who Anne was. He'd felt certain she would return. And now she had. He just wished it had been under different circumstances.

Tom bit off two pieces of duct tape and secured the ends of the makeshift diaper.

"I understand that you don't want to get this baby's mother in trouble," Anne said from behind him. "I'll do what I can for her. But it's imperative that this child be properly treated."

Tom wrapped the blanket around the howling baby and picked him up. He turned to face Anne. She wore a soft cream blouse over brown tailored pants, exuding an elegance that was far sexier than flash. Her unpainted lips were a pale pink, her eyes the soft gray of a dove's wing. But the light within them was as sharp and keen as an eagle's.

"I'll treat him properly," Tom said.

She surveyed the mess around her and shook her head. "You don't know the first thing about taking care of a baby."

"I'm learning."

''I'm sorry,'' Anne said, pulling a cell phone out of her shoulder bag, ''but I have to have the child care people pick him up.''

The howling baby's tiny hand groped Tom's chest. Tom gently caressed the little hand with the pad of his pinkie.

''Don't,'' he said.

The sudden command in his voice stopped Anne in the middle of dialing. Her eyes rose to his. ''This is not negotiable,'' she said in a professional tone.

The baby's hand closed around Tom's finger and held on tightly as the little boy howled out his sorrow. Tom felt a strong, urgent tug in his chest.

''You're right,'' he said. ''It's not negotiable. I'm the baby's father.''

CHAPTER TWO

ANNE COULDN'T BELIEVE she'd heard right. ''Did you just say he's *your* baby?''

''Yes,'' Tom said.

''You do mean your biological baby?''

''Yes.''

''But I thought you'd never been married.''

''I haven't.''

Anne stared at the man standing before her—an impossibly handsome, half-naked, big-time sinner clutching his love child to his chest. Unfortunately for Anne, it didn't diminish her attraction to him at all.

Look on the bright side, an irreverent voice inside her said. *At least now you know he's not gay.*

Tom watched Anne drop her cell phone into her shoulder bag and plop down on the chair she had earlier refused. Gone was the crisp, cool woman with all the answers. In her place was a very stunned one.

As a seasoned judge, she'd probably considered herself unshockable. But Tom could see that this news had thrown her.

''Why didn't you tell me you were the baby's father?'' she demanded.

''I thought I just did.''

''I meant sooner.''

''It wasn't an easy thing for me to tell you,'' Tom said. That was the understatement of the year.

She sighed again as though the room had run out of breathable air. ''What are you going to do now?''

''Take care of the baby,'' Tom answered simply.

The baby's crying erupted into a full-throated wail. Tom rocked the unhappy child, trying to think over the ear-shattering sounds. He made a mental note to write a special sermon full of accolades to be delivered next month on Mother's Day. He'd never realized until now how much mothers deserved it.

"What about the baby's mother?" Anne asked. "Where is she? And why did she suddenly saddle you with sole care of the child?"

"There are some things I'm not able to talk about."

"Not able to talk about? I would think confessing the baby is yours is about as damning an admission as it gets."

It was clear to Tom that Anne didn't often say things she regretted, but she had just now. Two pink ribbons stained her cheeks.

"I'm sorry," she said quickly. "That was out of line. It's not my place to judge you. Occupational hazard, I guess."

Still, at the moment, she didn't look like a judge. She looked like a disillusioned woman.

And Tom knew why. She had thought better of him. The last thing he had wanted to do was change that. But that's exactly what he had just done. And he knew in his gut that her disappointment wasn't generated just from the fact that he was a priest, but from the fact that she was attracted to him.

That knowledge pumped through Tom like adrenaline, lifting the heavy weariness of the sleepless night.

Anne was soon going to realize that since the baby was with his father, her concern as a judge had ceased. And when she realized that, she'd leave, no doubt never to return.

Tom had no intention of letting that happen.

"Do me a favor?" he asked.

Anne looked up cautiously as he approached. "What?"

"Hold the baby while I take a shower?"

She hesitated. "I don't have a good track record with babies. Every time I've held my sister's kids, they've wailed their heads off."

"That's no problem here. This one's already wailing."

Before she could think of another objection, Tom gently laid the crying little boy in Anne's lap.

She carefully closed her arms around the baby, gathering him gently against her. The infant's harsh wail ended abruptly. With a soft sigh, he settled his little head against her breast, closed his eyes and went to sleep, just as though he had done it a hundred times.

Blessed quiet reigned.

"You're as good as an African drumbeat," Tom said with a happy grin.

Anne flashed him a look that could have pounded a few tom-toms.

But when her eyes settled back on the baby, her lips drew into a soft smile.

"What's his name?" she asked, and her voice was suddenly a deep throaty sigh with a touch of wonder in it.

That change in her voice made Tom pause. "Tommy for now."

Anne heard an odd note in Tom's voice. But when she looked up, he had already turned and entered the hall leading to the rest of his quarters.

Tom Christen was proving to be one complicated, perplexing man. She looked again at the tiny bundle of warmth in her arms. And this was his sweet little baby. Incredible. She still couldn't quite get her mind around it.

Who was the child's mother? Where was she? Why hadn't Tom married her?

Even as she asked those questions, Anne knew she was being foolish. Her official interest in the case had ended the moment she learned that Tom was the baby's father. The smart thing for her to do was hand the baby back to him as soon as possible and get the hell out of there.

And since Anne prided herself on being a smart woman, that was exactly what she planned to do.

DR. FELIX DORN WARMED his stethoscope on his forearm before placing it on the tiny chest of the wailing baby. He leaned forward, his wispy white hair standing straight up as he listened intently to Tommy's heart and lungs.

The baby's thrusting hand grasped the edge of the doctor's horn-rimmed glasses, pulled them off his face and flung them onto the floor. The doctor ignored the interruption and continued his examination.

Anne picked the doctor's glasses off the floor and handed them to Martha Dorn, who was holding on to little Tommy while her husband examined him.

"What's wrong with him, Doctor?" Anne asked.

Tom noted the tiny crease of concern between Anne's eyebrows. He knew the moment he'd showed Anne the baby's rash that she would insist on rushing Tommy to the nearest doctor. Tom had counted on both her decisiveness and take-charge attitude. She hadn't disappointed him.

Dr. Dorn removed his stethoscope, calmly retrieved his glasses from his wife's outstretched hand and set them back on his nose. Although he and his wife had moved to Cooper's Corner to retire, Felix Dorn was not unwilling to see the occasional patient.

"The rash is roseola, Mrs. Vandree," Dr. Dorn answered. "It's a viral infection. Fairly common. He'll be grumpy for the twenty-four hours or so that he has it."

"What can be done for him?" she asked.

"Just be patient," Dr. Dorn said. "He's probably had the fever for several days. The rash is the last stage. He seems a bit thin."

"He gets hungry regularly," Tom offered, "but he doesn't take much from the bottle."

Dr. Dorn's white caterpillar eyebrows shot up. "Bottle?" He turned his sharp eyes on Anne. "Don't you know how important a mother's milk is for a baby's health?"

"I didn't give birth to this baby," Anne blurted out in immediate protest.

"An adoptive mother can still breast-feed," Dr. Dorn said, totally undeterred. "I'll give you a list of things you'll need to start taking, along with the techniques to get the milk flowing.

Now, when you shower, I want you to use a bath sponge to toughen up your nipples so that—"

"But I'm not the baby's adoptive mother, either," Anne managed to interject.

"Then what are you doing with this baby?" Dr. Dorn asked in confusion.

"Dear..." Martha spoke up, grabbing her husband's arm to gain his attention over the baby's screaming. "Anne brought the baby in to help out Father Tom. It's the one that was left at the church last night. The one Philo and Phyllis were telling us about this morning?"

"Oh, he's *that* baby." Dr. Dorn's glasses slipped to the end of his nose. His pale-blue eyes peered over the rims at Anne. "When a woman brings me a baby, I assume it's hers. Pity he isn't. You petite types are always the best milk producers."

The doctor turned back to Tom. "Let him eat as much as he wants, as often as he wants. The baby formula Philo carries at the general store will have to do, I suppose, since there's no one around to provide a mother's milk."

Dr. Dorn sent an admonishing glance at Anne, as though she was still somehow responsible for that. With silent amusement, Tom watched Anne exhale in frustration.

Martha Dorn handed the screaming baby to Tom.

"Keep him cuddled and feeling secure," Dr. Dorn said. "A baby bonds with his parents, especially his mother, by three months. This poor little fella is no doubt in separation anxiety on top of being grumpy from the roseola."

"What do I owe you, Felix?" Tom asked, handing the baby to Anne in order to get at his wallet.

The baby stopped crying the instant Anne wrapped him in her arms.

Felix and Martha Dorn turned to stare at her and the baby.

"Babies his age don't generally take to strangers," Dr. Dorn said in a tone that sounded a bit more like that of a suspicious detective than an easygoing country doctor.

"Is it true that you, *too,* arrived in town last night?" Martha

Dorn asked Anne, as though she were trying to make her inquiry sound merely conversational.

"He's got your nose," Dr. Dorn said as he looked from Anne to the baby.

"Both purely coincidental, I assure you," Anne said, not missing the open speculation shining out of both wrinkled, aged faces before her.

"If you say so, dear," Martha Dorn said just a bit too sweetly.

Anne glanced at the ceiling as though asking for help, or strength, or both. It took every ounce of Tom's control not to smile.

He held up his wallet, trying to catch Felix Dorn's attention.

"Don't be silly, Tom," Dr. Dorn said, waving away the offer. "You know I'm retired. I'm just happy to help out where I can."

"WOULD YOU DO SOMETHING for me?" Tom asked Anne as they exited the doctor's house and headed toward his car.

The look she flashed him left no doubt about how dangerous it was for him to be even thinking of asking her for a favor at the moment.

Tom bit his lip to hold back his smile. "I'd just like you to take a look at my shopping list to see if I've missed anything."

Anne shifted little Tommy to her right side as she glanced at the list Tom held out. "Just diapers and formula? How long will you have Tommy?"

"I'm not sure."

"Days? Weeks?"

"Could be. You think I'll need something else?" Tom asked in his most innocent tone.

"Well, to start with, baby cream, lotion, blankets… You'd better write this down."

Tom slapped his pockets. "Don't seem to have a pen on me."

Anne sent him the lethal look of a judge boring a hole in a defendant's feeble excuse. Tom smiled at her, hoping to be granted some mercy. It wasn't working. But Tommy's muffled little sigh against Anne's breast softened her expression. The kid had great timing.

"I'd best come with you," she said.

"Whatever you say," Tom replied as he held open the car door for her.

TOM CARRIED THE CRYING baby down the narrow aisles of Cooper's Corner General Store. He'd read once that the Occupational Health and Safety Act protected employees from excessive noise in the workplace. Obviously, OSHA had never recorded the decibels of a wailing baby or every parent would be issued mandatory protective ear wear.

"Here they are," Anne called out from a few steps in front of him.

As Tom watched, Anne picked up every one of the diaper packages to compare their features. He knew it would be a while before she made her selection. She had been just as meticulous with the other items on the shopping list she had carefully prepared. This was not a woman who made careless choices.

Tommy whacked Tom's ear with a flailing hand. Tom caught the tiny hand in his and stroked it gently. This business of being a parent was no picnic. It had only been one night and Tom was already done in. It wasn't from lack of sleep or even the baby's constant crying. It was from his inability to ease the little boy's sorrow.

Giving comfort was a big part of Tom's job. The knowledge that he was in over his head with this tiny baby was humbling.

Tom cuddled and rocked and wondered what magic Anne's arms carried that calmed the baby so quickly. Maybe he should try them and find out for himself.

Anne finally placed a large package of disposable diapers in their cart and checked it off her list. "Okay, we have the formula, bottles, baby wipes, soap, shampoo, cream, lotion, cotton swabs, blankets, diapers. He arrived in a car seat, so that's covered. Next is the crib."

"No need to spend money on a new crib," Lori Tubb said as she sidled up to Tom. "I've got a perfectly good portable one I use for my grandchildren, and serviceable sheets, as well. I'll drop them off at the church this afternoon."

"Thanks, Lori," Tom yelled over the baby's crying as he turned to smile at his parishioner.

Lori was short and rotund, with a sunny disposition, dark eyes and hair. She and her husband, Burt, were owners of the village's café and longtime members of the church's vestry, the body of laypeople who, along with Tom, were responsible for running the Church of the Good Shepherd.

"May I hold him?" Lori asked.

Tom nodded and handed the little boy to her.

The baby's cry immediately escalated into a screech. "Oh, my," Lori said. "Does he have colic?"

"Dr. Dorn says he's getting over a viral infection," Tom yelled.

Lori bounced the baby as she glanced at the contents of the shopping basket. She pulled out the blankets Anne had dropped in just a moment before. "I've extra blankets, so you don't have to waste your money on these. I'll just put them back on the shelf."

"You hold it right there, Lori Tubb," Phyllis Cooper, co-owner of the general store, said as she walked up behind her.

Lori turned to bravely face Phyllis, who was only a couple of inches taller but whose wild cloud of gray-blond hair made her seem a great deal more formidable.

"I was just trying to save Father Tom some money, Phyl."

Phyllis grabbed the blankets out of Lori's hands and dumped them back into the shopping basket. "You think Philo and me would charge Tom for these baby things? We know it's hard enough on him, assuming the care of this little abandoned boy."

"Sorry, Phyl," Lori said, sincerely contrite.

The baby's screams rose until they seemed to be vibrating the glass bottles on the shelves. A customer in the adjacent aisle headed for the door.

"Let me see if I can quiet him," Phyllis said as she took Tommy out of Lori's arms. Phyllis rocked and cuddled the little boy, but Tommy's unhappy tirade raged on.

"I'll take him outside," Anne said, lifting the baby out of Phyllis's arms.

But the instant Anne settled the baby against her chest, little Tommy's screaming stopped. All eyes turned toward her.

"You certainly seem to have a way with him," Lori remarked, her tone ripe with growing interest.

"How lucky for Father Tom that you just happened to be around," Phyllis said, her eyebrow lifting with possibilities. "I heard you were staying up at the B and B. You here to help Father Tom find this cute little baby's mother?"

"No, I'm just filling in the blanks on the shopping list," Anne said.

"Really?" Phyllis flashed Tom a speculative look before turning back to Anne. "I didn't know you and Tom knew each other that well."

"We don't," Anne said.

"Yet here you are, pitching in to help him," Lori added. "And on your vacation, too."

Anne's eyes dropped to her list. "You'll need something to carry him around in, *Father Christen,*" she said in her very formal judge's tone. "I doubt you'll want to use a towel again."

It was clear to Tom that Anne had caught the growing speculation coming from both Phyllis and Lori and was trying to cut it off in the bud.

Anne obviously didn't have a clue as to the kind of women she was up against.

"The baby carriers are on the next shelf," Phyllis said, pointing. "I'd recommend the over-the-shoulder sling. Keeps the baby close and frees the hands without giving you a backache. Any idea who the mother is, Father Tom?"

"Trudi saw her car," Lori said before Tom had a chance to respond.

"When was this?" Phyllis asked, swiveling around to face her.

"She was walking down Church Street last night when it whizzed right past her," Lori said.

Tom knew he didn't have to ask any questions at this point. Not with Phyllis Cooper around. She was as good as any prosecuting attorney when it came to grilling a witness.

"Did Trudi get the license number?" Phyllis asked.

"No, it was going by too fast," Lori answered.

"But she got a good look at the driver?"

"Just enough to see it was a woman."

"What did the woman look like?" Phyllis pushed some more.

"I tell you, Phyl, she didn't get that good a look."

"She had to have noticed whether the woman was young or old."

"Well, of course the woman was young. What mature woman would abandon her baby?"

"How is Trudi doing?" Tom interjected quickly, uncomfortable with the direction the conversation was suddenly going.

"Turning into a real good waitress," Lori said. "Glad you talked us into hiring her."

"She seems to take a lot of walks at night," Phyllis said. "I've seen her out in all weather."

"She works hard," Lori declared almost defensively. "I don't see anything wrong with her wanting a little time to herself."

"Young girls shouldn't be walking the streets alone at night," Phyllis said.

"She's perfectly safe in the village."

"Don't kid yourself," Phyllis warned. "You never know who could be pulling off the highway."

The general store's front bell tinkled as a couple came in, and Phyllis went off to wait on them.

"I'll check around the village to see if I can round up some baby clothes," Lori said. "Never can have enough."

"Would it be possible to send Trudi by with the crib?" Tom asked. "I'd like to talk to her."

"Sure thing," Lori said. "And remember, Burt and I have raised five babies of our own. You need any help, you come see us."

After Lori had left, Anne sent Tom an accusing look. "Either one of those women could have helped you prepare this shopping list."

"But you were the one who was there when I needed it prepared,'' Tom said as he pushed the shopping cart toward the baby carriers. ''Besides, Tommy obviously prefers you.''

''OKAY, I ADMIT my curiosity has gotten the better of me,'' Anne said as Tom put the last of the supplies in the back of his sleek, midnight blue sports car. ''Where did a priest get a Porsche?''

''An addiction from my previous life,'' Tom confessed as he closed the back. He walked around and opened the passenger side for Anne.

''What did you do in this previous life?'' she asked.

''I was in construction.''

Her eyes glinted up at him. ''I don't believe it.''

''Shall I invite you over to see my power tools?''

A reluctant smile tugged on the corners of her lips. ''I would think that a guy who wore a hard hat would be into trucks.''

''Known a lot of guys in hard hats, have you?''

Anne flashed him a warning look before leaning into the back to place the baby in his car seat. ''As strange as it is to picture you on the other end of a pile driver, I suppose it's as likely as your being a priest.''

''Oh? How so?'' Tom asked.

''Well, you have to admit you don't look like a priest.''

''What do I look like, Anne?''

She twisted toward him and the sunlight fused with her hair—copper alloyed with gold. Her eyes turned a misty pearl as she studied him in rapt concentration, as though trying to decide. She had no idea how stunning she was, or how stunned he was by her.

''Actually, you look like a bank robber I once prosecuted while I was working for the D.A.'s office,'' Anne said.

She turned away and busied herself with strapping in the baby.

''And you saw that he was acquitted,'' Tom said, unable to keep himself from baiting her.

''I saw that he got twenty years,'' she called over her shoulder. "Although, if he hadn't been so good-looking, I might have gone for twenty-five."

Tom chuckled. She was intelligent, self-assured, beautiful, irreverent and attracted to him. He couldn't think of a more alluring set of qualities.

The baby began to wail again the moment he was out of Anne's arms. Tom hated to hear his anguished sounds.

Circling the car, he got into the driver's side and started the engine, enjoying its pantherlike growl. Apparently, the baby did, too. Tommy stopped crying whenever the car was in motion. Just as he did when he was cradled in Anne's arms.

No doubt about it, the kid had great taste.

"Give me your professional opinion about something?" Tom asked Anne as he spun the car away from the curb.

"What?"

"How would you go about finding someone? In an unofficial sort of way."

"You mean the baby's mother, don't you?" Anne asked.

"Does it matter?"

"Seems strange you don't know where she is," Anne said.

"Does it?" Tom replied.

Anne turned to study his profile. "You answer a lot of questions with questions."

He snapped her a grin. "Do I?"

She was trying not to grin back. Trying hard. "Tell me something."

"Anything I can."

"Did you even know about Tommy before yesterday?"

Tom slowed to round the corner, carefully thinking about her question.

"No," he said finally.

"I figured as much," Anne said. "Did she dump the baby on you in order to embarrass you?"

"It's a confidential matter," Tom said carefully.

"So we're back to that again. What can you say?"

"I'd like to find her."

Tom felt Anne's eyes studying him again. He waited.

''The logical place to start is her last known address,'' Anne said after a moment.

''She's not there.''

''Family? Friends?''

''Dead ends, as well. I'm looking for more official channels, Anne, ones that can be accessed unofficially.''

''Running her name through the registry of motor vehicles?'' Anne suggested.

''I doubt she has a driver's license.''

''She was driving a vehicle.''

''Is it possible to trace that vehicle even if we don't have the license number?'' Tom asked, sidestepping Anne's implicit question.

''If we had a good enough description, I could ask the state police to be on the lookout for it and pull her over.''

Tom shook his head. ''I don't want her pulled over. That wouldn't help either her or the baby.''

Anne was quiet for a moment as she cast a look back at Tommy. ''I might be able to call in a favor.''

''Favor?'' Tom repeated, trying to sound as uninformed as possible until she made the suggestion he'd been leading her to.

''I could ask the state police to let me know if they see the vehicle, but not stop the driver.''

''Good idea, Anne,'' Tom said as he pulled into the church's parking lot. ''As soon as Trudi arrives with the crib, we'll get the vehicle's description from her. I'm glad I asked for your advice on this.''

ANNE REALIZED she'd been had. As she stood over the sink in Tom's kitchen, washing dishes, she could see how adroitly Tom had set her up every step of the way. First the doctor's, then the store, then tricking her into agreeing to find the baby's mother.

And now, somehow—she couldn't even remember the specifics—here she was cleaning up his kitchen!

If she'd had any doubts before, she had none now. Father Tom Christen was a very dangerous man.

Anne told herself that if it weren't for the baby, she'd leave right this minute. But little Tommy hadn't liked the new formula any more than he had the old, and had just spit it up all over Tom.

And was screaming at the top of his tiny lungs again. Poor little sweetheart.

She figured Tom was getting everything he deserved. But Anne was very worried about Tommy. How could his mother have left him when he wasn't well?

She set the last of the dishes in the drying rack and went over to lift the baby out of Tom's arms. As he had every time before, Tommy stopped crying, snuggled his little cheek against her chest and with a soft sigh went right to sleep.

Ah, the sudden quiet was wonderful!

Anne sat on a kitchen chair, cuddled the baby close and wondered at this odd role that had been so suddenly thrust upon her.

When her co-workers brought their babies to the office, she always said the polite things she knew a parent wanted to hear. But she never asked to hold their babies. And when she had helped her sister with her nieces and nephew, she felt very much an outsider—awkward and unwanted.

But she didn't feel awkward or unwanted now. Not with this surprising little baby who fit so perfectly into her arms. Since the first moment she'd held his warm little body next to hers, it had felt so natural to cuddle him and keep him close.

Why did Tommy stop crying only when she held him? And why was it she who felt comforted whenever she cradled him in her arms?

"You're a natural mother," Tom said from the chair beside her.

Anne kept forgetting how deep and rich Tom's voice was until it suddenly hummed through her ears and her blood.

"I have a ton of screaming testimonials to the contrary," she said. "Just ask my sister. And her kids."

"You were married for four years," Tom said. "Why no kids of your own?"

The surprise of his question beat like butterfly wings inside Anne's chest. Her eyes shot to his face.

"How is it you know about my marriage?"

"I asked Maureen about you."

His eyes were as clear and warm as a summer day and looking directly into hers. The butterfly in Anne's chest suddenly grew eagle wings.

The doorbell rang through the rectory.

"That will be Trudi with the crib," Tom said. "Be right back."

He was out of his chair and gone in a flash.

Anne took a deep breath and let it out very slowly. Her pulse was fluttering and her nerves were skipping. And all he had said was that he'd asked about her. This was definitely not a good sign.

Tommy whimpered in his sleep.

"It's okay, little guy," Anne soothed as she rocked the baby. "We're going to find your mommy. And then everything will be all right."

Hearing her own words brought a frown to Anne's face.

Tom would find the mother of his child. And when he brought her back to Cooper's Corner and reunited her with their baby, what then?

Would he marry her?

It's none of your concern, that wise voice inside Anne's head admonished. *So stop wondering. And stop letting that priest get to you.*

TRUDI KARR SEEMED OLDER than her eighteen years. She was short and thin, her hair the color of the mud that made the unpaved county roads around the village a quagmire. She wore jeans and a faded yellow sweatshirt. Her wary brown eyes never looked straight at Anne.

The three of them sat together in Tom's study—a cozy space with tall, narrow windows, a polished brass wood stove and walls filled with an eclectic assortment of books neatly stacked on sturdy pine shelves.

Trudi perched on the edge of her chair, her elbows braced on her bony knees.

Anne had seen young women like Trudi in her court. Their old faces had always made her sad.

"I'm sorry I haven't made it to church, Father," Trudi said. "I'm grateful you got me the job with the Tubbs and all, it's just..."

"You don't have to explain, Trudi," Tom said. "And you don't owe me anything. Whether you come to church or not is your choice."

The tension in Trudi's thin shoulders didn't abate, despite Tom's reassurance.

"I understand you saw the vehicle that drove by the church around eight o'clock last night?" he asked.

"Yeah. It passed me on Church Street, going real fast. Kicked up a mess of mud."

"Could you determine its make or model?" Tom asked.

"A rusty-red VW Bug—one of those real old ones, not the new models."

"License plate?"

"Massachusetts, probably. Sure I would've noticed were it different."

"You remember any numbers, letters?"

Trudi shook her head.

"Anything else about it, Trudi? Anything at all?"

"It had a bumper sticker on the back. Driver's side."

"What did it say?"

"Red Sox Rule."

"You a baseball fan, Trudi?" Tom asked.

"My older brothers had the games on TV all the time," Trudi volunteered, then looked down at her hands as though she had said something wrong.

Anne thought Trudi was exhibiting all the nervous habits of a witness on the stand who wasn't being totally candid. She wondered why.

"You have amazing eyesight," Anne said carefully. "Reading a bumper sticker on a car that whizzes past you at night on a road without any lights."

"Oh, I didn't read the bumper sticker last night. I read it when the car was parked in the church's lot yesterday afternoon."

"Yesterday afternoon?" Anne repeated, her voice rising in surprise.

"You've been a big help, Trudi," Tom said, quickly coming to his feet. "I'm sure Lori needs you back at the café. I'll get the door for you."

When Tom returned after seeing Trudi out, Anne was ready for him. "You saw Tommy's mother at the church yesterday."

"I didn't see the car," Tom said. "Do you have enough of a description of the vehicle to call the state police?"

Tom knew Anne wasn't satisfied with his explanation. Her gray eyes were as cloudy and cool as an overcast day.

"If I'm going to help you find this woman," she said, "I need to know more about her."

"I'll tell you what I can," Tom said.

"Let's start with her name."

"Lindy."

"And her last name?"

Tom shook his head.

"You won't tell me?" Anne asked.

"I can't," Tom said.

Her eyes aimed at him like two silver bullets. "Is she married?"

"No, Anne, she's not married."

"Lindy wants to marry you, though, doesn't she?" Anne asked.

Tom hesitated. He knew exactly where Anne was heading. Unfortunately, there was no way to stop her now.

"Yes."

"But you don't want to marry her."

"No."

Anne looked down at the baby in her arms.

"I don't know why I'm surprised," she said. "I've heard at least a hundred cases just like it in my court. He wants instant gratification. She wants romance with all the trimmings. And because they are so focused on their own wants, neither of them thinks about the life they end up bringing into the world.''

''It wasn't like that, Anne.''

Her eyes rose to his. ''No? Then tell me what it was like.''

He wished he could. God help him, he wished he could.

''I can't,'' Tom said.

The disappointment on her face was heavy enough to bury a man. Tom felt the weight of it like an anvil over his heart.

For a moment, he thought Anne was going to press him for the whole truth. But then she sighed as though in defeat and reached for her shoulder bag, to dig out the cell phone inside.

''I'd rather do this without an audience if you don't mind,'' she said, pointing at the phone.

Tom nodded and stepped out of the room so she wouldn't have a sense of his hovering. But he listened in from the adjoining hallway. He had to know if she was going to mention him or the baby.

A moment later she was chitchatting with some guy named Fred in the state trooper's office. After exchanging a few pleasantries, she asked Fred to keep an eye out for the old rusty-red VW Beetle with a woman driver. She said nothing about Tom or the child.

Tom was relieved until he heard her sign off.

''Let's have dinner Monday night,'' Anne said into the phone. ''Pittsfield is good. Yeah, I like it there. Seven o'clock will be fine. I love you, too.''

Anne loved some guy named Fred with the state police?

No. Tom didn't believe it. Fred had to be an uncle, or brother.

Not that it mattered now. Anne had lost what little faith she had left in Tom after his jarring admissions during their previous conversation. He had read that clearly in the freezing chill of her eyes. It would take a miracle for him to have a chance with her now.

Fortunately for Tom, he believed in miracles.

The telephone rang. He walked down the hallway to answer it.

Anne could hear Tom's side of the conversation as he spoke

on the kitchen telephone. He really had the most amazing ability to project his voice—even when he didn't seem to be trying.

He was being asked to console parents whose young daughter had just been diagnosed with terminal cancer. Tom told them he was on his way.

Anne wondered how anyone could bring comfort in a situation like that. It seemed to be asking a lot of someone to try. Maybe that was the problem. The job asked too much. Maybe that's why it was just too hard to meet all its demands.

Like the one that called for control over sexual urges. The one Tom had failed.

What disappointed her so much? Was it that he had had a child out of wedlock? Or that he didn't want to marry the mother of his child?

No, it was the fact that he had put his desires first—just like any ordinary man. Tom wasn't special, after all. And she had wanted him to be. Because she was so damn attracted to him.

It's better this way, that wise voice inside her said. *You know the truth. Now you can stop the silly fantasies about the guy and get on with your vacation.*

As soon as he got back from his visit to the distraught parents, that was exactly what Anne was going to do. And this time, she was not going to let herself be talked out of it.

CHAPTER THREE

ANNE AWOKE SUNDAY MORNING to a raven's angry croak. She slipped out of bed and crossed to the window. The raven was perched on a nearby tree, scolding a sleek ginger cat that was in pursuit of whatever had ducked beneath the deck below. The cat was clearly oblivious to the bird's tirade.

A prowling tom, no doubt, Anne thought with irritation.

She cracked open the window and leaned out. The raven eyed her curiously, then ignored her completely as it proceeded to preen its silky black feathers.

The morning mist drifted like a delicate silver veil through the meadow below. Ribbons of pink and purple light encased the sleepy village of Cooper's Corner like giant bows decorating a birthday present. The images were lovely, the air sweet with the kiss of spring.

But it was way too frosty for a thin nightgown and bare feet. Anne leaned back and shut the window.

She knew when it was time to retreat. And not just from a chilly morning.

If and when Fred called to let her know about the rusty-red VW Beetle, she would pass along the information to Tom as promised. But by telephone. There was absolutely no reason to ever see him again. And she wasn't going to.

Smart women stayed clear of unsuitable men.

Yesterday, she'd gotten carried away, become too involved in a business that shouldn't have concerned her. It had been a mistake. Not her first. Probably not her last. But one that she definitely was putting behind her.

Today was a brand-new day—the day when she really started her long-awaited vacation.

A gentle knock sounded at the door. Anne padded across the thick carpet to see who it was. Maureen stood in the hall, holding a tray with two cups of coffee.

"You are a great hostess," Anne said as she opened the door wide to invite Maureen inside.

"Newlyweds and friends get special treatment," Maureen replied with a smile.

They settled on the daisy brocade bedspread, backs braced against the headboard, softened with fluffy pillows. Anne polished off her coffee in one long delicious gulp. The rich liquid left a trail of warmth, more than welcome after her brief taste of the chilly morning air.

"Thanks," she said, returning the cup to the tray when she had finished. "I really needed that."

Maureen eyed Anne over the rim of her cup. "You didn't sleep well."

"The bags are that big beneath my eyes?" Anne asked, chuckling.

"I heard you pacing the floor. My room is just below."

Anne frowned. "Oh. Sorry."

"No reason to be," Maureen said. "The twins caught a cold. They kept me awake. The question is, what kept you?"

Avoiding Maureen's inquisitive gaze, Anne got up and meandered over to the window. What she had learned about Tom and the baby was not her secret to share. If Tom wanted to tell his parishioners, that was up to him. But no one was going to hear it from her.

"The view from this room is spectacular," Anne said. "I love seeing the snow-covered mountains soaring above the trees."

"Okay, you don't want to talk about it," Maureen said, rising off the bed. She picked up the tray and started toward the door. "Take your time coming down. I won't clear away the buffet until you're ready."

Anne felt a twinge of guilt for having cut off her friend. "Maureen?"

Maureen reached the door and turned to face her. "Yes?"

"Thanks for caring to ask," she said.

Maureen studied her silently for a moment. "He didn't get any sleep, either, Anne."

Anne's pulse jumped. "He?"

"The baby. Unless there's another 'he' you're interested in?"

"How do you know the baby didn't sleep?" Anne asked, pointedly ignoring Maureen's question.

"It's a small village," Maureen replied. "People around here help out when problems arise. Several women took turns dropping by the rectory last night, but none of them could stop the little guy from crying."

Anne felt the chill of the cold morning seeping through her nightgown. The coffee hadn't helped much, after all. She wrapped her arms around her chest.

How long could a baby go without rest?

"Phyl and Lori insist you're the only one he responds to," Maureen said. "Is that true?"

"When does the church open?" Anne asked.

"The Church of the Good Shepherd is always open," Maureen said. "And services will be starting soon. I'll be back in fifteen minutes to drive you over."

Before Anne could even think about reconsidering, Maureen was gone.

"Damn it," Anne muttered as she pulled off her nightgown and rushed toward the shower. "I do not want to see Tom Christen again."

Maybe if she said it loud enough, she might even start believing it.

THE VILLAGE CHURCH was packed for Sunday service. Farming families from miles around had come to join their neighbors in Cooper's Corner. Anne sat in the front pew next to Maureen. She wore a tailored blouse of deep blue, with slacks to match.

To Tom, she looked even lovelier than she had that first morning he saw her. Because this morning she had come to cradle a tiny, exhausted baby in her arms, no matter what she thought of its father.

And what she thought of Tom showed crystal clear in the frozen gray pools of her eyes.

Lent was the time to read scriptures full of the message of sacrifice. But as Tom stood in the pulpit and gazed down on Anne and the marvel of the sleeping baby in her arms, he found a far different message forming on his lips.

"The first Bible class I ever taught was made up of five- and six-year-olds," Tom began. "I had no idea how to explain scripture to them in terms they would understand. I decided maybe the best thing to do was to start with a question. So I asked them if they knew where God was.

"A thin girl with black braids told me that God was in the rain that made her grandmother's thirsty tomato plants grow. A boy with no front teeth lisped that God hung out under his bed, keeping the monsters away. A chubby-faced boy said he knew for a fact that God stayed in the pantry protecting the small brown mouse that his mother was always trying to trap. And, finally, a shy girl, barely five, leaned forward and whispered to me that she had seen God in her daddy's smile."

Tom paused to enjoy the soft murmur of appreciation flowing through the congregation before he continued. "Jesus said that unless we become as little children, we will not enter into the Kingdom of Heaven. His words made a lot of sense to me after listening to those little kids. They saw God everywhere they looked because that's where they knew God would be."

Tom gazed down into Anne's eyes—now a soft, warm velvet and staring directly into his own. "Finding heaven is as simple as opening our eyes and seeing with our hearts. That's what the little children in that Bible class taught me."

ANNE WAITED in the parish hall while Tom said goodbye to the last of his parishioners. Maureen had driven back to the B and B. Anne planned to walk back later. Right now she was thankful for a moment alone to try to sort through her emotions.

The message in Tom's story had sneaked past all her defenses and touched her heart. She'd never met a man before who could freely admit to being taught by children, much less show such strength doing it.

She had some previous assumptions that needed reevaluating. Maybe she'd grown into too much of a judge, become too quick to find fault. Everyone made mistakes. So what if Tom had a child out of wedlock and didn't want to marry its mother?

Okay, it was hardly exemplary behavior for a priest, but at least he was trying to care for his child. His sweet little child.

Anne looked down at Tommy, fast asleep in her arms. The moment she had arrived at the church that morning and taken him out of Phyllis Cooper's hands, Tommy had stopped crying, settled his tiny head against her and slipped into a sound sleep.

She had come to expect this from Tommy. What she hadn't expected was the sudden rush of pleasure when she felt the steady beat of his heart once again next to hers. She had missed him.

"Thanks for coming, Anne," Tom said.

Anne hadn't heard him enter the room, so intent had she been on the baby. She lifted her head with a start.

He was standing in front of her chair, looking long and lean in a black suit, clerical shirt and white collar. The contrast of his dazzling smile against the bronze of his skin was dramatic and nothing less than dynamite.

"I heard you had a rough night," Anne said, and was dismayed that her voice didn't sound nearly as tough as she'd intended.

"I've had better," Tom admitted as he slipped onto the chair beside her. He leaned across her to stroke Tommy's cheek with the pad of his index finger. She could smell the soap he'd used to wash with, a blend of clean pine woods, laced with a touch of enticing incense.

"I don't know how Tommy or I would have managed this morning without you," he said in that deep-throated voice of his.

No doubt about it, Tom was just as tempting as sin. But it was the open sincerity in his clear blue eyes that was the real threat to Anne's composure. She leaned back in her chair, away from his warmth, and reminded herself once again that she was a sober, sane judge and could handle this situation with the proper emotional distance.

"About your baby, Father Christen—"

"Please, Anne. Call me Tom."

"Why?"

"Because I can't wait to find out whether you use that very proper judicial tone when you say my first name or that incredible throaty sigh that slips out once in a while."

Tom watched the light of understanding turn Anne's eyes into dazzling pools of pure crystal.

She dropped her gaze to the baby. "This isn't a good idea."

But it was too late. Her beautiful, expressive eyes had betrayed her. Somehow she'd gotten past her disappointment in him. And for Tom, the weariness of two nights without any sleep simply faded away.

He rose and held out his hand. "I've packed enough formula and diapers for the day. And there's a basketful of food. We'll take it with us."

She looked at his offered hand but made no move to clasp it. "Where?"

"There are some people I'd like you to meet," he said.

Tom knew her choice at this moment was an important one for them both. He stood before her with his hand held out for what was probably only seconds, but felt like a lifetime.

Then, slowly, she slipped her right hand from around the baby and placed it palm down on his.

Her skin was warm and soft, the tone of her voice wonderfully tart. "I'm not doing any more shopping and I'm not doing any more dishes. And when this little cherub of yours needs feeding or changing, Tom Christen, he's all yours. Is that clear?"

"As a church bell," Tom said as he curled his fingers around her slim wrist and pulled her gently to her feet.

For a second she stood tantalizingly close, the warmth of her seeping into his senses. She smelled like rain-washed flowers, and the desire to hold her was a growing ache inside him.

Tom reminded himself that he was stronger than his urges. He stepped back, released her hand and led the way to the car.

"I'VE GOT AN ACE-HIGH straight, boys," the eighty-five-year-old lady with the humped back and thin, blue-veined hands said as she slapped her cards down on the table. "Read 'em and weep."

The other senior citizens sitting around Tom and Anne at the rickety old card table moaned in unison as they threw in their cards.

"She's cheating, Father," sputtered a thin, wrinkled man who Anne was certain had to be at least ninety. "Nobody wins eight straight in a row fair and square!"

Tom peered across the table at the smug grin on the old lady's face as she gingerly scooped up the pile of wagered matchsticks from the middle of the table.

"You dealing from the bottom of the deck again, Shirley?" Tom asked.

Shirley stared at Tom with the face of a born cardsharp. "Accusing an old lady of such a thing. You should be ashamed of yourself, Father Tom. Just for that you owe me another cupcake."

Tom shifted the feeding baby in his arms to reach into the basket at his feet. He drew out a chocolate-topped cupcake and slid it slowly across the table toward Shirley.

Shirley eyed the cupcake greedily. When she reached for it, however, Tom quickly pulled it back. As Shirley made a final, valiant grab, an ace slipped out of her sleeve.

"There! See? See?" shouted the old man.

"Oh, put a cork in it, Walter," Shirley said, totally unperturbed at having been caught. Her twinkling eyes returned to Tom. "Now, you going to hand over that cupcake, or am I going to have to arm wrestle you for it?"

Tom eyed Shirley for a moment as though sizing up his opponent. Then he pushed back from the table, stood up and carefully handed Tommy to Anne.

"Two out of three," he said as he started to roll up his sleeve.

Pandemonium at once reigned as the senior citizens at the

table began rolling wheelchairs and hopping on their canes in order to reposition themselves to get a clearer view. Matchsticks got dumped onto the table as they yelled out their bets to Anne, whom they immediately designated as their official bookie.

Anne had a hard time restraining her mirth—particularly when she noticed that the previously irate Walter was smiling happily as he bet all his matchsticks on Shirley. The formidable old lady was the odds-on favorite.

Tom and Shirley sat face-to-face, knee-to-knee, elbows on the table, hands clasped. Tom huffed and puffed and made a good show, but Shirley easily pinned him two in a row.

Shirley was smugly munching her cupcake and basking in the back slaps of the other seniors when Tom and Anne left the convalescent home a few minutes later.

"Does this go on every Sunday?" Anne asked as they headed for his car in the parking lot.

"First day I came to visit them they told me straight out that they knew the scriptures better than I ever would," Tom explained with a grin. "Said if I insisted on bothering them on Sundays, I'd better bring food and be ready to play some poker."

Anne chuckled. Tom was really very nice. And such a blend of contrasts. A sort of sexy saint and sinner all rolled up into one.

Every time she thought about that very personal message he had delivered to her earlier, she could feel the blood charging through her body. It astounded her that she could come so unglued just by learning of a man's interest in her. But then, as she was quickly discovering, Tom wasn't just any man.

"How's Tommy?" he asked.

They had reached the car, and Anne waited at the passenger door while Tom dug into his pocket for his keys.

"He's awake and looking at you," Anne said as she held up the baby.

Tom glanced over at Tommy. The baby's eyes were indeed wide and alert—and very blue. A wisp of pale-blond hair curled over his forehead. His light-bronze skin was clear and smooth.

It was the first time that Tom had seen the baby when he wasn't eating, in a fit of crying or passed out in sleep.

The little boy was beautiful.

When Tom gently touched the baby's cheek, the infant grabbed his finger and held on, looking right into his eyes. Tom experienced that tug in his chest that he had several times before, as if he was being pulled toward something warm and wonderful.

"I think he's feeling better," Anne said. "Maybe—"

She stopped in midsentence when an attendant from the retirement home suddenly raced up to Tom. He was a bantam-size man with perky white teeth and was holding out a slip of paper. "This message just came in for you, Father," he said.

Tom extracted his finger from Tommy's grasp, took the note and thanked the attendant.

The man turned to retrace his steps back to the retirement home. Tom quickly read the note, which brought a frown to his face.

"Problem?" Anne asked.

"I need to make a stop at the hospital," he said as he reached down to open the car door for her.

ANNE STOOD IN THE DOORWAY as she watched Tom bend over the elderly man in the hospital bed. There were tubes coming out of the man's chest and an IV stuck in his arm.

"So, Joe, we missed you in church this morning," Tom said, his manner light and playful. "I suppose you think I'm going to let you off the hook just because you're all hooked up here?"

Joe smiled. "Actually, Father, I do need you to get me off the hook for something," he said, his voice a heavy wheeze. "I need you to marry us."

Tom glanced to the other side of the bed, where a grave woman with gray-white hair stood, holding Joe's hand.

"Betty, you're not married to Joe?" Tom asked.

Betty shook her head as though in shame. "I know we told everybody in Cooper's Corner we were when we moved in together. But we couldn't. Joe's children were so against it. They thought it meant Joe didn't love and honor the memory of their mother. Please, don't be disappointed in us, Father.''

Tom smiled. ''I could never be disappointed in two people so committed to each other. Is the marriage ceremony what you both want now?''

''Yes,'' Joe wheezed, looking over at Betty as though she were the most beautiful girl in the world.

Betty smiled back as though Joe were her ardent young lover. ''Yes, Father,'' she said.

''Then it would be my pleasure,'' Tom assured them, drawing out the *Book of Common Prayer* from his pocket.

As Tom's deep, rich voice recited the marriage ceremony, Anne listened to Joe and Betty promise to love and comfort each other in sickness and in health as long as they both would live. There was no white dress, no flowers, no organ music, no candles. Just the full joy of love to light their faces.

And Anne felt tears stinging the back of her eyes.

It was later, when she and Tom walked down the hospital hallway to the exit, that she asked, ''How much time does Joe have left?''

''Not much,'' Tom said.

Anne heard it in his voice then. Tom felt for Joe and Betty. He had not found a nice, safe, comfortable place from which to view their pain. He was part of Joe and Betty's intimacy of suffering.

''Couldn't you get in trouble with your bishop for performing an illegal ceremony?'' Anne asked after a moment.

''Probably. Going to tell on me, Anne?''

Tom didn't sound worried. It struck Anne then that this was not a man who did the safe thing. This was a man who got into the full fray of life and let himself feel.

''I could issue a waiver of the three-day waiting period for a marriage license,'' Anne offered. ''They could make their marriage official.''

''It's official in their hearts,'' Tom replied. ''Has been for a long time. They just needed the comfort of saying the words aloud to each other in a ceremonial context.''

"Even if the ritual doesn't mean anything?"

"Ritual means a great deal," Tom said. "We're constantly seeking the tangible evidence to our intangible side. Ritual helps to put the bone and muscle on our beliefs."

Anne considered Tom's words and had to admit they had merit. "I suppose if you took all the ritual out of a courtroom, the law would lose a lot of its tangibility. How long have Joe and Betty been together?"

"Ten years," Tom replied. "They met when they were both in their sixties. Joe's wife had died of cancer. Betty's husband had left her years earlier. They totally surprised themselves by falling in love just like a couple of teenagers."

Yes, Anne had seen that rare kind of love on their faces. It was a shame it was so rare.

"Hungry?" Tom asked as they exited the hospital.

"A little," Anne admitted.

"There's a nice spot a few miles from here. We'll stop there for lunch."

Anne thought Tom meant a restaurant, but the nice spot turned out to be a sunlit meadow, very private and secluded within a copse of trees. The air was cool, but not unpleasantly so. Tom spread out a blanket on the grass. When Anne and the baby were settled on it, he brought the picnic basket over and sat across from them.

Reaching into the basket, Tom pulled out the last two chicken sandwiches, along with a thermos of hot chocolate. He handed Anne a sandwich and poured them each a cup of the chocolate.

Anne didn't know if it was because she had missed breakfast or because the fresh air was adding a special seasoning zest, but the sandwich tasted wonderful and so did the hot chocolate. She polished them off in record time.

She stroked the sleeping baby in her arms, enjoying the feel of him, the sun on her skin. The sky was clear as glass. The trees all around them were full of songbirds, and a hawk circled lazily overhead. From deep within the trees came the sound of water rushing over rock.

"Nature's always been the best cathedral," Tom said as he

lay on his side watching her, his comment perfectly mirroring her thoughts.

"Did you grow up in the country?" Anne asked, curious to know more about this very different man.

"Far from it. I was born in Boston, brought up in New York City."

"Yes, I suppose that's as far from it as it gets. Brothers? Sisters?"

"Only child."

"Maureen said the vestry was at first concerned that you'd never been married. They thought it odd."

"Do you think it odd, Anne?"

"You don't get to ask the questions now," Anne said. "It's my turn. So, why haven't you married?"

He hesitated before he answered, and she could feel his eyes on her. "I've been waiting for my soul mate."

"I hear that term a lot these days. Never been clear about its definition. So, what's the difference between a marriage mate and a soul mate?"

"None, if you've selected right."

"You know what I mean," Anne said, her eyes rising to his.

"A person who is *only* a marriage mate will see the mistakes in what you do. But a soul mate will *only* see the love."

Anne wondered if there really were relationships in which each partner only saw the other's love. "Sounds wonderful," she admitted. "And totally unbelievable."

"Wonderful, unbelievable things are called miracles, Anne. And they happen all the time."

No, Anne didn't believe in miracles. But a priest obviously had to. She also imagined he had to be extra careful to marry the right person. Was that why he wasn't marrying the mother of his child? He didn't believe she was his soul mate?

"What made you decide to become a priest?" Anne asked after a moment.

"It's a long story and best left for another time."

"Why not now?"

"Because as the lead in that story, I'm not always a sympathetic character,'' Tom admitted. ''I'd prefer you learn about some of my good points first.''

''You have some good points?'' she asked, not able to resist the opening.

That got a grin out of him. ''A few.''

''Name one.''

''Well, let's see. I don't rob banks.''

''The former prosecutor in me is impressed. Anything else?''

''I'm a good listener.''

''So was my beagle...after I got him fixed.''

Tom's laugh was deep and vibrant, and resonated like fine music inside her. A whole chorus of her own feminine chords was eagerly joining right in. She was going to have to be very careful. Tom was proving far too likable for her own good.

''My turn to ask questions,'' he said. ''Where are you from?''

''I never really know how to answer that question,'' Anne admitted. ''I was born in California, but I was only there the first couple of months of my life. My father was a career military officer. We moved every eighteen months.''

''The travel must have been fun,'' Tom said.

''Sometimes, but I lost a lot of friends and memories.''

''Memories?'' Tom repeated.

''The kind that come back when you pick up an old photo or something else from your past.''

Anne told him then about being invited to her college roommate's home for Thanksgiving and seeing all the stuff she had in her bedroom—dolls, toys, books, old school papers and report cards. Anne had never been able to keep any of those things. ''When you're always moving,'' she explained, ''you have to travel light.''

''I understand,'' Tom said, and oddly enough, Anne could see that understanding right there on his face.

Before she knew it, she was telling him about the places she had lived, how her father had finally retired and moved to Boston, the thrill of getting the news when she had been accepted into law school, and later, the recruitment call from the Boston prosecutor's office.

"I was with them for eight years," Anne said.

"Twice as long as your marriage," Tom commented. "You must have liked it better."

"When I put some really serious sinners behind bars."

"And when you didn't?" Tom asked.

"I don't like to think about the ones that got away with what they had done."

"No one ever really gets away, Anne."

"Maybe not, but it sure would have been nice to see them pay for their sins in this lifetime."

Tom rolled onto his back and looked up at the sky. To Anne it seemed pale after the rich blue of his eyes.

"So you decided to become a judge to see that those serious sinners got what was coming to them."

Anne laughed. "Hardly. I handle mostly probate, divorces, adoptions and deadbeat dads. Not exactly hardened criminals."

"Then something else made you change jobs?"

She hesitated for a moment. These were not things she normally talked about. Still, it was surprisingly easy to talk to Tom. She supposed that was part of what made him a good priest.

When he was a good priest.

"I was on the fast track with the Boston district attorney's office when the governor called with the offer of the judgeship here in the Berkshires," Anne said. "I was ready to turn it down."

"And then?"

"Then suddenly my marriage was falling apart and the job offer began to sound like a chance for a new start."

"So, taking the job here was a way to try to distance yourself from the pain," Tom said with understanding. "Did it work?"

"It helped," she admitted. "Although I never planned to stay in either the job or the Berkshires. I froze in these hills my first winter here. But before I knew it, a year had gone by and somehow the job had grown on me."

"How do you mean?"

His question wasn't casual. There was genuine interest in his voice, and Anne found herself trying to put into words what it really felt like.

"Law sets the standard for what's right and wrong. Every time I hand down a decision, I'm impacting lives, possibly changing them forever. I can't afford to be wrong. The job's exacting, humbling and exhilarating all at the same time."

"I know what you mean," Tom said.

Anne realized Tom wasn't just politely agreeing with her. She hadn't thought of it before, but it must be like that for a priest, as well—impacting lives, possibly changing them forever.

"If you don't want to talk about why you became a priest, can you at least tell me why you're in the Berkshires?"

"I came because my bishop asked me to, and the Church of the Good Shepherd accepted me. I've stayed because of the people."

"Anyone in particular?" Anne asked, wondering if he intended to tell her now about the mother of his child.

"No one in particular," Tom said. "And everyone in particular."

"That was helpful," she said with sweet sarcasm.

Tom flashed her a grin. "Last summer Phyllis Cooper came by with flowers for the altar. She found me making peanut butter and jelly sandwiches for those seniors we visited today. Every Sunday since, I've received a basket like this one. Clint Cooper donated the sandwiches today, made from the fresh chicken that Ed Taylor, a local farmer, supplies. Martha Dorn bakes the cupcakes Shirley likes so much. The superb hot chocolate is from the Tubbs' café. The basket, cup and utensils all come from Philo and Phyllis's general store. These people give from their heart, Anne, because they have so much heart to give."

And so, it seemed, did Tom. He was that combination of opposite qualities that Anne never would have imagined possible—a man capable of great commitment to his parishioners, but no commitment to the woman with whom he had conceived a child.

The realization that she was still strongly drawn to him, even knowing the latter, was dangerous to Anne's peace of mind, even her sense of self. Men didn't change, no matter how much women wanted to believe they would. She saw ample evidence of that every day in her court. If she let herself feel something for Tom, the likelihood was that he would treat her just like he was treating Tommy's mother.

"Don't believe it, Anne," he said.

She looked over at him and realized he had been watching her. "What?"

"Whatever it was about me that suddenly put that frown on your face," Tom answered.

The man was also a little too perceptive for comfort.

"Let me take Tommy for a while and give you a chance to stretch out," Tom offered.

Carefully, as though afraid to break the blessed spell of quiet, Anne handed Tom the sleeping baby. She lay on her side and watched the gentle way Tom cradled the baby to him, how he smiled as he tenderly stroked his son's hair.

Then Tommy stirred and stretched, opened his eyes, took one look at Tom and let out a wail. "Well, it was a nice twenty seconds while it lasted," Tom said good-naturedly.

He went about the business of changing the little boy's diaper, and Tommy continued to wail throughout the entire process.

"Maybe he does have colic," Anne said.

"He just wants you to hold him," Tom said.

"How can you be so sure?"

He scooted over to Anne and handed her the freshly diapered baby. Tommy immediately snuggled close within her arms and stopped crying.

"I rest my case, Judge."

Humor shone in Tom's eyes as the sun streaked gold through his hair. He suddenly reminded Anne of a blond Lucifer—the brightest and best of all the angels, before his fall.

Tom was close beside her—so close that she could smell the clean, woodsy scent of him mixed with that enticing spice of incense.

"The boy knows where he wants to be," Tom's deep voice said. "I don't blame him."

She could feel his breath against her hair as he spoke, the warmth of his long, lean body. Slowly, with focused intent, Tom's eyes caressed her light copper bangs, her high cheekbones, her too-short nose, her too-wide mouth. Only, when his eyes touched them, her features no longer felt flawed, but beautiful.

Anne had never been made love to with just a look before. Her face felt hot at the same time that chills raced up her spine.

"I promised my mother I'd never get involved with a Porsche man," she said, hoping Tom couldn't hear the hint of panic in her voice.

His eyes brushed the pink rising in her cheeks. "I'll put it up for sale tomorrow."

Suddenly Anne was finding it very difficult to draw in a steady breath.

"What will you ask for it?" she said.

His eyes focused intently on her lips. "Thinking of making me an offer?"

"Maybe I'd best check out the mileage first," she said, acutely aware that they were no longer talking about a car.

His eyes rose to hers. "Keep in mind, Anne. A little mileage often makes an engine run smoother and handle better around the curves."

His voice was way too warm and she felt way too hot.

"No need to worry," he said, as though reading her mind once again. "As much as I'm tempted to offer you a test drive, they're not in keeping with the policy of the management."

With one swift, fluid movement, he shifted back to the other side of the blanket.

Anne's heart pounded in her ears.

She was used to fending off physical advances. Hell, she could handle them in her sleep. But she hadn't been prepared for Tom's restraint. And she knew from every sizzling nerve ending in her body that it was a great deal more dangerous.

When she met Tom's eyes across the blanket, there was no mistaking the heat still in them. Or how perfectly he controlled it.

She had never met a man like him. She was beginning to think that might be because there were no other men like him.

Anne's cell phone screeched, distracting her thoughts. She sat up, dug the phone out of her shoulder bag, flipped it open and said hello.

"It's Fred," her friend's voice said in her ear. "I've got a possible sighting on that old rusty-red VW Beetle you were looking for."

"Great," Anne said, suddenly wondering if it really were. "Where?"

"One of the guys who came on shift a few minutes ago says he saw it going into a campground north of here the night before last. Ready for the directions?"

Anne dug out a pen and paper from her shoulder bag and jotted down the information Fred gave her. She thanked her friend and flipped the phone shut.

"The VW?" Tom asked.

"About forty minutes from here," Anne said, as she began to rise, the baby still in her arms.

Tom shot to his feet. He wore the look of a different man.

"You get the baby in the car. I'll take care of this stuff."

Then, with an efficiency that amazed her, he gathered the remnants of their picnic lunch and beat her to the car.

TOM DROVE THE PORSCHE into the campground thirty-two minutes later. They met no other cars on the road. It was late in the season for skiers and early for campers. All the trailer hook-ups they drove past were empty.

"You realize the sighting was the night before last," Anne said. "She may have come and gone."

"Let's see if there's anyone around," Tom said. "Hiking in this area is popular year-round. Someone might have seen her."

Anne sensed a focused intensity in Tom. Whatever his relation to the mother of his child, it was clear to Anne that he really wanted to find her.

The area was heavily wooded, and trees blocked out the warmth of the sun.

They saw an RV pulled off onto a side road and stopped. Anne felt the cold when Tom got out of the car to go knock on its door. She was glad she was staying within the warmth of the vehicle.

A thin, dark man wearing a noisy yellow shirt answered Tom's knock. From the shake of his head, Anne knew before Tom returned to the car that he hadn't seen the old VW Beetle.

Tom took the winding road farther up into the hills. They climbed slowly, looking out the windows for any sign of the rusty-red car. They stopped once more for Tom to ask questions at the door of another RV on the other side of the campground. But no one answered Tom's knock.

When the Porsche started to slide on the icy road, Tom turned the car around and headed back.

"It was a long shot that she'd still be here," Anne said after a moment.

"Yes," Tom agreed.

"Fred will call if there are any more sightings," she added.

"Yes."

Anne knew Tom was disappointed, and her words weren't helping. She gave up, settled back and let the quiet grow between them as she gazed out the window.

White pines and spruce, thick with age, lined the road. They were majestic in their grandeur, silent sentries to thousands of sunrises. Beneath their dense canopy of green, the forest floor was covered in a white sheet of frost.

Birds flittered in and out of the branches. Soon they'd be building nests. This was Anne's favorite time of year in the Berkshires—when new life boldly asserted itself, transforming the bareness of winter into the vibrant green and gold of spring.

She wasn't looking for it. Which was why when she saw it, she wasn't sure she had.

Anne came forward in her seat. "Stop!"

Tom's reflexes were instantaneous. The car came to a halt before Anne had time to take another breath.

He turned to face her. "What is it?"

"Back there. Between the trees. I saw a flash of something red."

Tom slowly backed up the car, following Anne's pointing hand. She peered out the window, waiting once again to glimpse that flash of red. But when they reached the spot where she thought she had seen it, there was nothing there.

She shook her head. "I could have sworn…"

Tom shifted the car into neutral and set the brake. "Wait here," he said as he slipped out of the driver's seat.

She watched as he walked over to the edge of the road. He peered into the thick underbrush, then dropped to his knees. A minute later he got up, walked a few paces down the road, then squatted again to survey the terrain.

He was trying to approximate the height range of her vision out of the passenger window, she realized. When he suddenly stiffened, she knew he had seen it. Without hesitation, he started down the steep slope.

Anne was out of the car in a flash.

By the time she had reached the spot where Tom had gone over the side, he was already pushing through the frosty underbrush in the deep gully below. She made a mental note to add mountain goat to Tom's growing list of talents.

Anne was freezing in the icy air, but she stood rooted to her spot on the road. About fifty feet in, Tom came to a stop and started clearing away fallen branches and debris. A moment later the fender of a rusty-red VW Beetle came into view.

Red Sox Rule, its bumper sticker read.

The vehicle was on its side. It took several minutes for Tom to clear away enough of the thick underbrush to be able to pry open the driver's door.

When he leaned inside, Anne held her breath. A moment later he straightened, drew out a cross from his pocket and bowed his head in prayer.

The breath in Anne's chest came out in a deep, sad sigh.

Up the road, inside the Porsche, a motherless baby began to cry.

CHAPTER FOUR

ANNE STOOD next to State Trooper Frederica Ferguson, watching the other state troopers and Tom climb up the steep gully, carrying the draped stretcher.

It was almost dusk, and the tall trees blocked out the last of the light like the closing lid of a coffin. A wind had come up and was whistling down the open road.

Frederica took off her parka and draped it around Anne's shoulders. "Why don't you wait in my car? Heater's on."

Anne shook her head. Tommy was wrapped in a blanket nestled next to her heart, sleeping soundly, warm and secure. "We're fine, Fred."

Her friend nodded. Frederica seemed personally oblivious to the cold. At six-three and weighing in at two hundred twelve pounds, Fred was the epitome of an Amazon woman. Next to her, Anne always felt like she was standing in a hole. But Anne knew that despite Fred's size and sometimes gruff manner, she had a gentle heart.

Anne had first met State Trooper Frederica Ferguson three years before, when Fred had offered to drive Anne through a heavy snowstorm to a fund-raiser. On the way to the benefit, a doe had dashed out in front of Fred's patrol car. She hadn't been able to brake in time.

Fred had gotten out of the car, knelt down in the snow and held the doe in her arms until it died. Then Anne had held Fred in her arms as they both cried. Anne learned that night that Fred was the oldest of four kids. She had been supporting them and her mother ever since her dad skipped out on the family when Fred was sixteen.

Anne also learned that Fred's youngest brother was headed for juvenile hall after having been caught stealing. Anne convinced a fellow justice to give him a second chance. The boy had been put on probation and was doing well.

She'd never told Fred that she had intervened. But somehow Fred had found out. Fred quietly made it her business to locate and serve Anne's court orders on the county's deadbeat dads. The gruff state trooper's success rate in getting those guys to pay was impressive. Word soon got around that if you brought your case to the bad-ass munchkin's court, your kids were going to get their child support.

Anne knew Fred would do anything for her. The feeling was mutual.

"How did it happen?" she asked her friend.

"The accident reconstruction specialists will have to determine the details," Fred said. "But I can tell you that she was going way too fast when she hit the curve. That VW had to have flown off this road to have landed so far down the gully."

"Was she…did she die quickly?" Anne asked.

"No seat belt," Fred said. "Never knew what hit her."

It was quick. At least that's something to be thankful for, Anne thought.

"Who was she, Anne?"

"Someone Tom knew."

"Tom?"

"The priest."

"Ah, so that's why he's here. What's the story with you two?"

"Story?"

"You ask me to keep a lookout for an old rusty-red VW Beetle and it turns up crashed in a gully," Fred said. "You must have known something like this was going to happen."

"I had no idea."

"Then why did you ask me to pass the word to watch for her vehicle?"

"It's…complicated," Anne said, wondering what else to say. Wondering what else she could say.

"Does it have anything to do with the fact that she didn't have any ID on her?"

"Her purse must have gotten thrown from the car during the crash," Anne said.

"It was right beside her on the seat," Fred corrected. "It just didn't have any ID in it."

"Why wouldn't she have ID?" Anne wondered aloud.

"I was hoping you could tell me," Fred said, and then looked pointedly at the baby in Anne's arms. "There were diapers and baby bottles in the back seat."

Anne did not meet her friend's eyes. "What about the vehicle?" she asked. "Can't you trace her through it?"

"Its plates were stolen off a junked Ford Ranger over in Springfield. The vehicle identification number wasn't legible. At the moment, we've got zilch."

Questions raced through Anne's mind, but there were no answers. Just a great deal of confusion and growing concern.

She turned to see the stretcher being hauled out of the gully onto the road. The state troopers thanked Tom for his help and proceeded to carry the stretcher toward the medical examiner's van.

Anne saw Tom's face in the dwindling light as he followed their progress. There was a grimness to his features that she had never seen before. And a sadness in his eyes.

A patrol car pulled up, lights flashing but no siren. A tall man with coffee-colored hair got out. Anne recognized Scott Hunter immediately. He went over to the stretcher. Before it was put in the van, Hunter unzipped the black body bag. Anne caught sight of a thin arm and waist-length, curly red hair before Hunter zipped it back up again.

A chill ran down her spine. Tommy whimpered in his sleep. She hugged him to her more closely.

"Hunter knows about our being on the lookout for this vehicle," Fred said, her voice now a whisper beside Anne's ear. "He also knows the driver had no identification. He'll be over here soon to talk to you and he's not going to take 'it's complicated' for an answer—not even from a judge."

Anne understood that Fred was trying to warn her. And with good reason. Scott Hunter's reputation for being thorough was well deserved. She braced herself as he started toward her.

But before Hunter had gone two steps, Tom cut him off and held out his hand. They spoke for a few minutes before they approached Anne together.

"Evening, Your Honor," Hunter said, nodding his head toward Anne.

She acknowledged his greeting with a returning nod.

"Who was the driver?" Hunter asked her, drawing out a pad and pen. He was not a man who beat around the bush.

"Her name was Lindy," Tom answered before Anne could.

Hunter turned toward him. "And her last name?"

"Can't help you there."

"Address?"

Tom shook his head.

Hunter turned back to Anne. "She was a friend of yours?"

"Never met her," Anne replied.

"Odd then that you were looking for her," Hunter said.

"Anne was doing me a favor," Tom said quickly. "I was concerned about Lindy's welfare."

Hunter turned back to Tom. "Why were you concerned?"

"It's part of my job to be concerned about church members," Tom said, as though that should go without saying.

"So she was from Cooper's Corner?" Hunter asked.

"Not to my knowledge," Tom said.

"You just said she was a member of your church."

"Anyone who visits the Church of the Good Shepherd is welcome."

"You must have had a special reason for being concerned about this visitor," Hunter said. "Otherwise you wouldn't have been trying to locate her."

"It was a private matter between a priest and a parishioner," Tom said.

Tom's expression was serene—and very secure. His tone had held no hint of apology. Or of the need to elaborate further.

Hunter looked from Tom to Anne, as though he suspected

collusion between them. His eyes came to rest on Anne and the baby.

"I didn't know you had a child."

"I'm taking care of him for a friend," Anne said. "It's very chilly, Lieutenant. The baby shouldn't be out in this air. So if you don't have any more questions..."

"No more questions," Hunter said. "For now."

But as he turned away, Anne called out to him, "I would like to know exactly how this accident happened."

There was no mistaking the official tone of Anne's voice. A moment before, she might have been just another witness to be interrogated. But now she was a judge using the full power of her office.

Hunter turned back to face her. "Father Christen has already made the same request. I'll contact your office as soon as we know anything more."

"I'm on vacation. I'd appreciate it if you'd call my cell number."

Anne gave Hunter the number and he jotted it down.

As soon as the state trooper had walked away, Tom turned to Fred and offered his hand. "Thank you for your quick response. I'm Tom."

Fred took his offered hand and gave it a shake. "Everybody calls me Fred."

"So you're Fred," Tom said, a different note in his voice.

Fred looked questioningly at him but didn't say anything. Instead she turned to Anne.

"You need me, you call," she said.

"Thanks, Fred." Anne slipped Fred's parka from around her shoulders and returned it to the state trooper. "For everything."

Taking Anne's arm, Tom started to lead her toward the Porsche. But before he had gone a step, Fred's fingers were digging a groove in his biceps.

Fred's whisper was fierce against Tom's ear. "If I find you've involved Anne in any trouble, that priest's collar isn't going to protect you. I can take you, Christen, and don't think I won't."

BY THE TIME Tom drove into the church's parking lot, it was dark. He cut the engine but made no move to get out.

He had been lost in his thoughts on the silent trip home. Knowing that life was eternal helped him to accept death, but it never made it easy. Especially since he had known Lindy—and failed her.

Now the baby's future rested solely in his hands. The responsibility weighed heavy on his mind and heart.

''Words are completely inadequate at a time like this,'' Anne said from the passenger seat, ''but for what they're worth, I'm sorry about Lindy.''

Her voice was a blend of softness and sincerity.

Tom turned to her. ''Your words are worth a lot, Anne. Thanks.''

The parking lot was not well lit. The light barely penetrated the interior of the car. But Tom could feel her eyes, intent on his face.

''I'd like to ask you something,'' she said after a moment.

Tom knew she had given him time to make peace with his thoughts on their ride home. He appreciated her sensitivity. Now he braced himself for the questions that he knew would come.

''Go ahead.''

''What did Fred whisper to you back there?'' Anne asked.

Tom hadn't expected that question. He had to hold back a grin as he remembered the threat from the large state trooper. ''She just wanted to let me know that she is a very good friend of yours.''

Anne seemed puzzled at his response, but didn't pursue it further. He figured she had something else on her mind. But once again she surprised him with what it was.

''I'll see the baby inside before I walk up to the B and B.''

''It's not safe walking in the dark,'' Tom said. ''I'll drive you there when it's time.''

''What do you mean, when it's time?''

''Come on inside, Anne. We'll talk about it over pizza and rice pudding.''

She hesitated.

''You don't have to worry,'' Tom assured her. ''I didn't make either of them.''

She was still thinking about it when the baby began to cry, coming to Tom's aid once again. ''All right,'' she agreed. ''But I can't stay long.''

ANNE HAD TO ADMIT the pop-in-the-oven pizza wasn't half-bad, and the rice pudding was wonderful—a gift from a parishioner. Tom had the baby fed and changed before they retired to the study.

After settling the little boy on her lap, Anne curled her feet beneath her on the soft sofa. Tommy sat up, each of his tiny hands grasping one of Anne's fingers. She was immensely relieved to see him looking so much better than he had that morning, when she had rescued him from his inconsolable crying.

Tom took a seat across from them on a lounge chair. The room was warm as toast from the wood stove, the glow from its fire the only light. A soothing instrumental piece played on the stereo.

''If you'd like to talk about Lindy, I'm listening,'' Anne offered.

''Not necessary, but thanks,'' Tom said.

Anne had held her questions to give Tom space and time to deal with his loss. But there were some hard things to face. And she could put them off no longer.

''What are you going to do about the baby?'' she asked.

Tom knew what he had to do. He just hadn't yet worked out how he was going to do it. ''I'll take care of him.''

''Alone?'' Anne asked.

''For the present.''

''It's not going to be easy.''

He smiled. ''If that's an offer to help, it's accepted.''

Anne decided she'd better let that pass for the moment. ''Will you contact Lindy's family?''

''No.''

''Why not?''

''I don't know where they are,'' Tom said.

"Why didn't you give Hunter her last name so that he could find them?" Anne asked.

Tom's eyes rested on Tommy in Anne's lap. Nothing of what he was thinking was reflected in the calm on his face.

"I never knew Lindy's last name," he finally said.

Anne came forward in her seat. "Excuse me?"

"She never told me her last name," Tom said, his voice perfectly even.

"Are you telling me it was just a one-night stand?" Anne asked.

Tom's eyes met hers. "One-night stands are not and never have been who I am."

The sincerity on his face was hard to doubt.

"What was it then?" Anne asked. "You can tell me."

"That's just it, Anne. I can't."

The doorbell rang. Tom left the room to answer it.

Not for the first time Anne wished she knew what was going on. Why was Tom being so secretive about his relationship with Lindy?

She heard the door to the rectory open, then a woman crying. Alarmed, she rose and carried Tommy down the hall. Just inside the front door was Betty, the woman from the hospital that afternoon. She was weeping in Tom's arms.

"Joe died an hour ago, Father," Betty sobbed. "I don't know what to do."

Tom's voice was strong and gentle. "I'll drive you back and we'll take care of things together."

Anne had no idea how Tom could face another death tonight. When he turned toward her a moment later, she didn't wait for him to ask.

"Go ahead," she said. "I'll take care of Tommy."

Tom flashed her a look of thanks and was gone.

Returning to the study, she sat down and rocked the sweet little boy in her arms. "I thought being a judge had its rough times. But between you and me, Tommy, I'd take it over being a priest any day."

Five minutes later the doorbell rang again. It was beginning to look like Tom was on call twenty-four hours a day. Anne rose again, balancing Tommy on her hip as she padded to the door in her stocking feet.

Martha Dorn stood on the doorstep. She didn't seem at all surprised to see Anne. "Is Father Tom free?" Martha asked.

"He had to go out on a call," Anne explained. "Is there a message I can give him?"

"We just heard about the car accident," Martha said. "That poor young woman. Was she really the mother of that sweet baby?"

Anne was stunned at how fast the news had traveled. The FBI's information-gathering techniques did not hold a candle to those of Cooper's Corner's. When Hunter started asking questions around the village, he would quickly connect the baby with Lindy.

Anne made a mental note to warn Tom.

"I'll be happy to take care of Tommy for the next couple of hours," Martha offered.

"I've got it covered tonight, Martha," Anne said. "Will you let the other ladies know?"

Martha positively beamed. She placed her hand on Anne's arm and gave it a companionable squeeze. "I'd be delighted to, dear."

Once she'd said good-night to Martha, Anne closed the door. She returned to the study and settled back on the sofa, with Tommy in her lap. That look on Martha's face made her uncomfortable.

Her own fault, she knew. But she hoped she had stopped the flow of all the well-meaning women in the village tonight. She didn't relish getting up to answer the doorbell again, and disturbing the baby. He was snuggled and yawning in her lap.

And no wonder, after no sleep the night before. Poor little guy. She was yawning herself.

If Tom weren't back in an hour or so, she'd leave him a note and take the baby with her to Twin Oaks.

TOM WALKED INTO HIS STUDY a couple of hours later, his thoughts heavy. But when he caught sight of Anne and Tommy on his sofa, his heart lightened and his lips drew back in a smile.

Anne lay on her back, her thick bangs and eyelashes casting deep golden shadows across her cheeks, her skin as delicate as a snowflake in the dying glow of the wood stove. The baby lay on his tummy across her chest. They were both sound asleep.

Tom stood watching them silently for several minutes until their image was so firmly fixed in his mind that he knew he would never be able to enter this room again without remembering them there—and smiling.

How different things would be if only Anne were Tommy's mother!

Still, as hard as it was to accept sometimes, Tom knew everything happened the way it did for a reason. He just had to do the right thing and have faith that a higher power would take care of the rest.

He opened the door to the wood stove and added several thick logs to the burning embers, then slipped off his shoes and sat on the lounge chair across from Anne and Tommy.

The rain that had started as a sprinkle on his drive home now beat a heavy staccato on the roof. It was barely nine. There was time. He could let them sleep. When she woke, he'd drive her back to Twin Oaks. Not because he wanted to, but because it was the right thing to do.

Still, it felt right having her here. He'd never imagined himself falling for a judge. But there it was. Beyond any rational analysis and all possible doubt, he knew he was falling for Anne.

How it could work between them, he had no idea. He just knew that it was up to him to convince her that it could, and would.

Tom leaned back into the soft cushions of the chair, smiling at her lovely face as she lay sleeping so soundly across from him in the dark room. He wondered what she would say if she knew of his plans.

Probably something witty and wildly irreverent. He grinned as he stretched back in the chair and contemplated the possibility of waking her with a soft kiss. Would she return it or punch him in the jaw? Maybe he should try it and find out.

The next thing Tom knew, he was opening his eyes to morning sunlight streaming through the windows. He shot upright and looked at the sofa. It was empty.

Anne had left and taken the baby.

Disappointment whipped through him. Until he heard the shower running. Tom smiled as he made a beeline for the bedroom.

ANNE STOOD UNDER the shower, letting the spray of warm water cascade over her and the baby. Tommy giggled in her arms.

"Like that, do you?" she asked, smiling into his face.

She rocked him like a football under the spray so he could feel the tingling sensation all over his body, and he giggled some more. It was such a delightful sound that she found herself giggling, as well. She was beginning to understand why parents mimicked their babies. A baby's delight in the simplest things was contagious.

She wasn't thinking about the rocking motion drawing her breast close to the baby's mouth until Tommy suddenly clutched her breast and latched on to her nipple.

Anne stopped rocking and became still, stunned and utterly spellbound as she felt the baby become such an intimate part of her. Something so familiar and compelling it felt like a genetic memory burrowed warmly inside her. And then the sensation from the baby's eager mouth and strong suction on her sensitive nipple shot through her breast.

"Ouch. Hold on there, little fella."

Gently inserting the tip of her finger into the corner of the baby's mouth, she rubbed his gums until he released her.

Tommy was not pleased and let out a howl to let her know.

Anne rocked him against her. "I'm sorry, sweetie. Really I am. But I don't have any milk to give you."

He stopped crying after a moment and Anne switched off the shower. She gave him an extra hug before she stepped out onto the bath mat and grabbed a towel to wrap the baby in.

Tom's white terry-cloth bathrobe was hanging on the door hook. As soon as she slipped into it, she found it had that same woodsy scent as his bath soap. Of course, it dropped to her ankles and she had to roll back the long sleeves, but it would have to do. She opened the bathroom door.

And gave a sudden start when she came face-to-face with Tom.

He was leaning against the bedroom wall, blocking her way, arms crossed over his chest, looking rumpled and unshaven and just as sexy as hell.

He gave her an appreciative once-over, from the ends of her wet hair to her bare feet. "That bathrobe looks familiar."

"You have keen powers of observation," she said, determined to project a calm she did not feel. "I need a shirt."

Tom shook his head with mock concern. "First you steal my bathrobe and now you want the shirt off my back?"

"I'd prefer a clean one out of the closet, thank you. Your son spit up his breakfast all over me and himself, and it seeped through my blouse."

"I thought you weren't going to feed him," Tom stated.

He knew perfectly well she had done it for him. Annoying male satisfaction just oozed out of his pores.

"Well, since you were snoring away, someone had to," Anne said, thrusting the towel-clad baby into his arms.

As Tom took the little boy, he flashed Anne a look that made her blood very warm. She forgot all about being annoyed with him.

"He giggled when I bathed him in the shower," Anne said, aware of an odd note of pleasure in her voice as she stepped farther into the bedroom.

"Who wouldn't?" Tom replied, the devil in his eyes as he plopped down on the bed with the baby.

Nervously Anne eyed her white lace panties and bra lying on the bed next to him.

"And his rash is gone," she added, circling around the bed to make a grab for her underclothes.

Tom watched her slip them into the pocket of the bathrobe, amusement glinting in his eyes.

Summoning her most commanding tone, as she pointed toward the door. "Out of here."

"Commandeers my bathroom. Steals my clothes. And now she's kicking me out of my own bedroom," he complained dramatically as he got up and carried the baby to the door. Tom stopped in the doorway to smile back at her. "It's nice having you here, Anne."

It wasn't until he had left and closed the door behind him that Anne's heartbeat started to approximate normal again. She realized that, for the first time, the baby hadn't cried when she'd released him into his father's hands.

Maybe Tommy didn't need her anymore now that he was well. The thought should have been a welcome one. But somehow it left Anne with a hollow feeling.

She was getting too attached to the little guy. And to his father. That wasn't smart. Tom hadn't been forthcoming about his relationship to Lindy. A man who hid things he'd done was generally a man who had done the wrong things.

It was hard imagining Tom doing wrong. Mistakes, yes. He was human. Deliberate wrongs? That didn't seem possible. He had too good a heart.

Anne slipped into her bra and panties and slacks and went to check on her blouse. She had hung it in the bathroom after washing it out. She felt it and found it still quite damp. It was going to take a couple of hours to dry.

She was definitely going to have to borrow a shirt.

Tom's closet was surprisingly tidy for a bachelor, with shirts and slacks arranged in neat rows on hangers. She had found the bathroom spotless and the bedroom in perfect order, as well. An uncluttered space that spoke of an uncluttered life.

She supposed it fit a priest. But she wasn't sure if it fitted Tom. Somehow, he seemed too complicated for such simple surroundings. There were no pictures or mementos anywhere, nothing at all personal. Where was the evidence of his past?

Anne took a dress shirt out of the closet and tried it on in front of the dresser mirror. The sleeves and shirttail were so long she looked comical.

She returned it to the closet and rooted around in the dresser for something else. She found a faded blue cotton T-shirt and tried it on. It was a little too snug for comfort, so she looked for something to wear over it. After selecting a sleeveless cardigan and pulling it on, she stood in front of the mirror once again.

The cardigan hid the snugness of the T-shirt, but it came to her knees. She slipped her hands into its pockets, trying to decide if she could pull it off. And found her hand coming into contact with a folded sheet of paper. Anne drew the paper out of the pocket and unfolded it. She read the rapid scrawl.

Tom,
I think someone's following me. Have to leave Tommy with you until I can be sure. I've thought about what you said. I know you think giving him up is the right thing to do. But I can't. I love him. And I love you.
Lindy

Anne had forgotten until this moment what Keegan had said about a note being left with the baby.

Was this what Tom had been hiding? That he had been pressuring Lindy to give up Tommy? Was he so afraid for his reputation?

Anne sank down on the bed. Of course, that had to be it. A priest needed respect from his congregation if he expected to remain their spiritual leader. Without that respect, he had nothing.

Despite whatever good deeds he might have done, Tom was bound to lose the respect of his parishioners if the facts of this situation were made known. Fathering a child out of wedlock. Refusing to commit to its mother. He might even be kicked out of the priesthood altogether.

But, still, how could Tom have asked the mother of his child to give up her baby?

Disappointment settled like a black cloud over Anne's heart.

She never should have come to the church yesterday morning. She never should have held the baby. She never should have agreed to help. And she definitely never should have looked into Tom Christen's warm blue eyes.

TOM GOT A DIAPER on Tommy, fixed himself a cup of instant coffee and sat down to wait for Anne to get dressed. But drinking the coffee soon became out of the question.

Tommy appeared to have discovered that he had strength in his leg muscles, and he was trying them out for all he was worth.

Setting his coffee on the table, Tom supported the little guy while he bounced to his heart's content. Not only wasn't the child howling, he was cooing and actually seemed happy. Two major victories as far as Tom was concerned.

Even if his lap had suddenly become a trampoline.

"So, you're feeling better, are you?" Tom asked, and wondered why the pitch of his voice had suddenly ascended to that of the cooing child's.

As the baby bounced and gurgled and spit at him, Tom took the time to study his tiny features more closely.

Tommy's head was very round and his ears were small and flat. In addition to his fair hair and big blue eyes, he had light-bronze skin, high cheekbones, a slender body and long legs.

All in all, a true credit to his genes. It rather amazed Tom that so much already showed in a body so small. The baby reached out and latched on to Tom's nose. Tom smiled at the little bundle of energy in his arms.

"Was Lindy a bad mother?" Anne's voice demanded from the entrance to the kitchen.

Tom twisted his head to look at her, surprised at her unexpected entrance and her out-of-the-blue question. Then he totally lost his train of thought when he saw that she was wearing one of his shrunken T-shirts. It hugged her slender waist and the fullness of her breasts like none of her tailored blouses had.

''Was she, Tom?'' Anne persisted.

''Yes, uh, I mean no—I believe she tried to be good to Tommy,'' Tom said, forcing himself to focus on her words. ''Why do you ask?''

Anne studied him for a moment as though she were seeing him for the first time. Tom did not like the reassessing look on her face.

''It's not important,'' she said, but Tom knew with a certainty that it was.

''I meant to tell you earlier,'' Anne said as she made her way to the back door. ''Word has gotten around the village about Lindy's accident. Hunter is bound to find out about her connection to the baby when he starts asking questions.''

Tom had figured that was inevitable. But at the moment, he was more concerned with what was happening with Anne. ''Where are you going?'' he asked.

''Twin Oaks. I'm leaving by the back way so as not to attract any unnecessary attention.''

''Everyone in the village already knows that you spent the night here,'' Tom said, trying to understand her sudden eagerness to leave.

Anne halted at the back door. He could see the surprise registering on her face. And then the dismay.

''When the baby woke me up last night and I saw you were sleeping so soundly, I didn't have the heart to… I mean, it didn't occur to me that… I'm sorry.''

''Don't let it bother you, Anne.''

''I know you're concerned for your reputation.''

''The people of this village know me,'' Tom said. ''And they'll know you were here for the baby.''

''Will they?''

''Passing gossip is a way of life for them, but they mean no harm,'' Tom assured her. ''These are really nice people here in Cooper's Corner, Anne. They would far rather believe good about someone than bad.''

''Wouldn't we all.''

Her tone was so odd, so distant. He tried to see what was in her eyes, but they darted down to her watch.

''I have to go. Checkout at the B and B is in just a couple of hours. I'll send back your shirt as soon as I have it laundered.''

She was already turning the doorknob.

Tom shot to his feet. ''Anne—''

''Don't bother offering to drive me. I'm walking. Fresh air will do me good. Bye. Take care of Tommy.''

Before Tom could say another word, she was gone.

CHAPTER FIVE

"SO, HOW'S THE STEAK?" Fred asked Anne over the table at the North End Ristorante in Pittsfield.

"It's good," Anne answered distractedly as she picked at the food on her plate.

"Then why did you order the fish?" Fred asked.

Anne stared at the grilled filet of salmon Milanese on her plate as though seeing it for the first time. She knew she'd been busted.

Giving up the pretense, she put her fork down, leaned back in her chair and faced her friend. "I'm sorry, Fred. I'm not very good company tonight."

"It's that priest, isn't it," Fred said.

"What makes you say that?"

"Anne, I've met the judges, attorneys and businessmen you've casually dated and then dumped after a couple of weeks. You never looked at any of them the way you looked at that priest yesterday."

Anne was acutely uncomfortable with Fred's assessment because she was afraid it was far too accurate.

"Talk to me, Anne."

No, she couldn't discuss Tom, not even with her very good friend. "I was thinking maybe I'd go back to work tomorrow."

"Don't do it," Fred said. "You need this time off."

"Could be I'm just one of those people who can't take vacations."

Fred leaned forward. "For weeks you've been telling me how much you were looking forward to gardening and catching up on all that leisure reading you never have time for."

"Yeah, well, I tried both today, and you know what I ended up doing? Cleaning the oven."

Her friend's tone turned grave. "That priest has a lot to answer for."

Fred didn't know the half of it.

"Maybe what you need is to get away," Fred suggested.

"I got away this last weekend, remember?" Anne said, not happy for the reminder.

"I mean really get away. Hop on a plane to the Virgin Islands or Jamaica or some other warm and sunny spot."

Anne stared at the sleet slashing against the restaurant's window. The temperature had taken a sizable dip with the night storm that had rolled in. She pictured herself lying on the beach under a warm tropical sun, palm trees swaying in the breeze.

"That might not be such a bad idea," she admitted.

"You could even hook up with some muscle-bound beach boy and have a wild, one-night stand."

Although Anne tried out the fantasy, it just wouldn't gel in her mind. "I'm not much for muscle-bound beach boys or one-night stands."

"So put a priest collar on him and make it an entire weekend."

Anne looked over at the grin on Fred's face and had to smile. "That's sacrilegious."

"That's what I was going for," Fred said happily. But her face quickly sobered and her shoulders stiffened when she looked at something behind Anne.

"Well, speak of the devil."

"Good to see you, too, Fred," Tom's deep voice said. "Although I'd prefer you call me Tom."

Anne whirled around to see him standing behind her. He was wearing a blue sweater and faded jeans that hugged his lean hips. His hair was wet with rain, his mouth drawn back in an easy smile.

Damn, he looked wonderful.

"May I join you?" he asked, and then slipped onto the empty chair closest to Anne.

"How did you know where to find me?" she asked, still not quite believing he was here.

"I saw your car outside," Tom answered easily.

"Why are you here, Christen?" Fred demanded from across the table.

"I brought the note I discussed with Hunter earlier," Tom said.

"Note?" Anne repeated.

Tom's eyes met hers. "Fred didn't tell you?"

Anne looked over at her friend. "Fred?"

"You're on vacation, Anne," Fred said, shifting uneasily in her chair. "Besides, this business is getting nasty and it's not your affair."

"This is my affair," Anne said, not ungently. "Now, what's going on?"

Fred exhaled heavily as she leaned back in her chair. "Turns out a couple of hikers up at the campgrounds saw the rusty-red VW Beetle on Friday night in a high-speed chase with a green van."

"Lindy was being chased," Anne said, leaning forward in her chair. "That's why she was going so fast when she lost control of her car."

Fred nodded. "Looks that way."

"What did the driver of the green van look like?"

"Hikers couldn't say," Fred answered. "Vehicles went by too fast."

Anne turned to Tom. "You know who was chasing her?"

"No. But when Hunter called me with the news, I thought I'd better hand over the note Lindy left."

Tom drew it out of his pocket and gave it to Anne. She unfolded the paper and reread the note that she had found in the pocket of the cardigan that morning.

So, he was turning over the note to the police, despite the implications in it. Anne felt a sense of relief. At least Tom drew the line at how far he'd go to protect his reputation. On a scale of one to ten, she supposed he deserved a point or two for that.

"She suspected someone was following her," Anne said simply, not letting on that the note was not news. ''Does Hunter know about the baby?''

''He knows that Lindy left him with me,'' Tom said, and Anne could tell from the way Tom worded his reply that Hunter still didn't know that the baby was Tom's.

Anne leaned forward to place the note in Fred's waiting hand.

''Why didn't Hunter call me?'' Anne asked Tom, while Fred scanned the note's contents.

''He probably did,'' Tom said. ''Every time I've tried to call today, I've gotten the message that you were unavailable.''

Anne remembered now. She had turned off her cell phone. Tom had been there when she had given the number to Hunter, and she didn't want to chance his having remembered it. Which he obviously had.

She had told herself that she never wanted to see or talk to him again. But now that he was here, she knew that she had lied.

''Where's the baby?'' Anne asked.

''Maureen Cooper is watching him for me. Anne, I need to talk to you.''

Tom was looking at her with an intensity that unnerved her.

''Now?'' she asked, and realized her voice had cracked on the word.

Tom glanced at Fred as he got to his feet. ''No offense, Fred. But it's a private matter.''

Fred didn't look pleased. ''You haven't finished your meal, Anne.''

Tom held out his hand to Anne. ''It's important.''

Anne remembered the last time he'd held out his hand to her. And how wonderful it had felt when he clasped his strong fingers around her wrist and pulled her to her feet.

The next thing she knew, her hand was once again encased in his strong grasp and she was being drawn out of her chair. He tightly interlaced their fingers, as though worried that she might change her mind. The warm, hard feel of his palm pressing into hers shivered up her arm.

"I'll phone you later," Anne called over her shoulder to Fred as Tom pulled her toward the door of the restaurant.

Anne had left her coat in her car, and the icy sleet-soaked air assailed her the moment they stepped outside. "Where are we going?" she asked.

"Your place."

"Why?"

"Because if we stand out here much longer, we're going to get soaked."

Tom kept a firm clasp on Anne's hand as he led the way to her car and handed her inside.

"I'll follow you," he said, before closing the door. And then he just vanished into the dark, wet night.

During the drive to her town house in Pittsfield, Anne watched the Porsche's headlights in her rearview mirror. She was a jumble of unwanted emotions. She was angry with Tom for pulling her out of the restaurant. And disappointed with herself for going. And worried at how good it felt to see him again.

She didn't know how she was going to handle this private conversation he seemed determined to have with her. She wanted so badly to be indifferent to him. But she wasn't indifferent.

Every time she had tried to concentrate on reading or gardening that day, images of him had crept in to steal away her thoughts. The shape of his mouth, his smile, the blue of his eyes, the deep timbre of his voice, the way he walked with such sinuous grace. She hadn't been able to concentrate on anything but him.

Smart women did not make stupid mistakes about men. And damn it, she was a smart woman. It was time she started acting like one.

She pulled into her garage and turned off the engine. She was just about to open the driver's door when Tom appeared beside the car and opened it for her. Looking up at him, she wondered how he'd had time to park his car and make it here so quickly.

Tom held out his hand to her once again. This time, however, she didn't take it. She was going to keep her distance from this guy if it was the last thing she did. She got out of the car by herself and led the way into the house.

Anne entered her kitchen, knowing Tom was just behind her. She dropped her shoulder bag and keys on the counter and headed for the living room, the most formal space in her home. She switched on a table lamp and rested her arm across the white marble mantel over the fireplace. It was her intention to keep this conversation short. She waited for him to begin.

He stood in the middle of the room. His eyes roamed over the gleaming green marble floor, the profusion of healthy houseplants that adorned the windowsills and wicker planters, the light green and gold cushions of the softly tailored furniture, the bright splashes of colorful tulips in the paintings on the walls.

Tom's resulting smile was one of appreciation. "It's warm and bright and very much you."

Anne didn't want to be pleased with his approval of her home or her, but she was.

His eyes searched hers. "Why did you leave so abruptly this morning?"

Careful to project nothing but an impersonal tone, she replied, "I said goodbye."

"You walked up to the B and B, got in your car and just drove off," Tom said. "Maureen told me you didn't even come inside, but called her from your cell phone to ask her to pack up your things and hold your bags."

"I don't see why it's any of your—"

"Anne, what's wrong?"

Tom's normally calm features were creased with concern. His hands, usually relaxed by his sides, were rustling against his jeans. There was a palpable tension in him that Anne had never seen before. She felt the pressure in the room building, and it took an effort of will to remain calm.

"Tommy's fine now. You don't need me."

He took a step toward her, his eyes like blue lasers, boring into her. "That's not why you left."

Anne felt the mantel at her back. She had the overwhelming

sense of being trapped. Not just physically, but emotionally. She needed to vent. And she needed to know.

"Why were you pressuring Lindy to give up your child?" she asked.

Tom stared at her, confusion in his eyes. When it cleared, he took another step toward her. "You found the note from Lindy this morning. And you left because the message in it hurt you."

Oh, no. He was not going to get her to admit that. Anne knew she couldn't let him see how much her disappointment in him had hurt her.

Once men knew you cared, they did their worst damage.

"You told me a baby belonged with its mother, remember?" Anne challenged.

"I remember."

"But you didn't mean it. You didn't want Lindy to keep Tommy."

"You don't understand."

"You told me she was a good mother."

"That wasn't it."

"Then what was it?"

"All I can tell you is that I wanted what was best for Lindy and the baby."

"And for your reputation?"

He let out a heavy sigh. "So that's what you think."

"The facts are rather hard to ignore. Look, I don't want to judge you, but—"

"But you are," he interrupted.

"If I'm wrong, then tell me where I'm wrong."

"I'm not able to."

"You expect me to take you at your word without any explanation?" Anne demanded.

"I don't expect you to, Anne. I'm asking you to."

"Why?"

Tom's silence had an edge to it, as though it were filled with a savage patience as he searched for the right words. "Anne, the things that are worth the most in this life are those that command the deepest faith from us and for which we have no explanations.''

Anne turned toward the mantel and fingered a picture of her that sat there. She was sixteen, dressed for a dance, excited, eager, innocent. Those days were long gone.

''When I was twenty I had faith in the long, lanky cowboy to whom I was engaged,'' she said. ''He told me I was the only woman in the world. He turned out to have a girl at every rodeo. When I was twenty-eight I married a Boston homicide detective and had faith in his promise to forsake all others until death do us part. Three years later I discovered he had a girlfriend on the side.'' Anne turned around to face Tom and found him standing directly in front of her. ''I don't put my faith in men anymore.''

''I'm not just a man, Anne. I'm a priest. I stand by my vows.''

''What exactly does that mean?''

Tom stepped closer. He cupped her shoulders, holding her lightly, as though she were a priceless piece of porcelain. Anne felt the sudden, gentle heat of his hands.

''It means I can't always tell you everything you may want to know,'' Tom said. ''But you can have faith in what I do tell you.''

Anne looked up into his eyes. They were so deep, so blue, so warm. ''What are you telling me?''

''This,'' Tom said as he slowly bent his head to hers.

The initial touch of his lips was nothing more than an intriguing brush of warmth, but it sent a delicious shiver into Anne's breasts right down through her thighs. When the smooth heat of his mouth pressed delicately against hers, Anne felt the leap of her pulse.

Then his mouth settled firmly against hers with a soft, sweet hunger that poured through her core, and her senses went wild.

His was a tender sensuality, exquisite in its intensity, unlike anything she had ever known. Nerve endings she had no idea she possessed shot vividly to life. The heat from his mouth, the warmth of his breath sent her heart dancing against her ribs.

Anne's lips parted of their own accord as she lifted her mouth to his for more. The tip of his tongue slowly caressed the sensitive edges of her parted lips over and over again until they hummed with pleasure. His tongue dipped into her heated softness, tasting her, tantalizing her.

Her knees grew weak as she breathed out his name, an exhalation of pure pleasure. "Tom..."

"That's how I've wanted you to say my name." His voice was deep and throaty and delicious.

His mouth pressed firmly against hers. He tasted smooth and hot, like a night of sweet, dark passion. The intensity of her response rippled inside her. She was suddenly, acutely aware of a secret well of elemental hunger raging within her core.

What this man could say with just a kiss was incredible. Anne knew then that she had wasted her time with cowboys and cops. It was priests who knew how to kiss!

She wanted more of him. A lot more. She leaned forward, intending to have it.

But his mouth drew back from hers and the warmth went with him. Anne opened her eyes and found she was looking directly into his. A blaze of sheer blue heat.

Both of Tom's strong hands clutched her shoulders now as if he was holding on to a lifeline. His voice was a velvet whisper, with nothing of its normal deep strength. "This is how I feel about you."

His words seared her aching insides. Anne was shaken, not just physically but emotionally. She wanted him. And he knew it. What's more, he wanted her. It blazed in his eyes.

"Do you understand what I'm telling you?" he asked, his breath coming out in a strangled sigh.

Anne was beginning to. He had kissed her to prove to her that despite the strength of his desires, he had control over them. He would not take her, no matter how easy it would be. She could trust him.

Anne realized then that she was shaking. She groped for the back of the couch.

Tom released her shoulders and stepped back. Anne clutched the fabric as she sank onto the cushions. Tom sat beside her, but did not touch her.

"Dear heavens, can all priests kiss like that?" she asked when she had regained a sufficient lungful of air.

"Don't know," Tom said, his own breath not quite even. "Haven't kissed any."

She glanced up at him. He might be a priest, but that self-satisfied grin pulling back his lips was all man.

"My weakened condition might have a lot to do with what just happened," Anne said, determined to wipe that grin off his face.

"Weakened condition?" Tom repeated with a note of genuine concern.

"I didn't have a chance to eat, remember?"

Tom smiled as he rose to his feet and held out his hand. "Then the very least I can do is take you out to dinner."

She laid her palm on his. It was warm and strong and felt so right against her own. He pulled her to her feet in one powerful, effortless move that made her legs grow weak again.

"On second thought," she said, "let's see what I have in the kitchen."

TOM SAT ON A BAR STOOL at the center island of Anne's mint-green and cream kitchen and watched her toss a salad of romaine and baby lettuce, sliced apples, chopped tomatoes and hazelnuts, then top it off with a generous shower of finely shredded cheddar cheese.

Her movements were graceful and sure. The overhead light played on the fiery copper strands of her hair, caressed the snow white of her skin. He studied the delicate curve of her cheek and chin, the generous line of her mouth, the full curves of her breasts, the slender turn of her waist.

She was so lovely to look at, she took his breath away. There had been times during the day when he'd wondered whether he'd ever see her again. Even tonight when he'd finally found her at the restaurant, he hadn't been sure they could work out whatever it was that had driven her away that morning.

They probably wouldn't have if he hadn't kissed her.

The irony of it wasn't lost on Tom. He was a man who had

disciplined himself to use the power of words in place of physical displays, only to find himself in a situation where he could not speak. He could only show her how he felt.

Her response had been heaven. It had taken every ounce of his self-control to back away and prove to her that he could be trusted.

He knew it was asking a lot. She had given her trust twice before to men and been burned. But Tom needed her to trust him.

As much as he tried to tell her and show her, he still wasn't convinced that she understood what it meant for him to be a priest. She was a judge, used to weighing all the evidence before making a decision. He would never be able to give her all the evidence.

If Anne did not have faith in him without evidence, they would have no future.

Tom wrestled with that plaguing thought as he thoroughly enjoyed the dinner she prepared. He couldn't remember the last time he'd eaten. He was as hungry as she was. The salad was excellent, as were the roast chicken with raisin sauce and the freshly baked buttermilk rolls.

"And she cooks, too," Tom said appreciatively after swallowing the last bite.

Anne was sitting on the bar stool next to him, sipping her after-dinner coffee. "No, what my mom does is cook," she corrected. "Apple pies and bread from scratch. What I do is follow a few favorite recipes."

"What I do is open the freezer compartment," Tom admitted. He took a swallow of his own coffee. It was as delicious as the meal. "Your mom is a homemaker?"

"All her life. Which is why she doesn't really understand this need I have for my work. Still, she accepts me as I am."

"Then she is special," Tom said. "Often the hardest thing to do is accept people as they are, not as you want them to be. What about your dad?"

"He doesn't care much what I do."

Tom heard an unusual note in Anne's voice. "You don't get along with your dad?"

"We've grown apart a lot in the last year."

Tom wondered what she was thinking. Her eyes, so very clear and openly expressive at times, had begun to cloud over.

"You don't plan on telling Hunter that Tommy is yours, do you?" she asked.

"Not if I can help it."

"Now that Lindy is dead, Hunter's going to expect you to turn the baby over to Child Care Services."

"Any suggestions?" Tom asked.

She gave it a moment of thought. "Child Care Services just wants what's best for him. I'll convince them that you'll provide a good foster home for Tommy until other arrangements can be made. Is that what you want?"

"It would help a lot. Thanks, Anne."

She stared at the cup in her hands. "Hunter would have sent someone to pick up Lindy's note, or you could have dropped it at his home in Cooper's Corner. You didn't have to deliver it to Fred."

"If I hadn't insisted, I wouldn't have had an excuse to see you."

Her eyes met his and a soft smile curved her lips. "How *did* you find me at the restaurant?"

"I overheard you making plans for dinner with Fred."

"You mean you eavesdropped on my conversation."

"Next time I'd appreciate it if you'd mention the restaurant," Tom said with a note of feigned complaint. "I had to check out a dozen others before I finally saw your car in the parking lot at the North End Ristorante."

Anne was trying to look peeved, but she couldn't quite pull it off. "I don't think Fred's going to forgive you for dragging me out of there. It was my turn to pick up the check."

"I tried to find you sooner, but not knowing your address was a problem," Tom said. "And then there were the funeral services for Joe this afternoon."

"Oh," Anne said. "So soon. I would have been there if I'd known."

Tom put his hand over hers. Her skin was soft and warm and matched the expression in her eyes. She had an extremely kind heart beneath that very tough air of authority she wore so well. He found the combination irresistible. A little too irresistible at the moment. He drew his hand away.

"Mind if I use your telephone?" he asked.

Anne slipped off her bar stool to reach the portable phone sitting on the kitchen counter. "You don't carry a cell phone, do you?"

"They always seem to intrude at the wrong moment."

She passed the phone to Tom, but before he made his call, he felt he'd better explain. "When I handed Tommy to Maureen this evening to come look for you, he started to cry."

Anne's eyes widened in immediate concern. "Why didn't you bring him?"

"Too damp and cold. I didn't want to risk his getting another virus."

He punched in the number for Twin Oaks. Clint Cooper answered and informed him that his concern wasn't misplaced. Tommy had been crying steadily since Tom left him several hours before. Tom thanked Clint and hung up the phone, giving Anne the report.

"He must know you're his father now, Tom. Just like Dr. Dorn said. When a baby his age gets used to being with his parents, he has difficulty accepting care from strangers."

"Except he took to you the first time you held him," Tom said.

"It's strange, isn't it?"

"Not to me," Tom said. "His heart is in tune with yours."

"And how do you explain that?"

"I don't try to explain miracles," Tom admitted as he brushed aside a silken strand of copper hair from her cheek. "I just know them when I see them."

A small smile lifted the corners of Anne's lips. "I'll walk you to the door."

When they got there, Tom turned to her and gently cupped her shoulders. "Come see me tomorrow?"

She nodded. "After I talk with Child Care Services."

"Don't turn off your cell phone again, Anne. I'd rather not go through another day like today."

He brushed his mouth lightly across hers, needing to taste her sweetness one more time. The soft sigh of surrender on her parting lips licked flames clear through to his solar plexus. He'd had no idea a woman's sigh could do that to him. He was going to have to drive home with the windows open and the air conditioner on in thirty-degree weather.

For the tenth time that night, Tom reminded himself he was stronger than his urges, then he pulled back from her warmth and forced himself to leave.

"ARE YOU GOING TO BE ABLE to trace the green van that was chasing her?" Maureen asked Scott Hunter as she spoke to him from the private phone in her office.

"Pretty slim chance," Hunter said. "The hikers only got a quick look at both vehicles."

"And you still don't know who she was?" Maureen asked.

"Lindy's the only name the priest could give me—or would give me. We've taken her prints and put them through the system. They're performing the autopsy now. The accident investigation team is at the site. We should have some answers soon."

"Sounds like you have everything in control," Maureen said, knowing from her previous experience as a New York detective that Scott was right on top of things.

"Maureen, I don't think this woman's death has anything to do with Nevil's threat against you, but I'll follow up every lead."

When Maureen was with the NYPD, she had helped to send murderer Carl Nevil to prison. His brother Owen had been out for revenge ever since. Scott Hunter was one of the few people in Cooper's Corner who knew of the man's attempts on her life. Scott was a good ally and friend.

"I appreciate your keeping me in the loop, Scott."

"Truth is, I had an ulterior motive for calling," Hunter admitted. "How well do you know Tom Christen?"

"Pretty well. He arrived here around the time Clint and I did. Why do you ask?"

"He knows something about this dead woman he's not telling me."

"You sure?"

"Yeah. He pulled his priest thing on me."

"Well, he is a priest, Scott. He's got rules to follow, too."

"And I've got what could be a murder here. Maureen, if you have any influence with the guy—"

"Anne Vandree is who you should be talking to if you want someone with influence over our Father Tom. He's asked me about her a couple of times now. Unless I miss my guess, he's got a thing for our pretty judge."

"She'll be a big help," Hunter said sarcastically. "She didn't even tell me the kid she was holding at the crash site was the dead woman's."

"She didn't?" Maureen smiled. "Well, well. That's not like our proper judge at all. And just three days ago Anne was such a nonbeliever in that love stuff. How the mighty have fallen."

"Excuse me for interrupting your glee over the matchmaking, but I have an investigation going on here and I could use some help. You're friends with Anne. Why don't you try talking to her?"

"Okay," Maureen agreed. "But I can't promise it'll help. Last time I attempted to broach the subject of Father Tom with Anne, she was suddenly off talking about the beautiful scenery."

"Still, it can't hurt to try. I'll call you as soon as I have any news. And Maureen?"

"Yes?"

"Watch your back. Even if this investigation has nothing to do with him, that bastard Nevil is out there somewhere. We don't want any more accidents."

IT WAS LATE Tuesday morning when Anne arrived at the Church of the Good Shepherd. She found Tom in the parish hall, rehearsing a choir made up of preteens. The singing sounded slightly off-key, as if the voices of the boys hitting the fragile high notes were changing right in the middle of the hymn.

And yet it was a happy sound, as exuberant as their youth, full of hope and untapped resources. Anne sat on a chair in the back, enjoying their energy, as they finished the hymn.

Tom told them they did great with such enthusiasm that even the hardest nut among them was smiling. He got them to promise to continue practicing before meeting again the next week, then dismissed them to go back to school. The kids took off at a run, stampeding out the door like a herd of rhinoceroses.

As Tom turned, Anne saw Tommy in a baby holder wrapped around his chest. The little boy was sound asleep. Anne shook her head, amazed that the baby could sleep through both the choir rehearsal and the stampede.

Then she remembered this was the child who slept through the noise of car engines and native drumbeats.

Tom smiled as he saw her and quickly closed the distance between them.

Something squeezed inside Anne's chest at the sight of his smile. All night long she had tossed and turned, reliving his incredible kiss. Yet she didn't feel at all tired today. She felt alive—more alive than she had felt in a very long time.

When Tom reached her, he brushed a kiss against her hair. "You smell wonderful."

Her silly heart flip-flopped in her chest.

"Sorry I'm late," Anne said, knowing she needed to get a grip and fast. She was way too old and experienced to be getting this soft and mushy over a man. "After squaring things with the child care people, I had to go to court to have my clerk draw up the papers. Here's your official custody order for Tommy. You sign at the bottom."

Tom took the papers she held out and flashed her a smile that melted the polish off her toenails. He rested his arm lightly across her shoulders.

"I have a baptism now. Come with me?"

"Sure," she said, perfectly aware that he could have asked

her to a funeral and she would have skipped to the site singing. As long as he was going to be there.

You're getting carried away. Don't be a fool. It was that wise voice inside her. But Anne just didn't feel like listening to it today.

She sat with Tommy on her lap while Tom performed the ceremony. The smiling new mother held her tiny baby girl, just a fragile swirl of dark hair surrounded by a froth of pink dress. The father stood beside them, a look of pride on his face that Anne hadn't seen in a long time on someone that young.

The rain came down in torrents outside, but inside the church it was calm and quiet. Soft light poured through the tall, stained-glass windows. Dark pools filled the corners. Candlelight warmed the baptismal font, and Tom's rich voice recited the ceremonial words as he anointed the baby's head with sparkling drops of water.

Anne was filled with a sense of peace as she witnessed this ancient ceremony. These were the scenes she would never see in her job as a judge. The joy of exuberant preteen singing. The faces of happy parents as they gave thanks for the precious life they had brought into the world.

And the look in Tom's eyes, so calm, content and full of purpose.

I'm not just a man, Anne. I'm a priest.

And this was part of his being a priest. This celebration of life—and gratitude for it.

The cell phone in her shoulder bag rang, an ugly cacophony in the presence of such peace. Anne was beginning to understand what Tom meant about intrusions. She cradled Tommy in her arms as she hurried into the parish hall to take the call.

"It's Fred," her friend's voice said after Anne answered.

"Hi, Fred. I'm sorry about last night. I—"

"Anne, forget about last night. I have something to show you. Can you come down to the station?"

"Now?" Anne asked, not missing the very serious tone of her friend's voice.

"Right now, Anne."

She knew that Fred wouldn't be so insistent unless it was something really important.

"Okay," she said. "I'll be there as soon as I can."

"Good. And, Anne, come alone."

Before she could ask why, Anne heard a loud click, then the dial tone.

CHAPTER SIX

"IF HUNTER FOUND OUT I was sharing this with you, he'd have my hide," Fred told Anne. "He issued us a warning this morning. No one is to discuss this case. Nothing about that green van chasing her has been given to the press."

They were at the Cheshire State Troopers Barracks in a back office with the door closed and locked. Fred had hustled Anne inside the moment she had arrived.

"Why the secrecy?" Anne asked.

"Hunter thinks it could be tied to one of his ongoing investigations. He always gets this way when a case has even the slightest connection to Cooper's Corner. He's sent all the physical evidence to the crime lab in Sudbury."

"You said over the phone you had something to show me?" Anne asked.

"First, you need to read the autopsy report," Fred said, handing it to Anne across the desk. "We have to get through these quickly. I only have a few minutes before I have to get them back into the file."

Anne took the report from Fred's hands and scanned the entries. "Lindy died from massive head trauma," she murmured. "Not surprising, from what you described of the accident."

"Keep going," Fred said.

Anne nodded and bent over the report. The notations on the autopsy record confirmed that Lindy had recently given birth. When Anne looked at the statistics and discovered that the dead woman had been five-eight and yet weighed only a hundred and ten pounds, it didn't surprise her to also read that Lindy had very little breast milk.

But something else did surprise Anne. She read that information aloud.

''Evidence of several old fractures on her ribs, two on her arms, several on both legs, one to her collarbone, and an old concussion to the right temporal lobe. Fred, this sounds like an abused woman.''

''Make that girl and you've got it right,'' Fred said.

''Girl?'' Anne repeated as her head shot up.

Fred slipped another document across the table toward Anne. ''She was Lindy Olson, a sixteen-year-old Boston runaway. Her mother reported her missing eighteen months ago, when she was only fourteen and a half. Told the police she didn't care if the brat ever came home. Claimed she was nothing but trouble.''

Anne looked at the missing person's report in her hands, at the picture of the tall, slim young girl with the lovely heart-shaped face, long curly red hair and sad dark eyes. Sorrow surged through her, laced with sharp anger. ''No wonder Lindy ran away. What kind of mother could feel that way about her own child?''

''The kind that never should have been a mother,'' Fred said. ''She's as worthless as the bastard that got the kid pregnant.''

The bastard that got the kid pregnant!

Anne had been so caught up in the other revelations that she had momentarily missed that message entirely. Now the full force of what she had just learned hit her—and hit her hard.

''Anne?'' Fred's voice seemed to come from far away. ''Anne, what's wrong?''

It was only through a supreme effort of will that she forced herself to face her friend. ''I have to go.''

''You're as white as a sheet.''

''I...I'm suddenly not feeling too well.''

Pushing herself to her feet, she walked stiff-legged toward the door. Fred was at her side in an instant, grabbing her arm. ''Anne, sit down before you fall down.''

Anne forced herself to take a deep breath. She placed her hand on Fred's arm. ''No, all I need is a little air. You'd best get those reports back before they're missed. I'll call you later.''

As she fled the brick building, Anne could feel Fred's eyes on her. She didn't bother to open her umbrella as she sloshed through the slanting gray rain toward her car in the parking lot. She pulled open the Camry's door, slid behind the wheel and slammed the door shut. But when she tried to put the key into the ignition, her hand was shaking so badly she couldn't.

She dropped the key on the seat and rested her wet head against the steering wheel. As she shut her eyes against the rain battering the windshield, she wished she could shut out the battering pain of her thoughts.

So this was what Tom had been hiding. Dear God.

An hour ago the world had been such a clean, sweet place—full of children's happy voices and parental pride and a man she had begun to believe in.

Now it felt as though lice were crawling on her very soul.

She never would have imagined this of Tom. Never. She thought she had seen inside him these last few days, and what she had seen was a man of heart and kindness. Even now, despite the evidence Fred had shown her, a part of Anne still couldn't accept that Tom would do such a thing.

His words came back to her, kept repeating over and over in her mind. *I'm not just a man, Anne. I'm a priest. I stand by my vows.*

Anne vividly remembered his kiss of the night before. He had wanted her. And he had to have known from her response that she had been willing. But he had restrained himself. He had shown her he could be trusted. Could the man he'd revealed himself to be last night really have impregnated a fifteen-year-old girl?

It just didn't make sense. Anne knew she was missing something here—something critical. She had to find out what it was. And there was only one person with the answer.

Straightening in her seat, she picked up her key and inserted it into the ignition.

TOM LOOKED AT THE CLOCK for the third time in the last ten minutes. It had been nearly two hours since Anne's abrupt departure. The only thing she had told him was that she had to see Fred.

With decreasing success he tried to keep his mind on his counseling session with a young couple who wanted to be married. They were both nineteen, still living with their parents. The husband-to-be planned to attend college in the fall but had no idea what he wanted to major in. His intended bride was going to get a job if she could find one she liked. They didn't want to start a family for at least five years, yet neither had given any thought to birth control. They were another tragic divorce statistic in the making if he didn't get them to see how unprepared they were for marriage.

When Tom glanced out the window and saw Anne's silver Camry pull into the church's parking lot, he breathed a sigh of relief.

Quickly he scooted the young couple out the back door, telling them to return only after they had completed the household financial report and birth control plan he'd given them as homework.

Tom opened the front door before Anne had a chance to ring the bell.

"We need to talk," she said as she moved past him into the room. The sharpness of her voice could have cracked a Brazil nut.

Every muscle in his body tensed. Tommy started to fuss in the baby sling that kept him snug against Tom's chest.

"Then we'd best do it in the kitchen so I can feed the baby," Tom said, leading the way.

Anne stood by the sink, as silent as stone, while Tom prepared the formula and Tommy's fussing escalated into a cry. Tom knew that whatever Anne had learned from Fred was at the root of this dramatic change in her. He had a pretty good idea what it was.

Tommy refused the nipple several times before Tom got him to take it. When the baby finally settled down to feed, Tom looked up from his seat at the table and waited for Anne to begin.

Her face had become a stoic mask, her eyes chips of gray slate. "Did you know Lindy had a birthday last week?" she asked.

Tom shook his head and waited.

"She was sixteen," Anne said, and the words hung in the air like a rope around his neck.

Tom exhaled a heavy breath. "I never knew how old she was."

"Is that supposed to be some kind of excuse?" Anne's voice was suddenly so cold—so very, very cold.

"No. Just a statement of fact. Please sit down, Anne."

"I'll remain standing, thank you."

"Will you listen to what I have to say?"

"If I weren't willing to listen, you'd be talking to Scott Hunter right now."

So she was here to give him a chance to explain, despite what she had learned and what she must think of him. That had taken some faith on her part. Hope filled Tom's heart—the first hope he had felt since opening the door a few minutes before.

Tommy stopped feeding, thrust the bottle aside and began to cry. Tom burped him and the little formula he had consumed came right up.

The baby had been difficult ever since Tom had picked him up from Maureen Cooper the night before—almost as though he was still mad at Tom for leaving him for those few hours. Now his crying rapidly escalated into a scream.

"Let me try," Anne offered, stepping forward.

Tom handed her the baby and she snuggled him gently against her chest. Tommy's cries subsided. He stared up at her, his big blue eyes wide. Anne smiled at him and slipped onto a nearby chair. "Give me the bottle," she said, her voice suddenly soft as she held out her hand, continuing to smile down at the baby.

When Tom passed the bottle to her and she offered it to the baby, Tommy took it without hesitation. As Tom watched her work her magic with the child, he felt an ache to hold them both within his arms.

"I believe you were about to explain yourself," Anne said, still not looking at him.

Tom knew she was keeping her voice soft for the baby's sake. He got up and poured himself a cup of instant coffee. It tasted terrible and scalded his tongue. But it was strong and wet, and his mouth suddenly felt very dry.

"It's hard to know where to start," Tom said.

"The beginning," Anne responded softly, still looking at the child.

"I received my religious education at the General Theological Seminary in New York City," Tom began. "My first assignment was a parish in Boston."

He could see it now in his mind's eye, the transition from the quiet Chelsea oasis of cloistered lawns and flower gardens within redbrick buildings to the bustling working-class district of Boston teeming with traffic and the loud cacophony of all its untidy humanity.

"The rector of the parish was a scholarly man and a masterful fund-raiser," Tom said. "He set out to teach me all he knew. But it was the homeless, the drug addicts, the prostitutes, the mentally ill—society's shamed and discarded, who showed up to eat the food we set out each day in the soup kitchen—who taught me the most. From them I learned the power of compassion."

Anne heard Tom's sincere gratitude for those lessons woven deep within his words. Her eyes rose to his.

"Then, one day, a boy—no more than eleven—stood in line with the rest," Tom said. "The scared look in his eyes immediately told me he was a runaway."

He paused. Even now he could still see the boy's face clearly—too clearly.

"I sat with him while he ate, asked him if I could help," Tom continued. "He was leery at first. After a while he relaxed a bit and told me his name was Kyle. He also told me that no matter what I said or did, he wasn't going home."

"Why?" Anne asked.

''There were cigarette burns on his arms. Someone at home was using him as an ashtray.''

Tom saw the sharp sadness flash through Anne's eyes. ''What did you do?'' she asked.

''I took Kyle home with me. Eventually, he told me the whole story. I got his okay to report his abusive stepfather to the police. I promised Kyle they'd take the guy away. The police arrested the stepfather. Kyle's mother came to the church to pick him up, all teary-eyed and thankful to have her son safely back.''

''So it ended well,'' Anne said.

''No, his stepfather made bail and beat Kyle to death with a baseball bat.''

Anne flinched.

''The next runaway who came to the soup kitchen was a girl of thirteen,'' Tom said. ''Her pimp dropped her off.''

He went on to describe the girl with the big brown eyes and bruises covering both her arms. It hadn't been easy for Tom to win her trust. When he heard about her nightmare of a childhood, it chilled his heart. He worked hard to convince her that she had options other than prostitution. He promised he would see her safely to a state-run boardinghouse, and eventually she let him take her there. A week later Tom found out that she'd died from a drug overdose. The drugs had been supplied by another girl at the boardinghouse.

A shudder ran through Anne's shoulders as she heard the fate of the girl. Tom hadn't wanted to shock her or cause her pain, but he was afraid he had just done both.

''Anne, I'm only telling you about these children in order to explain why I wasn't so eager to return the next runaways I found to their families or to the state.''

Anne nodded but said nothing.

''It seemed like every other week after that, I'd see a new one in the soup kitchen,'' he continued. ''I wanted to find a safe place for them to stay. So I convinced one of my parishioners to donate an old warehouse. It wasn't much to look at but it had light, heat and plumbing.''

Tom's shelter for runaways gradually took shape in Anne's

mind as he described how he and the kids had haunted garage sales and convinced people to donate discarded appliances and furniture and even power tools. He'd taught the runaways basic carpentry skills, and in no time they had built separate bedrooms for themselves. Their sense of pride in what they had accomplished transformed them, as well as their living space. The five runaways he began with soon burgeoned into twenty-two.

"I promised them that if they kept away from drugs, alcohol, gangs and prostitution, they were welcome," Tom said. "I even got my parishioners to employ them in odd jobs so they'd have a little pocket money."

"You weren't afraid they'd use it to buy drugs?" Anne asked.

"Having a job where they learned responsibility and earned money from honest labor was emancipating for them—and a strong contributor to a sense of self-worth. A kid needs a strong sense of self-worth to stay away from drugs."

"What about school?" Anne pressed.

"I did some basic remedial math and reading with the ones who needed it, but mostly what the kids wanted and needed was the sense of belonging they got when we sat down at the table together every night."

"Like a family," Anne said, not finding it difficult to picture Tom sitting at a table with a bunch of smiling kids.

After hearing the experiences of their fellow runaways, some had realized they didn't have it so bad, after all, and had asked him to take them home. He was happy to do it. But for the remainder, going home would never be an option. They weren't wanted there and they knew it.

"Did you consider that these kids could have been placed in foster homes?" Anne asked.

"They were emotionally and physically abused preteens and teens with attitudes. Anne, we both know that those kinds of kids are virtually impossible to place."

She agreed with a troubled nod.

Anne's phone rang and Tom reached into her bag and retrieved it for her. He took Tommy out of her arms as he handed her the phone.

The baby had finished feeding, so Tom flipped a fresh towel over his shoulder and proceeded to burp him. He spit up less this time. Anne told Maureen Cooper that she was in the middle of something and would have to call her back.

"Where does Lindy fit into all this?" she asked as she closed the cell phone.

Ah, Lindy. Tom held the baby with one hand as he chugged down the last of the bitter tasting coffee with the other. Compared with his thoughts it was sweet. He set his cup on the counter.

"Lindy showed up at the soup kitchen one afternoon. She wore a torn, skimpy outfit and was limping. One of the women parishioners who prepared the food asked Lindy if her pimp had hurt her. When I saw the shocked look on Lindy's face, I knew that despite her appearance, she wasn't a prostitute."

Tom had talked to Lindy for hours as that snowy afternoon turned into evening. He'd tried to convince her she'd be safe at his shelter. But Lindy was very distrustful, even more so than the other runaways he'd met. She finally agreed to go because it was so bitterly cold out and her only other option was sleeping on the street.

Slipping onto the kitchen chair next to Anne, Tom settled the baby against his shoulder. "The other girls at the shelter later told me that Lindy had been beaten and kicked out of the house by her mother. The mother's latest boyfriend was showing too much interest in Lindy and the mother was jealous."

"Lindy told them that?" Anne asked.

"Apparently. She never said a word to me about her past then or later."

Anne learned from Tom that it had taken two weeks at the shelter before Lindy started to relax and realize she was safe. Tom was trying to figure out which one of his parishioners he could approach to get her a job when the parish computer went into meltdown. Without a word, Lindy sat down at the terminal and fixed it.

"She must have been trained in computers," Anne said.

"She told me she had taken a couple of classes," Tom said. "But I also think she just had a natural talent."

Tom put her to work in the parish office. In no time at all she had transferred all of the parish's paper records to the computer database, was zipping out letters and answering the telephone like a pro.

"As the months went by, I didn't know how I had ever done without her," Tom admitted. "I said those very words to her. Only too late did I realize my mistake."

"Mistake?" Anne repeated.

"Lindy was very leery of men. That was why it had been so difficult for me to convince her she'd be safe at the shelter. It didn't take much imagination to realize she'd been sexually abused. But it didn't occur to me that being kind to Lindy would be misinterpreted."

"She thought you were in love with her," Anne guessed.

"And she thought she was in love with me."

"When did you find out?" Anne asked.

"She came into my office one afternoon and started to take off her clothes. I asked her to stop. When she told me she loved me and wanted me, I tried to explain to her that what she was feeling was gratitude—not love. When she persisted, I had no option but to leave the office."

"You left?"

"Yes, Anne. I realized then that I had been wrong to let her work at the parish." Tom exhaled heavily. "I should have realized it from the first."

Anne heard the deep sadness in Tom's voice as he described his conversation with Lindy the next day. He had tried to explain to her that he respected her too much to touch her in any way that would be improper. He told her he'd found her another job, away from the parish house. But Lindy didn't want the other job. She begged him to let her stay with him. When Tom explained that it wouldn't be possible, she became upset. Before she stalked out of the parish house, she telephoned the bishop and told him about Tom's shelter for runaways.

"You never told your bishop about the shelter?" Anne asked.

''I knew neither he nor the rector would approve. When the bishop found out that I was taking care of homeless, underage kids, he demanded I close the shelter at once and turn the children over to the proper authorities.''

''Did you?'' Anne asked when Tom paused.

''I tried to convince him that the only real chance for the kids was the support of adults who cared.''

Anne knew what Tom would tell her next—that his plea had fallen on deaf ears. The bishop could not condone violating the law under any circumstances. He'd given Tom twenty-four hours to close the shelter. Tom went to talk with the kids. He hoped to get some of his parishioners to take them in, but Lindy had gotten there first and convinced them that Tom was turning them over to Child Care Services. They had vanished into the wind.

''I'm confused why Lindy would turn on other runaways that way,'' Anne said after a moment.

''I had hurt her,'' Tom said. ''She was trying to hurt me back by sabotaging what she knew I cared about—providing the kids with a family.''

''Did you ever see them again?'' Anne asked.

''No. Lindy had spread the word on the street. None of the kids even came back to the soup kitchen. That's why when the bishop asked me to interview for the vacancy at the Church of the Good Shepherd in Cooper's Corner, I agreed.''

''You felt you had failed in Boston.''

''No, Anne, I *knew* I had failed in Boston. I told the search committee here all about the illegal shelter I had run for the homeless kids. And how I had let the kids down. The committee conferred quietly for a few minutes before their chairman, Felix Dorn, stood up, looked me right in the eye and said that the Berkshire Hills were full of survivors looking for a fresh start. And if I would like to join them, they would be proud to have me as their priest. That was just over a year ago.''

''And what of Lindy?'' Anne asked.

''I did not see Lindy again until she presented Tommy to me for baptism last Friday afternoon.''

''Are you telling me you didn't impregnate her?''

"That's exactly what I'm telling you."

Anne's face was suddenly full of light. Tom didn't think he had ever seen anything more beautiful than her smile of relief.

"I could kill you for lying to me before," she said.

"Anne, I've never lied to you."

"Of course you did. You told me you were Tommy's father."

Tom took a deep breath and slowly let it out. "I am."

The smile washed off Anne's lips like water. "Are you playing word games with me?"

"No, Anne. I'm telling you the truth. I will always tell you the truth."

"Well, if Lindy wasn't Tommy's mother, who is?"

"There are some things that I am not able to discuss."

"What's to discuss? I just want to know who Tommy's mother is."

"I can't say."

"Tom, you can tell me," Anne said, her voice a sudden plea. "I need to know. Please."

"I...can't."

The disappointment darkened her eyes and her voice. "Why can't you?"

Tom wanted to tell her. God knew, he wanted to be able to see her lovely smile again. He wanted everything that he knew was possible between them. With all his heart he wanted it. He would have given anything. No, *almost* anything.

"I can't explain, Anne. Please understand. I would if I could."

Anne rose to her feet. "I left my blouse here yesterday. I'm going to get it now."

And then I'm leaving and I won't be back. She hadn't said the words, but they were written all over the dark distress and disappointment on her face. She headed out of the kitchen.

"Anne..."

She didn't turn around. A second later she was gone.

Tommy started to cry. Tom hugged him. "I know how you feel, little guy. Believe me, I know."

The doorbell rang. Tom did not want to answer it. He wanted

to go after Anne and find the words to convince her to stay. But he knew he had no words now that could do that.

The obstacle that stood between them was not one he could move.

The doorbell rang again. He had to answer it. The Church of the Good Shepherd was always open to those in need. He could still help others, even if he couldn't help himself. Tom's step was heavy as he went to see who was there.

ANNE FOUND HER BLOUSE hanging up in Tom's closet. It had been ironed. She let out a sigh that hurt. She didn't want to be touched by anything that Tom did.

But she was touched by everything he did. When she listened to how he had put himself in jeopardy with both the church and the police by personally taking responsibility for those runaway children, she had seen a depth of courage and kindness in him that she'd never seen before in a man.

She tried to swallow the hard knot of disappointment sticking in her throat. After showing her all that, how could he do this to her now? All she had asked him for was the answer to a simple question. What was behind this stubborn secrecy that he held on to so tightly?

Well, whatever it was, she didn't care anymore. She was fed up with his evasions. A man who couldn't be completely honest with a woman wasn't worth the anguish.

What kind of relationship could any two people hope to have when openness and honesty were missing? She didn't have to wonder. She'd had two of those relationships already in her life.

The doorbell had sounded a moment before. As she stepped into the hallway, carrying her blouse, Anne could hear male voices coming from the living room. She was glad that Tom had company. Now she could slip out through the kitchen door and not have to see him. Ever again.

Then she heard Tommy let out an anguished cry.

Anne rushed to the end of the hall and looked into the living room to see what was wrong.

Two men were standing just inside the entrance with Tom.

The short, burly one had a balding, broad head, shrewd eyes, and wore a custom-made silk suit. Anne conservatively estimated its cost at six months of her salary. A gold Rolex winked from beneath his sleeve. His voice was an annoying bark.

"I'm Attorney George Shrubber. This is my associate, Chet Bender."

Chet Bender was a moose of a man with a mop of thick black hair and feral eyes. He stood at least six-five and probably weighed two hundred fifty pounds.

"Associate?" Tom repeated.

"I'm a private investigator," the moose said with the high, squeaky voice of a mouse.

Tom regarded the two men silently for a moment as he bounced a fussing Tommy in his arms. "Why are you here?" he asked, and Anne noted an unusual coolness in his manner and tone.

"May we sit down?" Shrubber proceeded to make himself comfortable on the couch without waiting for Tom's response.

Bender, the moose, stayed standing, watching Tom and the baby with his small, piercing eyes.

"Father Christen, I understand you knew Lindy Olson pretty well," Shrubber said.

Tom's expression reflected nothing but his self-assured calm. "Is that what you understand?"

"Come on, Father," Shrubber said, his voice now an irritating bark. "We know she worked for you at the Boston parish. And we know that she left her job a year ago when you...well, how shall I say this? Were asked to look for another parish?"

Shrubber smirked, as if he found that funny. Anne had the immediate and unwelcome image of a pit bull in pants. With every passing second, she liked this attorney less.

"And how exactly do you know all of this?" Tom asked.

"Bender, here, is a very good private investigator. Would you like to know what Lindy did after she left her job at the Boston parish?" Shrubber inquired, obviously baiting him.

"Is that what you've come to tell me?" Tom asked, still rocking the fussing baby.

"She went to work as an aide at a Boston hospital," Shrubber said. "Of course, she wasn't legally old enough. But she had stolen some ID. And, as you know, she could pass for a lot older than she was. You did know she wasn't yet fifteen when she worked for you?"

"Get to your business, Shrubber," Tom said, and there was no mistaking the lack of warmth in his tone.

"While Lindy was working as a hospital aide, she got knocked up," Shrubber continued. "Probably by one of the orderlies. Doesn't matter. Thing is, she lost the baby and sort of went nuts. She stole a newborn from the maternity ward."

Anne listened to the attorney's explanation. It seemed plausible. The autopsy report showed Lindy had given birth, but her baby could have been stillborn.

"Whose baby did she steal?" Tom asked.

"That doesn't matter," Shrubber said.

"It matters to me," Tom said.

"Rolan and Heather Kendrall are the parents. Naturally, they were devastated, and approached me for help."

"Why not the police?" Tom asked.

That would have been Anne's next question.

"The Kendralls are very sympathetic people," Shrubber said. "Lindy had been Mrs. Kendrall's aide in the hospital. Mrs. Kendrall knew she had lost her own baby. She didn't want to have the girl end up with a police record."

"Sounds strange that she would put the welfare of a baby-snatcher above that of her baby," Tom said.

"She wanted the matter handled sensitively," Shrubber replied.

"Are you implying that's why she went to you?" Tom asked.

"Both Rolan and Heather were afraid that if Lindy felt pursued by the police, she might just go off the deep end and hurt the baby or herself. The Kendralls are personal friends of mine. They knew I had access to a good private investigator and would handle the matter discreetly. Still, it took a while for Bender here to pick up Lindy's trail."

Shrubber looked from Tom to the baby. His flash of teeth was not a smile. "But Bender did finally find her."

"If you have a point to make, make it," Tom said.

"The point is," Bender said, taking a step toward Tom, "that's the Kendralls' baby you've got."

Anne noticed a perceptible change in Tom's stance. His legs were slightly spread, as though he was braced for something. Despite the considerable difference in their heights, he looked the burly private investigator straight in the eye.

"This is not the Kendralls' baby," Tom said. "This is my baby."

"You're a priest," Shrubber said, coming to his feet as though in righteous indignation. "Priests can't have kids."

"He's an Episcopal priest, Mr. Shrubber," Bender said, as though embarrassed to have to explain this fact to his boss. "They're allowed to marry and have kids. They're sort of like Roman Catholic light."

"He didn't have that kid," Shrubber said, his temper showing. "Lindy Olson left that baby with you, Christen, when she found out Bender was closing in. I know it and you know it. Now I'm taking him back to where he belongs."

Tommy's fussing rose to a full-fledged cry at the angry voices.

"You're not taking my baby anywhere," Tom said, his quiet words accelerating like strokes of a piston gathering speed. "Now get out of here."

For a very long moment, the men stayed exactly where they were, staring at Tom.

"We can do this the easy way, Priest," Shrubber said, taking a small step toward Tom. "Or we can do it the hard way."

Anne was suddenly very afraid. The tension in the room was palpable. She fully expected these men to pounce on Tom at any second and forcibly take the now screaming baby from him. And she had no doubt, looking at the calm, determined expression on Tom's face, that he would resist them.

She didn't know what to believe about Tommy. She didn't know what to believe about Lindy. She didn't know what to believe about these two men. Only one thing emerged crystal clear in Anne's mind at that moment.

She believed in Tom.

If he said the baby was his, then the baby had to be his.

Anne boldly stepped into the room. "You were just told to leave," she roared in a tone that had quelled many a courtroom.

Shrubber and Bender whirled around to face her.

"And who in the hell are you?" Shrubber demanded.

"Anne Vandree, Associate Justice of the Berkshire Court."

Shrubber's eyes took in Anne's petite frame as though he were sizing up her mettle. The guy didn't know the first thing about mettle. Something that was probably meant to be a smile, but emerged much more as a sneer, drew back his lips.

"Why should I believe you are who you say?" Shrubber demanded.

Anne sent the attorney a lethal look, the kind she reserved for his particular brand of scum. Her voice descended into its deadliest delivery. "I don't have to prove anything to you. The state police are on their way. They know me. It's your credentials they'll be checking when they arrest you for trespassing."

Bender shot a nervous glance at Shrubber. Anne knew that he was looking to his boss for his next instructions.

Shrubber blinked, a quick reassessment of both Anne and the situation flashing through his eyes.

Anne took another step toward him. "I don't know what the judges are like where you come from, but here in the Berkshires we throw the book at outsiders who barge into private homes making threats."

"We didn't barge in," Bender said, his squeaky voice clearly on the defensive. "Father Christen let us in."

"I just heard him tell you to get out," Anne said.

"I don't think you understand the gravity of this matter," Shrubber said, his tone suddenly far more conciliatory. "If the state police do arrive, the matter will be taken out of my hands and I'll have to file official charges."

"I'd be interested to know how you can file charges against

a man for refusing to hand over his child,'' Anne said, boldly advancing another step.

''That is not his child,'' Shrubber said.

''Oh, yes it is,'' Anne replied, marching over to stand beside Tom, not taking her eyes off Shrubber for a second.

''And just how do you know that?'' Shrubber demanded.

Anne took the screaming baby out of Tom's arms and hugged him to her. Tommy clung to her as she gently hushed his anguished sounds.

''Because I'm the baby's mother,'' Anne announced with a fierceness that shocked even her.

CHAPTER SEVEN

THE ROOM WAS ABSOLUTELY quiet. Shrubber and Bender stared at Anne, astonishment frozen on their faces.

Still, it was Tom who was the most astonished of all. Since Anne had charged into the room just minutes before, he'd been absolutely captivated by her. He knew she was tough. She'd shown that to him often enough. He'd just never realized how tough until now. It was pure joy to see her take on Shrubber and his goon of a P.I. and reduce them to size intellectually and emotionally.

What thrilled Tom most was why she was doing it. The faith she had to have in him to defy this attorney's claim so vehemently had stalled the breath in his lungs.

But it was her last statement that had completely stopped his heart.

"That's your baby?" Bender squeaked.

"That's what I said," Anne repeated as she planted a brief kiss on Tommy's brow. The baby was now quiet and as good as gold in her arms, a perfect testament to her claim. Bless his little heart.

"You've made a big mistake," Anne continued, her tone still carrying the full force of a left hook to the jaw. "You'll be making an even bigger one if you're still here when the state police arrive."

Bender looked decidedly uneasy as he peered at his boss. Shrubber was glaring at Anne as though still not quite sure what to believe.

Tom realized that Anne must have met lawyers like Shrubber many times in her court. She knew the kind of man she faced.

Shrubber, on the other hand, still had no idea with whom he was dealing.

But he was getting an inkling.

Shrubber finally looked away from Anne to Tom. Tom stared at the man as he would at any cockroach he found crawling in his living room.

The lawyer turned to his P.I. "Come on. We're finished here."

Tom kept his eye on them as he followed the two men to the door, making sure they were on their way to their car before closing the door and throwing the bolt.

Anne let out an audible breath of relief.

Until she turned around and saw Phyllis Cooper standing in the hallway, holding out a piece of paper, her eyes staring at Tom and Anne like two balloons about to burst.

"I, uh, knocked on the back door, but no one answered," Phyllis said. "This is the list of those making meals for Betty over the next few days. There were so many volunteers, I had to turn people away."

Tom had never seen Phyllis Cooper looking so shocked. He knew exactly how she felt.

"Appreciate your help, Phyl," Tom said, careful to keep his voice calm and even. "Just set the list on the kitchen table."

Phyllis nodded, her eyebrows wiggling in delight as she gave Tom and Anne one last look before turning and heading for the kitchen. Anne didn't move, didn't even blink until the sound of the back door closing reached them. Then she whirled around to face Tom.

"How long was she standing there?" she asked in a strangled voice.

Anne's tone—so full of deadly force just a moment before—was now about as fatal as a feather.

"Long enough to hear you announce you're the mother of my child," Tom said as calmly as he could.

"Oh, dear God."

Tom carefully arranged his expression into serious lines. "If that was the beginning of a prayer, give it your best shot. It'll take nothing less than divine intervention now to keep Phyllis Cooper from spreading the news of what she just heard.''

As Tom saw the sudden frown on Anne's lovely face, he had to fight the strong urge to kiss it away. All of his doubts about their being able to overcome the biggest obstacle against them had completely vanished during the last few minutes.

She had believed him—despite the all-too-plausible story Shrubber had told. Believed him without the explanation she had demanded from him, pleaded with him to give her only moments before.

Believed him and stood by him.

Tom had to hold in the excitement that threatened to burst from his heart.

''This is terrible,'' Anne said with a disheartened sigh. ''What if it gets back to your bishop?''

''I'll be in serious trouble,'' Tom agreed, trying his best to sound grave. ''And I doubt this conduct will sit well with your fellow justices. I'm afraid there's only one way you can save our reputations now.''

''How?'' she asked.

''Marry me.''

''This is no time for jokes,'' she said.

''What makes you think I'm joking?''

The wonderfully startled look on her face was more than Tom could resist. He circled his arm around her and drew her close to his side. He could feel the skipping beat of her heart against his ribs. His own had begun to pound. He bent his head to hers until they were just a breath apart.

''Marry me, Anne.''

He felt her shiver against him, saw the fire and silver sparks igniting in her eyes. He brushed his lips across hers, tasting once again the sweetness that was all her own. When she sighed and closed her eyes, his heart pounded faster.

With infinite care, he wrapped his arms around her and the baby. He gently kissed her closed lids, her cheeks, her lips.

Anne melted against Tom, the sudden heat of his body turning her bones to jelly, her brain to mush. As his tender kisses claimed her lips, then traced a path to her ear, she felt encased in a breathless heat. When his mouth found the side of her neck, a moan that was half prayer, half oath broke from her.

"Was that a yes?" he asked in a heated whisper as he nestled kisses against the sleek, slender column of her throat.

"What?" Anne asked. She couldn't focus on who she was, much less his question, not with the incredible new sensation of hot liquid chills coursing through her.

She knew she was forgetting something, something she was afraid was very important. But it was so hard to think with the seductive scent of him filling her, his touch fanning the fire inside her. She felt as helpless to fight it as a baby.

Baby! The sudden thought shocked her down to her shoes. She had totally forgotten she was still holding the baby!

Anne pulled back, her thoughts sizzling like scrambled eggs in hot butter as her eyes shot to Tommy. But her concern was for naught. He was fine, nestled between her and Tom, bright eyed, curiously pulling at the pearl buttons on the blouse draped over her arm.

Only then did she realize that Tom had one arm securely around her and one around the baby.

"Anne?"

His voice was a hoarse note above her hair. She lifted her head to his and sighed. Surely a woman could get lost—or was it found?—looking into eyes that warm.

The doorbell sounded like a cannon going off. Anne jumped within the circle of Tom's steady arm.

"I have to answer that," he said, but didn't make a move to release her. And Anne had absolutely no inclination to move away from either the compelling heat of his body or that in his eyes.

The doorbell rang again.

"I hope I can assume it's not the state police," Tom said, only half jokingly.

"I would have called Fred if I had had time."

Tom pulled Anne with him as he headed into the study. "Then I'm glad you didn't have the time. There's a staircase leading down to the workshop behind this bookcase,'' he said as he walked over to the wall and flipped a hidden switch. The panel popped open. ''Wait there with Tommy.''

''Why?''

''In case that's Shrubber and his P.I. with second thoughts.''

Anne shook her head. ''I'm not leaving you here alone to face them.''

Tom smiled. ''I normally don't go for the beautiful, reckless type who insist on coming to a guy's rescue,'' he said as he took Anne's arm and eased her firmly toward the opening in the panel. ''But in your case I'm definitely going to have to make an exception.''

After planting a brief, hard kiss on Anne's lips, he flipped on a light inside the stairwell, pushed her through the open panel and closed the bookcase in her face.

Anne bristled at his high-handed manner. He really had some nerve.

Beautiful, he had called her.

Tom's compliment, followed by the feel of his hard, claiming kiss, hummed through Anne's blood. And made her smile.

Still, she had absolutely no intention of moving from this spot until she was sure Tom was all right. She leaned against the panel and listened. After a moment she was reassured to hear muted female voices coming from the other side.

Only then did she deem it safe to grasp the banister and descend the stairs into what Tom had called the workshop. She didn't know what she'd been expecting, but what she found when she got there totally surprised her.

TOM HAD FORGOTTEN about the financial committee meeting. As its members poured into his living room, he quickly explained that something had come up and he would have to reschedule. After he had seen the last of them out the door, he hurried to join Anne in the workroom.

She was standing next to the wood shelves, looking up at the carved wooden inscription mounted on the wall.

"'By the work, one knows the workman,'" she read, then turned toward him. "La Fontaine said that, didn't he?"

"Yes," Tom said.

She turned back to the shelves, fingering the carved wooden models. Tommy was also reaching for them. Anne was careful to keep his eager little hand from getting too close.

"These are models of malls," she said. "You built them, didn't you?"

"First the models, then the malls," Tom said.

"But obviously not on the end of a pile driver," she said, turning to him.

"I was the general contractor on the projects."

Her smile was approving. "The brains behind the brawn. Why the models first?"

"To test out the architect's plan. Even the best architects can overlook the heating, lighting and plumbing practicalities in their eagerness to be innovative. A model points out those deficiencies and saves the expensive fixes that have to be done afterward."

She turned back to the shelves. There was a delight of discovery written over her face, coming through her voice. "The detail in these is amazing. I can even read the sign on the entrance to the Gap. You must have been wonderful at it. And it had to be financially rewarding. Why aren't you still doing it?"

Tom wished she hadn't asked that question. Was she disappointed that he had given up the opportunity to make money for the chance to make a difference in the world?

"The world isn't suffering from too few malls," he said after a moment.

When she glanced over her shoulder at him he could see a bit of color in her cheeks. "Being a priest means a great deal to you, doesn't it?"

"It's not just my profession, Anne," Tom said simply. "It's who I am."

There was a deep quiet on her face as she studied him for a moment.

She gestured toward the table saw and various power drills.

''You designed and built this room and the stairs leading up to the entrance behind the bookshelves.''

''Constructing it was a good challenge, not to mention good exercise when we were inundated with snow this last winter. And it gives me a place to work on the church repairs that are always cropping up.''

''I wonder if your parishioners appreciate all your talents. You do impressive work.''

''I'm glad you like the room.''

''I wasn't talking about the room.''

She smiled and Tom realized then that she meant his job as a priest. The tightness that had wound in his gut during the last few minutes eased.

Tommy cooed in Anne's arms and flailed his hands. Anne caught one of his little fists and gave it a kiss.

''Shrubber lied about Lindy and the baby, didn't he?'' Anne asked, a frown appearing between her eyebrows.

''Tommy is not the child of Rolan and Heather Kendrall,'' Tom said carefully.

''Can we prove that if it comes down to it?'' Anne asked.

''We're going to have to try,'' Tom said.

''Tommy's real mother could verify it, couldn't she?'' Anne asked.

''Anne, that is not an option.''

She shrugged, clearly disappointed, but didn't press the point. ''I wish I had gotten a look at his car. You realize it had to have been Bender in that high-speed chase with Lindy?''

''They left in a black Lexus,'' Tom said.

''If it had been a green van, I'd be calling Fred right now.''

''It's best not to involve the police at this time.''

Tom knew that he was asking her to trust him yet again. Without explanation. She studied his face, and after a moment nodded.

''Okay,'' she said. ''Where do we go from here?''

She'd never know how much her trust meant to him. He had no words to tell her.

"We need to find out more about the Kendralls, as well as Shrubber and Bender," Tom said.

"I still have contacts with the D.A.'s office in Boston. The people there know most of the lawyers around. And the ones they don't know, they can find out about. Tom, are you concerned Shrubber's coming back?"

"It's hard to know what he might do. If he knew about the hikers seeing Lindy in a high-speed chase with a green van, I don't think either he or Bender would have chanced coming here in the first place. But I didn't hear that mentioned in any news report about her death."

"Hunter has kept that information away from the news reporters," Anne said. "Fred tells me he's put a tight lid on the case."

"Did Fred tell you anything useful about the VW Beetle Lindy was driving?" Tom asked.

"Just that it's untraceable."

"Interesting," Tom said as he walked up to her and Tommy.

"How?"

"Just interesting." He placed his hand on the small of her back and guided her toward the stairs.

"Are we going somewhere?"

"Boston. That's where the answers are."

"Now?" Anne asked as she started up the stairs.

"As soon as we pack."

"Pack? Wait a minute." She whirled around. "How long are we going to be in Boston?"

She was standing two steps above him. Their faces were level with each other. It was just too good an opportunity to pass by. Tom lightly brushed his lips against hers. Her sweet taste was fast becoming addictive.

"At least a few days," he murmured against the softness of her mouth.

Her sigh was a warm breath. "Are you trying to completely compromise both our reputations?"

"Both our reputations are already completely compromised," he reminded her.

She pulled back to look him in the eye. "Tom, you have no idea how sorry I am about that."

"Don't worry about it."

"I have to talk to Phyllis and explain that I only said I was the baby's mother because I was trying to keep Shrubber and Bender from taking Tommy."

"And what are you going to say when Phyllis asks you why you didn't want them taking Tommy?"

"Well, because he's your baby, of course." Anne heard her words and grimaced. "Scratch that. She'll ask me who the baby's mother really is and I won't be able to tell her. Which means I can't tell her Tommy is yours. Dear heavens, what can I tell her?"

Tom kissed the tip of Anne's suddenly scrunched up nose. "You don't have to tell Phyllis anything."

"Tom, this is not something that's just going to go away. We're not two foolish teenagers who could be forgiven for a moment's stupidity. We're a priest and a judge. People look to us to set an example for responsible behavior. How could I ever admonish another couple in my court for what everyone will believe I've done? How could you continue to preach respect for the institution of marriage?"

"Anne, the solution is simple. I asked you before and I'm asking you again. Will you marry me?"

He watched the light shift and shimmer in the clear crystal depths of her eyes. Then they clouded over once again.

"I wouldn't do that," she said.

"What wouldn't you do?"

"Make fools of us both."

"Anne, I've never proposed to a woman before in my life. Never had the slightest inclination to. But now, with you—"

"Your inclination is to do the right thing," Anne said, cutting him off. "I understand that. But getting married to someone you don't know is not the right thing."

Tom moved to hold her, but she retreated to the next step.

"Tom, we've seen each other off and on for less than four

days. Nobody can know anyone in so short a time. I've been married. Believe me, it's not a mistake I'm making again, ever."

"But, Anne—"

"You told me you were waiting for your soul mate. Hold out for her, Tom. It's the only chance you have of ending up in that minority of marriages that make it."

Her voice, moments before so breathless, was back to its full force. Tom's heart gave a sigh.

He had rushed her. He shouldn't have. She wasn't an impulsive teenager who would let herself be swept off her feet. She was a woman with a level head on her shoulders and a heart that had been broken twice before. What's more, her arguments were sane and logical.

But Tom wasn't feeling very sane or logical. For the first time in his life he was violently in love. And it wasn't easy holding back what was in his heart. Still, he was going to have to.

Anne was not ready to listen to a declaration of love.

She turned and headed up the stairs. "So where are we going to stay in Boston?" she asked.

"A private home."

"Separate bedrooms?"

Tom let out a heavy breath. "Since you had to ask, I guess you're right. You don't know me."

"ANNE, I'M GLAD YOU answered," Maureen said.

Anne was hurriedly packing for Boston when her cell phone had rung. She held it against her ear with her shoulder as she shoved lotions and creams into her cosmetic case.

"Maureen, I'm sorry. I know I promised to call you back, but—"

"Don't worry about it," her friend interrupted. "You've obviously had a lot going on. Just tell me if it's true."

"If what's true?" Anne asked.

"That you and Tom had that adorable baby together."

Anne groaned. Maureen chuckled in her ear. "Yes, my friend, you two are the talk of the town—or in this case the village. So, when did this all happen?"

"Maureen, I..." What the hell could she say?

"Black robes can hide a lot, Anne. But you weren't wearing yours when we had lunch together six months ago. And if you were pregnant then, I'm Gwyneth Paltrow. What's going on?"

"I...can't say."

"It has something to do with that dead girl, doesn't it?" Maureen asked, all lightness gone from her tone. "Who were those two men who came by to see Tom this afternoon?"

Anne shook her head in dismay. Was there anything that happened in Cooper's Corner that the residents didn't end up learning?

"Maureen, I hope I can tell you all about this someday, but today is not that day."

"This talk isn't good for Tom," Maureen said in that same serious tone. "If you can tell me anything that could help stop it...?"

Maureen just wanted to help, and it bothered Anne that she couldn't explain. But this still wasn't her secret to share.

"I have to go out of town for a while," Anne said. "I'll call you when I get back. Things may be clearer then."

Once she said goodbye to Maureen, Anne flipped her cell phone closed. She hoped things would be clearer. They were nothing but a muddled mess at the moment, just like her emotions.

She couldn't stop thinking about Tom's proposal. The unexpected surprise of it still had her reeling. She'd never imagined that he would be prepared to go so far to protect their reputations.

Thank heavens she had the good sense to see the situation for what it was.

Tom was attracted to her. He made no secret of it. But she knew that he never would have asked her to marry him after knowing her only four days if she hadn't so foolishly claimed to be the baby's mother and put them both in this difficult situation.

Every time she thought back to that fateful moment when she stood in front of Shrubber and Bender and blurted it out, she wondered if she had gone insane. She hadn't even known she was going to say it until she heard her words reverberating in her ears. Even now she had no idea what had gotten into her.

All she had thought about was that she had to stop those men from taking Tommy at any cost. She just hadn't thought about the cost being Tom's reputation—and her own.

She could weather it, she supposed. Judges weren't held to the same personal high standards as priests. But what of Tom?

Was she compounding her error by agreeing to go off with him like this?

The doorbell rang. That would be him. She stared at the packed bags on her bed.

Tell him you're not going. Look what's happened to you already around this man. Don't be a fool. You don't know what's in Boston. You could get embroiled in even more of a mess.

It was that wise voice inside her again. Giving her such good advice. One of these days, she was really going to have to take it.

TOM AND ANNE STOPPED for dinner halfway to Boston at a family restaurant. A six-year-old was having a birthday party with all his friends. Anne found herself smiling. She hadn't heard so much noise since she'd spent Christmas morning at her sister's place with all twenty-eight of her in-laws. Of course, that was before her sister's divorce.

They were back on the highway with only the purring engine of the Porsche as a backdrop when Tom asked her the question he had asked once before. "Why no kids, Anne?"

She looked out into the black night at the distant lights of the towns streaking by them. This wasn't a subject she cared to talk about. But he had cared to ask. And suddenly she found herself telling him.

"Bill and I both wanted kids right away. After three years of no luck, we agreed it was time to find out what was wrong. I was right in the middle of a big case, working sixteen hours a day. I scheduled my battery of tests for the next month. A week later I called and cancelled the tests, when Bill proved he wasn't the one at fault.''

''He had his semen analyzed?'' Tom asked.

''He got his girlfriend pregnant.''

Tom was quiet for a moment before asking, ''How did you find out?''

''Bill told me. Sounded damn proud about it, too. They had been using protection for the entire year he had been seeing her, and he still was man enough to impregnate her. His exact words.''

Tom said something under his breath.

''I didn't catch that,'' Anne said.

''I was asking for forgiveness.''

''For what?''

''For what I was just thinking of doing to your ex.''

Anne smiled, oddly touched. It was strange to think of Tom having violent thoughts toward anyone. But kind of nice in this case. And such a relief that he hadn't responded with the cloying sympathy for her that her family had.

Pity was so damn denigrating.

They arrived late at a brownstone in the Back Bay. When Tom walked up the stairs, Anne expected him to ring the bell. But instead he drew out a key and inserted it into the lock and opened the door. He turned on a light in the entry and stepped aside for her to pass.

The house was lovely inside—shining oak floors, bay windows, a graceful curved banister leading to the second floor.

''Who lives here?'' Anne asked as Tom led the way into the living room and set her bags on the sofa.

''I do when I'm in Boston.''

''This is your home?''

''It was left in trust to me. The kitchen's that way. The bedrooms are upstairs. I'll carry these bags up in a few minutes when I return with the rest of the things.''

As Tom headed back to the car, Anne looked around with new interest. So this was where Tom had lived before he became a priest.

The living room was dwarfed by its enormous built-in bookshelves, a bona fide fireplace and overstuffed furniture in deep browns and golds. Above the fireplace was the portrait of a couple that had to have been painted a hundred years before.

Anne drew closer to it. The man had ragged features. But he also had blond hair and blue eyes and the same distinctive bronze skin that Tom possessed. The woman's coloring was darker, her features finer. Tom's great-grandparents?

Too bad people didn't smile in those days when they had their portrait painted, Anne thought. So much of what was inside a person came out in their smile.

She carried the sleeping baby in her arms into the kitchen. It was compact, gleaming white, with glass panel cabinets and a separate walk-in pantry. Just off it was a half bath. Next she ascended the stairs and found two bedrooms with an adjoining full bath.

The furnishings had bold, clean lines with a definite masculine touch, but there were no personal mementos to tell her about the man who lived here. She opened cabinets and closets and drawers, yet all she found were extra linens for the beds and towels for the bath.

It wasn't until she stepped into the second bedroom that she spied it sitting on the dresser—an old framed photo of a smiling young couple. The woman was slender, with bright blue eyes and golden-blond hair. The man with his arm around her looked exactly like Tom.

Anne turned the framed picture over and read the handwritten scrawl: "Tom and Julie on their third wedding anniversary."

TOM MADE TWO TRIPS to the car before he had all their luggage in the house. It would have been one trip if it had just been his and Anne's things. But he was learning fast that babies didn't travel light.

He found Anne in the second bedroom and set her things on the cinnamon comforter.

"You made a wise selection," he said. "This room has the softer mattress."

"This is your father, isn't it?" she asked, holding up the old photo.

"He *was* my father," Tom answered. "And she was my mother. They're both dead."

"I'm sorry." Everything about Anne's face and tone put real meaning into those two words. "Your mother was beautiful. And your dad looked exactly like you."

"If that picture is any indication."

"You don't remember?"

Tom leaned against the bedpost. "My parents were sky divers—part of a professional team that also included my grandfather, uncle and aunt. They were flying back from a jump when their plane hit bad weather and crashed. Everyone aboard was killed."

"When was this?"

"When I was five."

Anne could see him. A little towheaded boy suddenly alone in the world. It made her unbearably sad.

"Who took care of you?" Anne asked.

"I went to live with my grandmother in New York," Tom said. "Do you have everything that you need?"

She gazed down at the sleeping infant in her arms and was reminded anew of his recent loss.

"Mind if I keep Tommy with me tonight?" she asked.

Tom stepped away from the bedpost and came toward her. He leaned over and planted a light kiss on her forehead. "Tommy would love it. I'll bring in his things."

He was back at the door when Anne called out to him. "Tom?"

He stopped and turned. "Yes?"

"I never had any doubt about the separate bedrooms," she said.

Tom flashed her a soul-searing smile and left.

ANNE LAY IN BED that night with Tommy close beside her. He was awake, kicking his little feet and sucking on his fingers. She had tried putting him in the portable crib, but he'd immediately begun to cry. He missed being close to her. She had missed being close to him, as well. He needed contact with her now and she was going to be there for him.

Leaning over to kiss his little head, she took pleasure in his sweet baby smell, the warmth of his body snuggled so close to her own.

When Anne had realized that she was the infertile one in her marriage, she had faced the fact in the same way that she had faced the fact of her husband's betrayal. She had put them both behind her and focused on the things over which she had control.

She refused to define her life by those things she couldn't have. She had met betrayed women who could talk about nothing but their ex-husband's infidelity, and she had met infertile women who moaned and moped and obsessed about the babies they would never have.

She had sworn not to become one of those unhappy, pitiful creatures. And she hadn't. She had focused on all the wonderful things open to her and had carved out a full life for herself.

She had a job she loved. A home she loved. And she had friends she loved.

Only now...now there was this tiny baby that she loved.

Anne didn't know how this sweet, good thing had happened. She didn't know when her feelings had blossomed to fill that empty space in her heart. Until now, she never even knew it had been empty.

She loved this little boy. And she knew in the deepest part of her heart that he loved her. Tom had told her that Tommy was his and that he hadn't impregnated Lindy. She believed him. That meant Lindy couldn't have been Tommy's mother. He belonged to some unknown woman. Anne forcibly reminded herself of that fact. She was going to have to be prepared to give him up to his mother when the time came.

She would be prepared. She would love Tommy for the time he was with her, and she would be ready when it was time for him to leave.

But when would it be time? Did Tommy's mother know where her baby was? Was returning Tommy to her one of the reasons Tom had come to Boston? What did he feel about the mother of his child? And what had happened to Lindy's baby? Did he die, as Shrubber had claimed? How did Lindy get ahold of Tommy?

And why wouldn't Tom tell Anne about any of it?

"I wish I knew what was going on," she crooned softly to the baby as she hugged him to her. "I wish to hell I knew."

CHAPTER EIGHT

ANNE THREADED HER WAY through the familiar corridors of One Bulfinch Place, the Suffolk County district attorney's office. She had called ahead to her friend Pat Hosmer so that she would be expected.

Pat had been Anne's mentor when she first came to work in the D.A.'s office. Pat was a workaholic and a great prosecutor, and Anne respected her highly. She also counted her as a friend.

The older woman greeted them at the door to her office, where Anne performed the introductions. After patting the baby in Tom's arms, Pat beckoned them inside. A sleek woman in her midforties, with unruly black hair and dark intelligent eyes, she walked like a cat on a mantel as she circled her desk to reclaim her seat.

Elbows on her desk, Pat turned her attention to Anne as soon as she and Tom had taken the offered chairs.

"I can't believe you're still in the Berkshires," she said. "You cost me twenty bucks in the office betting pool."

Anne just smiled, but Tom asked, "Betting pool?"

Pat shifted her eyes to him. "None of us believed Anne could stay away. She enjoyed putting the bad guys behind bars too much. You should have seen her in court. The defense attorneys she went up against never knew what hit them."

"I can imagine," Tom said, a smile lifting his lips.

"I gave her two months in those hills." Pat's gaze returned to Anne. "Now here it is, four years later. Damn, it's good to see you. Oh, sorry, Father."

"No problem," Tom said.

''It's great to see you, too,'' Anne said, and meant every word.

''So, Anne, you said on the phone you needed a favor. How can I help?''

Anne leaned forward. ''I've come to ask about some people, Pat. Are you familiar with an attorney by the name of George Shrubber?''

Pat nodded immediately. ''Yeah, I know of him. He'd be sitting in a cell for bribery and suborning perjury three years ago if this office could have made it stick.''

''Tell me about it,'' Anne said.

''Shrubber was defending a guy accused of blowing up his boat for the insurance money,'' Pat began, leaning back in her chair. ''We had the guy cold. Then, on the last day of trial, Shrubber brought in a surprise witness who swore the defendant was with him at the time the explosion was set. The jury let the defendant off. Later we discovered that Shrubber had paid the witness to lie.''

''How did you find out?'' Anne inquired curiously.

''We subpoenaed the bank records. When the witness was squeezed, he came clean.''

''I don't understand why you weren't able to make the charges stick,'' Anne said.

''The detectives didn't read the witness his rights. Judge threw out his confession. Shrubber went free.''

Anne groaned. ''I hate those cases.''

''Don't we all,'' Pat agreed. ''Still, coming so close to getting caught must have thrown a scare into Shrubber. He hasn't shown his face in a courtroom since.''

''What's he doing now?'' Anne asked.

''Last I heard he was specializing in private adoptions.''

''Civil law?'' Anne asked, clearly surprised.

''Yeah, I know,'' Pat said. ''Doesn't sound too smart after specializing in criminal law to suddenly switch to civil. But any lawyer who tries to win cases by bribing witnesses and suborning perjury isn't smart. What's your interest in him?''

''I'm checking him out for a friend,'' Anne answered, then

quickly moved on. ''Do you know anything about the private investigator Shrubber uses? A big, squeaky-voiced guy by the name of Bender?''

''Can't say as I've heard of him.'' Pat scooted over to the computer keyboard on the edge of her desk. ''Give me his first name and I'll run him through the files.''

''Chet,'' Anne said.

Pat typed the name in and waited for a response. ''There's no Chet Bender with a private investigator's license in Massachusetts. If he's working as one, he's doing it illegally. Let me see if I get a hit on a criminal record.''

It took another minute for those files to appear on Pat's screen. ''No record on him. You say Shrubber's using him?''

''Yes,'' Anne answered. ''They're working together on a case for a couple named Rolan and Heather Kendrall.''

Pat shook her head. The Kendrall name obviously didn't ring any bells for her, either.

''Do you have a local address on Shrubber?'' Anne asked.

''Let's see.'' Pat proceeded to access more computer files. ''According to the assessor's office, he has two places.'' She printed out the sheet that listed them and handed it to Anne.

Anne knew that was all they were going to be able to get from Pat's sources. She thanked her friend and they left.

''I wonder why Shrubber lied about Bender being a private investigator?'' Anne said as she and Tom headed for the parking lot.

''Could be he doesn't care if Bender has a license,'' Tom suggested. ''From what your friend Pat told us, Shrubber doesn't appear to be on the upper rungs of the attorney's ethical stepladder.''

''I was hoping we might learn more.''

''Let's try a source of mine,'' Tom said.

Anne turned to him, unable to resist. ''Divine?''

Tom smiled. ''I don't think I'll have to resort to that one just yet.''

''WELL, IF IT ISN'T my favorite priest,'' the burly, mustachioed man bellowed at Tom good-naturedly as he and Anne stepped aboard the yacht. It was anchored in Boston Harbor and its skipper was anchored to a deck chair, his heels resting on a table as he swigged from a bottle of beer. As soon as he caught sight of Anne, however, he shot to his feet. Beer sloshed onto his sweatshirt and pants—a fact that didn't seem to concern him unduly.

''Whoa, and you brought an angel with you,'' he bellowed anew. ''Welcome aboard, sweet thing.''

''Down, Andy,'' Tom said as he extended his hand to the man. Andy pushed Tom's hand away and grabbed him for a bear hug.

''If this is your wife and baby and you're just getting around to telling me, I'm throwing you overboard, Rev.''

Tom extricated himself from the bear hug. ''I've offered but she's not buying. Anne Vandree, this is Andy Horne, the best architect in Boston bar none.''

Andy grinned at Anne and offered his hand. ''Turned him down, huh? You got good sense, gal. That's sure a pretty baby you got there. I love babies. Marry me and we'll make some more.''

Anne laughed. This was not a man to be taken seriously.

He invited them to sit and pointed to a cart that contained an assortment of beverages. Anne selected a bottle of sparkling water and Tom took orange juice.

''Orange juice,'' Andy snickered with good humor after Anne and Tom were seated opposite him. ''Priesthood is undoing you, Tom. You should have seen him in the old days, Anne. Hell, he could drink me and six other guys under the table.''

''Do tell?'' Anne said as she looked over at Tom in surprise.

''No, don't tell,'' Tom warned Andy, ''or I'll have to throw *you* overboard.''

''Sorry, Anne,'' Andy said, exhaling dramatically. ''I'd like to take the chance for you, I really would, but I've seen what the Rev here can do when he gets riled up.''

Anne stared at Tom's profile. It seemed as if every minute brought forth yet another revelation about him.

''Andy, you know everybody who's anybody in the social

circles around here,'' Tom said quickly, clearly eager to get on another subject.

''Just about,'' Andy agreed, taking another swig of his beer.

''Ever hear of an attorney called George Shrubber?''

''Sure, I know the guy. He married Mimi Witchem about five years ago after representing her in some legal matter. Everybody knew it was for her money. When she finally tumbled to it a couple of years later—and he started having some legal problems of his own because of shady dealings—she kicked him out.''

''Any kids?'' Tom asked.

''Neither were interested. Mimi paid Shrubber's expenses while they were married, which I understand were staggering, but he didn't get a dime once they were divorced.''

''You know what Shrubber's doing now?'' Tom asked.

''Nope. Once Mimi dumped him, he just faded away like a bad dye job. You've got to have some strong family and some strong money behind you to keep up with the clowns in this social circle I hang with.''

''Does that circle happen to include Rolan and Heather Kendrall?'' Anne asked.

Andy nodded. ''Sure does, angel. Now, Rolan's from old money. He also claims he can trace his lineage back to one of those Indians at the Boston Tea Party. But between you and me, I think Rolan's just blowing smoke from the old teepee—or in his case, toupee.''

''And his wife?'' Tom asked.

''Oh, Heather's a bona fide beauty queen. Rolan was pushing forty when he found her on some Fourth of July float. Miss Firecracker or Miss Rocket, something like that. Big, beautiful, buxom blonde. She was nineteen. That was about ten years ago.''

''They live around here, Andy?'' Tom asked.

''Beacon Hill. Of course, they have a summer home on the Cape. And another getaway on the Costa del Sol in Spain.''

''They have any kids?''

Andy chugged more beer. "Never known you to be so interested in kids before."

"Humor me, Andy," Tom said.

"The Kendralls tried for years with no luck. Artificial insemination, in vitro, the works. Then, must be nine months ago, Heather showed up in maternity clothes to a yacht club dance, beaming to beat the band. Surprised everybody. They had a boy, I understand."

"Have you seen their baby?" Anne asked.

"Not yet. Heather started attending social functions again just a few weeks after delivery, though. She looks amazing. Still has that beauty queen figure."

"Who's Heather's doctor?" Tom asked.

"Miles Mason. He's a respected fertility expert and a member of the yacht club. But Heather didn't go to him even once during her pregnancy. And let me tell you, Miles is not pleased. Every time I see the guy he's bitching about how much he did for that couple and how little thanks he got."

"Do you know what doctor Heather saw through her pregnancy?" Tom asked.

"No idea."

"The hospital where she delivered?"

"I know these people socially, Tom. Those kinds of details don't generally come up in polite conversation. I wouldn't have known about their fertility problems or her not having gone to Mason if that old boy didn't have such a big mouth. Now, you going to tell me why you've suddenly got all this interest in the Kendralls?"

"No," Tom said, finishing his orange juice.

Andy shook his head. "Yeah, just what I figured. You never tell me any of the juicy stuff anymore." He turned to Anne. "You should have known him before he put that collar on. Boy, the stories I could tell."

But before Anne got a chance to hear any, Tom had scooted her off the yacht and out of earshot.

"SO YOU USED TO DRINK six—make that seven—guys under the table?" Anne asked, her eyes alight with humor as they got out of the Porsche in front of Tom's brownstone, where they'd returned to feed and change the baby.

"Andy likes to exaggerate," Tom said.

"What happens when you get riled up, Rev?" she asked.

"Not much. What I want to know is why Heather Kendrall suddenly switched to another doctor when her fertility specialist finally succeeded in getting her pregnant," he said, deftly changing the subject as they walked up the steps to the entry.

"Maybe Dr. Miles Mason did something to make her mad. Or maybe she just decided to go to her family doctor for follow-up care once she was pregnant."

"I'd be interested to see the birth record of the Kendralls' baby," Tom said as he reached into his pocket to take out his door key.

"Since we can't be sure where Heather delivered her baby," Anne said, "the best place to look would be the state's Vital Records Office. That's in Dorchester. After the baby's fed and we grab some lunch, we could—"

"Tom!" a voice yelled from behind them.

Anne whirled around to see a heavy-boned man with a shock of white hair sprinting up the sidewalk toward them. He wore clerical black and a white collar and definitely not the type of shoes suitable for his current jog. Tom waited at the top step until the man reached them.

"Good morning, Harry," Tom said.

Harry nodded as he leaned on the ornate black iron railing, clearly winded. He had dark eyes that glimmered on either side of a patrician nose. Tom gave him a moment to catch his breath before he turned to Anne.

"Anne, may I present the Right Reverend Harry Barrett, Bishop of the Episcopal Diocese of Massachusetts. Harry, I'd like to introduce—"

"—Anne Vandree, Associate Justice of the Berkshire Probate and Family Court," the bishop spouted before Tom had a chance to. He had gotten his breath back. "A pleasure to meet you," he said to Anne as he extended both his hand and a ready smile.

Anne shook the bishop's hand, surprised that he knew her. She never forgot a face. If she had seen him before, she was sure she would have remembered. How had he recognized her?

The bishop immediately turned back to Tom. There was something flickering in his eyes that belied the nonchalance of his manner. "I need a few words with you, Tom."

Tom nodded and turned to open the door. Anne could tell by the exchange of looks between the two that this was not going to be a conversation to which she was invited.

"You'll excuse me while I take care of the baby," she said when they had all stepped inside, not waiting for either of them to try to think up a polite excuse to get rid of her.

"Thanks, Anne," Tom said, and she knew he wasn't just thanking her for assuming the care of Tommy.

She retreated into the kitchen, where she set Tommy's bottle of formula to heat on the stove. It wasn't until she laid him down on the counter to change him that she remembered the diapers were upstairs in the bedroom.

"Come on, little guy," she said as she swept the baby back into her arms. She carried Tommy out of the kitchen toward the stairs, but halted when she heard the bishop's voice clearly through the closed door to the living room.

"Tom, you know I have respect for you," Harry said. "Even when we've disagreed, I've embraced our differences of opinion as healthy exchanges between men of reason."

"I've always appreciated that about you, Harry."

Anne knew she shouldn't listen further, but she couldn't make herself move away from the door. Clearly, something was on the bishop's mind, and she wanted to know what it was.

"I've never faulted your spirit," he continued. "The soup kitchen you started has done a world of good. Even when you ran that illegal shelter for those runaway kids, I knew your heart was in the right place."

"Thank you."

"But having a child out of wedlock with this judge—this, Tom, is not behavior becoming a priest."

"Who told you I had a child with Anne Vandree?"

''For heaven's sake, Tom, word is out all over the diocese that Ms. Vandree announced it herself. Are you telling me she lied?''

Anne waited for Tom to respond, but he said nothing.

''Is that little baby I just saw her holding your son or not?'' the bishop demanded.

''He's my son,'' Tom admitted.

''For heaven's sake, Tom, I've already received a half dozen calls this morning from Adams to Andover. Did you think you could keep something like this secret?''

Anne waited for Tom to tell the bishop about the baby's real mother and explain the circumstances, but he offered nothing in response to the bishop's question.

''Look, Tom. You've done a fine job in Cooper's Corner this past year. Every time I talk to the vestry at the Church of the Good Shepherd, they say only good things about you. And I suppose it's a testament to their support of you that none of them called me about this matter. But they all must know. How long do you think you can keep the support of those good people with this kind of behavior?''

Again Anne waited for Tom's explanation. Again there was none.

''I checked up on Judge Vandree,'' Harry said after a quiet moment.

So that's how he knew her.

''She has an excellent reputation and is well respected,'' the bishop continued. ''Do you know of anything in her disfavor?''

''Absolutely nothing,'' Tom said. ''They don't come any better than Anne.''

Tom's words created a circle of warmth around her heart.

''All right,'' Harry said. ''If you don't care about what people say about you, aren't you concerned with what they're saying about her?''

''Yes, I'm concerned,'' Tom admitted.

''Well, you're certainly not showing it. Tom, she's had your baby. She's staying here in your house with you. Why haven't you done the right thing and married her?''

After a long moment, when Tom still didn't respond, Anne heard the bishop exhale heavily. "Tom, this is very hard for me to say to you, but you're giving me no choice. I have to ask for your resignation."

Anne knew she couldn't let this happen to Tom. Being a priest meant too much to him. Every nerve in her body suddenly shook with the need for action. This was her fault and she was going to correct it. Whatever it took.

She pushed open the door and stepped inside the room. "No," she said in a tone that brooked no argument.

Both Harry and Tom whirled around to face her.

"Ms. Vandree—" the bishop began.

"Tom is not at fault," Anne said, quickly cutting him off as she stepped farther into the room. "I am. He asked me to marry him. I said no."

"And may I ask why?" Harry said.

"Because I was married once before. I didn't want to make another mistake."

"And what of that baby you're holding?" the bishop asked.

Anne looked down at Tommy, who was making gurgling sounds and drooling all over her blouse. She smiled. "Tommy could never be called a mistake."

"Ms. Vandree, I appreciate your honesty," Harry said. "Naturally, you must make the decision dictated by your conscience. But your refusal to marry Tom doesn't change the fact that he has had a child out of wedlock. As this diocese's spiritual leader, I cannot allow an unmarried priest to send such a message to his—"

"Tom and I are getting married," Anne interrupted.

"Excuse me?" the bishop said.

"That's one of the reasons we came to Boston," she quickly improvised. "To make plans for the ceremony."

The bishop turned to Tom. "Why didn't you tell me this?"

Anne looked at Tom and found him staring at her. Fortunately, whatever he was thinking or feeling didn't show on his calm countenance.

"Would it have made a difference?" Tom asked smoothly as he turned toward the bishop.

"Of course it makes a difference," Harry assured him, smiling. "We all make mistakes, Tom. I won't attempt to minimize yours. But the important thing now is that you and Anne will be married."

Anne knew then that she had staved off the worse and bought them some time. She let out an internal sigh of relief.

Until she heard the bishop's next words.

"There's no reason for you and Anne to be tied to that three-day waiting period. My driver is parked down the street. He'll take us to the clinic for your tests and then on to the city clerk for the waiver filing. After that my good friend Judge Franklin will be happy to sign a certificate to allow the marriage license to be issued immediately. I'll perform the ceremony myself. Why, I can have you two married before dinnertime."

Anne stood stone still in her shock, unable to even blink.

"I can't wait to call back those parishes tonight and tell them that you are married," the bishop continued. "I see no reason to mention that the ceremony only took place today, do you? Let them just assume you've been married. Yes, that would be best."

Inside Anne's head, all sorts of alarms were going off. It took her a moment before she realized that one wasn't inside her head. It was the smoke alarm in the kitchen. She had forgotten she'd left Tommy's formula heating up on the stove.

Great. She'd not only just set fire to their future, she'd set fire to Tom's house.

THE NEXT FEW HOURS passed for Anne as though she were somehow floating outside herself, watching a movie of someone else's life.

None of it seemed real. Not the needle puncture that drew the blood from her arm. Not the yawn of the bored clerk that sent them off with their waiver. Not the smiling Judge Franklin, who issued the license. Not even the bishop's jovial wife, Connie, who whisked her off to pick out a simple white dress.

A very faint voice inside an isolated corner of Anne's mind kept repeating something—something it seemed to think was important. But the thick, heavy layer of unreality muffled its message.

And then, as though suddenly becoming conscious in the middle of a dream, Anne realized she was standing beside Tom, facing a candlelit altar in Boston's famous Old North Church.

She stared through glazed eyes at the church's historic interior, the original high box pews and gleaming brass chandeliers winking at her with a timeless beauty. The first set of church bells ever brought to America was here. Paul Revere had been the neighborhood bell ringer. On its soaring white steeple, Robert Newman had signaled the approach of the British regulars with his lanterns, "One if by land, and two if by sea."

On that memorable day, a declaration of war had been made.

And now, here in the deepening twilight, the bishop was asking Anne if she would begin a new life with Tom as her husband in the declaration of consent.

"To live together in the covenant of marriage, to love him, comfort him, honor and keep him, in sickness and in health, and forsaking all others, be faithful to him as long as you both shall live?"

Anne could not say the words. She had never made a promise in her life that she hadn't meant and kept. And this promise, asked in the hallowed walls of this, the oldest church in Boston—dear God, this promise was the most important of all.

An army of sluggish, silent seconds marched by.

And then, into that stretching silence, Tommy started to cry.

Tom rocked him but it was no use. The baby bellowed. Tom leaned over and whispered in Anne's ear. "Will you, Anne?"

"I will," Anne said as she turned to take Tommy out of his arms. But whether she had just agreed to hold the baby or marry Tom was muddled in her mind.

As Anne cradled Tommy and the little baby slipped into silence, she heard the bishop asking Tom what he had just asked her.

Tom didn't hesitate, but immediately answered, "I will."

Anne floated out of both mind and body through the rest of the ceremony as that all-prevailing sense of unreality swept in to claim her once more. At one point she vaguely remembered repeating something after the bishop, but what it was she had no idea.

The next thing she knew, the bishop was pronouncing them husband and wife and she and Tom were coming out of the church into the last rays of a golden April sunset.

Harry clapped Tom on the back. ''Congratulations. Beautiful ceremony even if I do say so myself.''

''And it's so nice that you could be married in the same church where your parents exchanged their vows,'' Connie said to Tom.

Where his parents had exchanged their vows?

''Connie and I want to take you out to dinner to celebrate,'' the bishop said. ''What do you say?''

''Thanks, Harry,'' Tom answered, ''but it's been a long day. We'll take a rain check.''

The bishop patted Tommy on his little head. ''Sure.''

Connie gave Anne a brief hug. ''The ladies of the parish dropped by to stock your kitchen this afternoon,'' she said near Anne's ear. ''You and Tom and the baby should have enough for a few days.''

Anne thanked Connie. At least she hoped she did. She wasn't sure what she was saying or doing anymore.

It wasn't until they were in Tom's car and alone that the dreamlike state finally faded and Anne began to fully realize what had just happened.

''You don't mind that I turned down the bishop's invitation?'' Tom asked.

''I'm grateful,'' Anne said. ''I'm not up to polite dinner conversation at the moment.''

She looked down at her hands, noticing for the first time the beautiful solitaire diamond engagement ring with the matching gold band on her finger. They fit perfectly. She stared at them, trying to remember when Tom had slipped them on there. But it was a blank.

"They were my mother's," Tom said.

His mother's rings. The same church where his parents had been married. A stab of remorse pierced Anne, and her words came out slightly strangled. "I didn't mean for it to go this far."

"I know," Tom said. "For a moment back there in the church, I thought it was all over. Anne, I know this has happened too fast for you, but we'll work through it."

"A few months of pretend marriage and then a divorce," Anne said with a sad sigh. "It's the only thing we can do now."

She knew she sounded miserable. She was miserable.

"I keep telling myself that what we just did was necessary so that you could remain a priest. But, I think…I think we might have paid too high a price."

Tom was silent for a long time before answering. "A good dinner will help things look brighter. Neither of us has had anything to eat since breakfast."

He drove straight to the restaurant, an intimate bistro in the Back Bay. The waiter greeted Tom by name and took them to a private room in the back. The candlelit table was already set with appetizers. When the waiter brought out a heated bottle of formula for Tommy, Anne realized Tom must have made the arrangements that afternoon.

Tommy didn't want his formula no matter how much Tom coaxed, but Anne soon realized she was starved. She polished off the poached salmon entrée, steamed vegetables and apple cobbler dessert with appreciation. When she sat back, the world did look a bit better.

The baby sat in Tom's lap, amazingly quiet as he stared at the candles, his little face looking flushed in the flickering light. Tom sipped his coffee.

"You're feeling better," he said when Anne's eyes rose to his.

"I don't know how you found time to arrange for all this, but thanks."

"It was while Connie took you shopping for your dress. You look beautiful in it, Anne."

As though seeing it for the first time, Anne gazed at the shimmering silk dress that softly clung to her from throat to knee.

"I don't feel beautiful," she said. "I feel like a fraud. When do you suppose word will get back to Cooper's Corner?"

"No doubt the first call Harry makes when he gets home."

Anne reached into her purse. "I'm turning off my cell phone right now." She flipped it open and pushed the button. "I can't imagine what they'll think."

"I don't care what they think," Tom said. "I care what you think."

Yes, he did care. Worry was written all over his handsome face.

"I think I've gone off the deep end." Anne gave a rueful shake of her head as she dropped the cell phone back in her purse. "Yesterday I told an attorney I was Tommy's mother. Today I told a bishop that we came to Boston to get married. You know the last time I lied before that?"

"You lied to Shrubber and Harry for me," Tom said, ignoring her rhetorical question.

"I was eight," Anne said. "I told my mother I had finished my homework so I could watch a favorite TV show. She discovered I'd lied, of course. Told me that if I couldn't tell the truth, no one would be able to trust me. I determined right then that I was going to be a truthful person. I was not going to lie. People were going to be able to trust me."

"I trust you, Anne."

"Well, I don't trust me. I don't even know who I am anymore. I used to be able to rely on my mind. Over the past few days it seems to have gone to sleep. It's getting so I'm afraid of what I'll say or do next."

"What you've done over the last few days has come straight from your heart," Tom said quietly.

"If that's true, then I'm in need of some emergency bypass surgery."

Tom searched her eyes for a moment before he leaned toward her. "The head can only tell you what you think, Anne. It's the heart that tells you what you feel. Are you really so eager to dismiss its importance?''

Anne was suddenly very aware of Tom. His eyes were a deep twilight, the light in them like a homing beacon. His smell was warm and clean and inviting. The touch of his skin against her arm was searing.

Her head swam as her pulse wobbled.

She was so caught up in the swirl of reaction that for a moment the reality didn't register. That wasn't Tom's skin on her arm.

Startled, Anne pulled back. She placed a hand on Tommy's brow. ''Tom, the baby feels hot. He hasn't eaten and he's been lethargic for the last hour. Something's wrong.''

Tom lifted the baby out of his blanket and felt his face, frowning. ''The thermometer's at home.''

''Forget the thermometer,'' Anne said, shooting to her feet. ''We're taking him to the emergency room.''

TOM WATCHED ANNE as she went up to the nurses' desk and demanded to know why the examination of Tommy was taking so long.

She was wonderfully intimidating. She had the nurses scurrying back to see what was causing the delay.

Even his current worry over the baby couldn't diminish the happiness Tom felt.

He would have stopped their marriage from taking place today if he'd had any doubt about Anne wanting to marry him. But he hadn't. She had lied for him twice during the last two days. A highly principled woman like Anne would have done that for one reason and one reason only.

She loved him.

That Anne was unaware she loved him rather amazed Tom. For a woman as smart as she to overlook such an obvious explanation for her behavior could only be attributed to the fact that she'd distanced herself from her true emotions for too long.

The price she paid for the betrayal of her husband? For the

pain and disappointment when she'd learned she was infertile? Probably both.

Tom told himself all she needed was time to tune in—to her feelings, to him, to the choice her heart had made. All it would take was time.

He could give her time. He planned to give her a lifetime.

The doctor, a bulky blond woman with tired eyes, carried the screaming Tommy out of the examination room.

"He has an ear infection," she said.

"How serious is it?" Tom asked.

"He'll have a temperature and be lethargic for a while. But you needn't worry. I'll give you a prescription for drops. I don't normally see babies this young with this kind of infection, though. Do either of you smoke?"

"No," Anne said. "Why?"

"Babies who breathe in secondhand smoke are more prone to ear infections," the doctor explained. "Are you breast-feeding him?"

"No," Anne said.

"It's really important for a baby to have breast milk," the doctor said. "It contains the antibodies that help ward off infections like these. If you're interested, we have a lactation consultant here this evening. I'd be happy to call her—"

"Thank you," Tom said, cutting the doctor off. "That won't be necessary." He saw no reason for Anne to have to go on the defensive again, especially not tonight, with concern for Tommy already clouding her eyes.

"It's all right, Tom," Anne said, surprising him. She turned back to the doctor. "May I see her now?"

The doctor nodded. "This way."

After Anne returned from her consultation, they picked up the eardrops at the hospital's pharmacy and headed home.

"Do you mind if I keep Tommy with me again tonight?" she asked.

Tom knew then that Anne's thoughts were all for the baby. She had totally forgotten that they had been married just a few hours before. And that this was their wedding night.

He had hoped…ah, what he had hoped!

Still, he knew when she spoke about getting a divorce that she had not taken their marriage ceremony seriously. He had promised himself that he would give her time. All the time she needed. And he would keep that promise.

''Sure, you can keep him with you,'' Tom said.

What he was going to do tonight, he did not know. Maybe a cold shower or two. Or three.

CHAPTER NINE

AFTER ANNE HAD BATHED herself and the baby, she settled on the bed with him in her lap and spread out the lactation instructions before her.

She'd never known how important breast milk was for a child until she read the scientific reports. Human breast milk contained at least a hundred ingredients not found in formula. A baby's immune system, IQ, eyesight—everything was enhanced if he were breast-fed.

There were lots of supplements offered for an adoptive mother. Anne had gotten them from the lactation consultant and taken them earlier. But what had been recommended most strongly for generating milk in the breast was suction action on the nipple.

She had no idea how long Tommy would be with her. Logically, she knew she was being foolish to even try this. But she had to do something. She couldn't let him keep getting sick because he wasn't getting the optimal nutrition he needed.

Anne sat up and unbuttoned the top of her white lace nightgown. She cradled Tommy to her and brought him close to her exposed breast. Gently she rubbed her nipple against the baby's lips. Tommy didn't need any more invitation. He latched on. This time Anne made sure the positioning was right—his mouth wide open, the nipple far back.

He looked up at her with such love and trust as they bonded flesh to flesh. Anne's heart melted. But it took only a moment for the suction to bring pain.

"Ooh-ah," she moaned, as she gently detached him from her nipple.

Tommy's disappointment came out in a loud and immediate howl. Anne felt a little like howling in disappointment herself as she rocked him gently to her. She was just too sensitive.

When the knock came on the door a second later, she yelled, "Come in," without thinking.

Tom entered. "Is everything all right?"

Anne exhaled heavily as Tommy's cries finally subsided. She gave the little boy a reassuring hug before looking up. "Yes. It's just..."

Anne forgot what she was going to say. Tom was standing beside the bed, his hair wet from his recent shower, wearing nothing but pajama bottoms. His lean, bronze body was beautiful in the glow of the lamplight.

But it was the heat in his eyes and where they were looking that had Anne's pulses racing.

It was only then that she remembered the front of her nightgown was still open and her breast exposed. She felt the warmth in her cheeks as she fumbled with the fabric.

"Were you trying to breast-feed Tommy?" Tom asked.

"You wouldn't believe how important it is," she said, struggling to button the gown with one hand. She looked down at it, not at Tom. "The food value is far superior to formula. Even the way a baby sucks milk from a breast is different. An infant strips milk from a real nipple with his tongue. With a bottle, a baby's tongue just serves to limit the flow of milk. Sucking at the breast promotes good jaw development and encourages the growth of straight, healthy teeth."

She was babbling and she knew it. But she was embarrassed. And edgy. And very aware of Tom.

"You stopped because it hurt," Tom guessed.

Anne nodded. "Of course I don't have any milk, but the suction action is supposed to stimulate a part of the brain to get it started."

"Anne, you don't have to do this."

"He needs it, Tom. It's important to him."

She lifted her head. Tom's eyes were looking directly into hers, gently searching.

"I want to do it for him," she admitted with a soft sigh.

Tom studied her quietly for a moment. That calm, contained expression was all Anne could see. Whatever thoughts were behind it were hidden.

"Do you want me to help?" he asked.

Anne frowned up at him. "How could you help?"

"I'll show you if it's what you really want. Is it?"

Anne didn't hesitate. "Yes."

He slipped onto the bed and moved behind her. Anne felt herself tensing as her nerves sparked to attention, alert, restless.

"You can trust me, Anne," he said, and the breath of his words moved against the back of her hair as his hands rested lightly on her shoulders.

She could feel the drawing heat of his body, the clean scent of his skin, the gentle warmth of his hands. Her shoulders relaxed as the tenseness faded away.

"There's an East African tribe that has a custom that has always fascinated me," Tom said as his hands started to slowly massage her shoulders and back. Anne felt as soothed by his rich, relaxed voice as she was by the languid sweep of his fingertips over her muscles.

"As soon as a woman realizes she wants a child, she leaves the village and goes to sit alone beneath the spreading branches of a shade tree," Tom continued.

His touch was so light, giving, freeing. Anne closed her eyes as his clever hands stroked her neck, then swept into her hair to knead her scalp, sending a luscious warmth down her spine.

"Under this tree, the woman waits, carefully listening until her heart can hear the song of the child that wants to be born." Tom's deep murmur hummed as he eased Anne back against his chest.

She relaxed against the hard heat of him with a sigh. He lightly kissed her hair as his hands continued to massage her neck and shoulders.

"And when she hears the song of the child who wants to be born, she sings it to herself," Tom said, his voice now as hypnotizing as his broad caresses. Anne's muscles melted as her senses overflowed with pleasure.

This felt so good. So very, very good.

"Then the woman returns to the village and teaches the song to her partner so that when they come together, they both invite this child to be conceived in their act of love," his velvet voice whispered beside her ear.

Delicious chills danced down her neck.

"That's the way every child should be welcomed into the world," Anne said with a smile. "What a great custom."

"Humm," Tom agreed, feathering kisses down the side of her cheek. When she felt the heat of his breath against her ear, a jolt of pleasure shot through her.

Anne was tingling. Tingling all over.

Tom's hands swept across her shoulders to the sides of her arms, a warm, deep, imprinting touch that she felt right down to her toes. When his hands swept back up her arms, his fingertips lightly brushed the sides of her breasts.

Anne's skin quivered as heat fizzed through her.

Then his mouth brushed kisses along the side of her neck, shortening her breath. Anne moaned and rolled her head forward as she offered him access to the sensitive back of her neck. He took it eagerly, with hungry, hot, openmouthed kisses that melted her spine.

He eased his hands down her sides, then circled her breasts, gently caressing, enticing. Blood charged through her and flames licked a path through her stomach. She could feel her breasts swelling with desire, her nipples aching to be touched.

His kisses burned her neck as he slowly undid the buttons of her gown, pulling it back to expose her breasts. The sudden cool air on her heated skin halted the breath in her lungs.

When his hot hands enclosed her bare breasts, she moaned and arched against him, filling his palms with her aching fullness. His fingers feathered across her hardened nipples and hunger rippled through her.

His breath was hoarse against her ear. "The baby."

The baby?

"Try him on your nipple now."

Anne had forgotten all about the baby! She shifted Tommy in her lap and brought him to her breast. This time when Tommy took her nipple in his mouth, there was no pain, only pleasure.

As the baby suckled Anne's breast, Tom pressed more searing kisses down her neck and throat, and his hand glided over her gown, across her flat stomach to caress the swell of her hip, the length of her thigh. The firm press of his hand burned through her lace nightgown to set her flesh on fire.

Anne could concentrate on nothing but the incredible sensations radiating through her body with each kiss, each touch of his hand.

She was on fire. And it was glorious.

Tom told himself he had aroused Anne so she could suckle the baby without pain. But he knew in his heart that he was doing this just as much for himself.

He inhaled her sweet scent until he was drunk with it. Kissed the honey from her skin until he was high. Let his hand trace from her full breasts to the swell of her hip to her slim thigh until he was throbbing with need.

It was pure, agonizing torment to keep it up without going further, but he would not take what she did not offer. No matter what it cost him.

And what it was costing him was a searing pain in every cell of his body. He forcibly reminded himself that he was stronger than his urges. And fervently prayed that he was right.

When a soft cry broke from Anne's lips, Tom immediately drew back, shifting her in his arms to see her face. "Is it hurting?" he asked, and knew his voice was nothing but a ragged whisper.

"No, no," she said. "The baby let go."

Tom looked down at the sleeping infant in Anne's arms. He gently picked Tommy up, got out of bed and laid him carefully in the crib.

"How did you know this would work?" Anne asked.

When Tom turned back to her, she saw his full arousal for the first time and gave a stunned start. She hadn't thought about what his touching her might be doing to him. His eyes smoldered as he drank in her flushed face and exposed breasts.

"I'm not just a priest," he said in a husky whisper. "I'm also a man."

Was he ever. Her eyes skimmed over the rapid rise of his muscular chest, glistening with a fine perspiration. Then her gaze lowered to his flat, clenched stomach and the large bulge below.

"Anne, I need to make love to you more than I need to breathe. But if you want me to go, I will."

Her head shot up. Faultless restraint shone in his eyes, despite the desperate need radiating out of his body, etched on his features like pain.

He had told her she could trust him. And when he gave her his word, he meant it. She knew with an absolute certainty that all she had to do was tell him to go and he would.

That knowledge did strange things to Anne. She suddenly felt utterly and completely defenseless against the overwhelming desire spilling into her blood and singing in her heart.

"Stay, Tom," she said, and her voice was deep and husky with need.

He was back beside her on the bed in a heartbeat, his mouth firmly and fiercely planted onto hers. God, he tasted wonderful. Anne closed her eyes and circled her arms around his shoulders. Her sigh escaped into his parting lips as her body melted against him.

Anne's response was so full, so complete, it burst like fire in Tom's blood. He pulled her to him, luxuriated in the feel of her flesh against his, devoured her mouth with all the need that had grown so deep inside him. She tasted like an April dawn, sweet and full of promise. He wanted that promise. And its fulfillment. Now.

Anne's senses spun, her thoughts scattered to the air.

He was branding her with a heat that seared her to her soles. This was nothing like his delicately sensual kiss of two nights before. She knew now that had been a mere preview of passion.

This was the passion.

And it sung in her bones, beat in her blood as her own passion rose to meet it. His mouth was pure fire, hot and hard. The cry that escaped her lips was unadulterated entreaty. He swallowed it and demanded more, tasting her deeply, tantalizing her with the heat of his mouth until she was trembling all over.

His lips and body burned into hers, branding her with their fierce claim. Anne's blood beat hot and fast, rushing through her body as intense pleasure rose in her core.

And then he released her mouth and bent his head to her breast, licking the nipple, bathing her with his breath, tugging the peak with his mouth, suckling her, burning fire into her bones.

As he heard her whimper of want, of need, blood hammered through Tom so hard that he could barely draw in breath. He shifted to her other nipple and suckled its sweetness as he lifted her and laid her back on the bed.

With hands that shook, he pulled off her nightgown, then sought the giving softness of her skin. He was too hot and too hard and she was shivering beneath his touch. He had to slow down. But he couldn't. Her hunger wouldn't let him.

Her hands pulled him to her as he trailed moist, heated kisses over her breasts, down her belly. She was satin, with the flavor of sweet cream. He could not get enough, quickly enough.

His hand spread her silken thighs, sought the sensitive flesh between. Feeling how hot and wet she was tore the breath from his lungs. As he caressed her sultry folds, she shuddered and called out his name, and his heart hammered his rib cage.

Anne melted in the heat of his kisses on her breasts, in the glittering fire that licked over her mind and body, consuming both.

The low sounds escaping her throat were ones of desperation. Her body was shaking, demanding with an intolerable craving. His firm fingers, then his wet tongue stroked her moist center, probed her, pushed her past all caring for anything else. The fierce pleasure swept through her and she ignited, arching against him, bursting with fulfillment.

And then his mouth was on hers and he was joining their bodies, pressing into her sleek depths until he could go no farther. She wrapped her legs around him and held on. The sensation of having him inside her, filling her so completely, fitting every part of her so perfectly, was incredible.

They moved together, breathed together, hearts beating together. Each glide of muscle and bone was as one in a rhythm of intimacy, a synchronized meshing of bodies and souls.

Anne had never imagined such feelings could exist. She and Tom were joined. And for the first time in her life, she really understood those words. The pleasure was glorious, mind shattering, heaven. And Tom was bringing it to her, sharing it with her.

He made a sound deep in his throat that became her name as he gave himself to her. With a muffled cry of discovery, she soared into uncharted worlds of sensation.

As the subsequent minutes blurred by in stunned succession, Anne wondered dazedly if she were ever going to be able to breathe evenly again. Tom still lay on top of her, braced on his elbows to keep his full weight from crushing her. His breath sounded as labored as her own.

And he still filled her completely.

Damn, he was good at this. Too good. His intimate knowledge of a woman's body spoke of experience. A lot of experience.

"I'm new to this kind of nuclear explosion," she admitted. "How long does it take for the fallout to settle?"

"I don't know," he said, humor and wonder weaving through his tone. "This is a first for me, too."

That made her happy. Insanely, foolishly happy.

He kissed her ear. "Anne?"

"Yes?"

"I didn't mean for it to be so fast. But it's been a long time for me, and having you in my arms is the answer to a prayer."

"It's been a long time for me, too," she admitted. "And if you had gone any slower, I might have had to hurt you."

His deep laugh rumbled warmly through him, and her.

He leaned down to kiss her neck, sending a delicious shiver across her skin. "Maybe we can take it a bit slower this time."

''This time?'' she asked, finding her breath catching at the mixture of heat and hunger in his voice.

His answer was a smile as he molded his lips to hers.

''YOU'RE MARRIED?'' Fred asked, her tone several octaves too high.

Anne still lay in bed, despite the fact that it was after ten in the morning. Between making love and taking care of the baby, neither she nor Tom had gotten much sleep.

When the baby had stirred them at six for his bottle, she'd fixed omelettes for Tom and her. But after that hunger had been satisfied, the other hunger had risen again. That incredible, insatiable hunger.

Now Tom was down in the kitchen, heating the baby's formula.

''Yeah, I'm married, Fred,'' Anne said, unable to get the goofy grin off her face. She ached in every cell of her body. And she'd never felt better.

''Why?'' Fred wanted to know.

Damn good question.

''It seemed like the right thing to do at the time,'' Anne said.

''Anne, you have not been yourself since you met that priest.''

Wasn't that the truth.

''He's embroiled you in that mess with the runaway dead girl. He's got you telling people that baby is yours. And now this guy's snooping around, asking questions about you.''

Anne straightened in the bed. ''What guy?''

''Some private investigator. He's been to the courthouse quizzing the clerks and bailiffs. Wanting to know if you were pregnant a few months ago.''

Bender. It had to be Bender.

''What did the people at the courthouse say?'' Anne asked, alarm racing through her.

''They called me. I told them to give the guy nothing.''

Anne sighed in relief. ''Did I ever tell you how great you are?''

"Yeah, yeah. Anne, he's going to find out that baby isn't yours. Why are you saying it is?"

"I'm trying to protect the little guy, Fred. Look, there's something going on here I don't fully understand. But I intend to. And until I can discover the truth, that baby is staying with me and Tom."

"Where does the priest fit in?" Fred demanded.

"He's the key to the mystery," Anne said, and the literal truth in her words caused her to frown.

"Anne, I don't like this. You hardly know this guy and you've gone and married him. This isn't like you at all."

And didn't she know it. "It's only temporary, Fred. Just until this thing with the baby gets sorted out."

"Look, I've got vacation coming," Fred said. "I can be there in a few hours. Just say the word."

"Thanks, Fred, but no. I've turned off my cell phone. You have the number here now. Call if there's any news. If all goes well, I should be back in the Berkshires in a few days."

"And if all doesn't go well?" Fred asked.

"Have faith, Fred. That's what I'm operating on."

Anne hung up the phone, feeling a great deal less lighthearted than she had at the beginning of her conversation. Fred's words keep ringing in her ears. *You hardly know the guy.*

It many ways, it was the truth. And yet in other ways she felt as though she had known Tom forever. Especially after the night they had spent in each other's arms.

That totally unbelievable night.

It was Tom's thoughtfulness, his total focus on her pleasure that undid Anne every time. She'd never realized what a boring, self-focused lover Bill had been.

She had no doubt now that what was inside a man came out in his lovemaking. And what was inside Tom was nothing short of magic.

Still, she was operating on faith.

Faith that Tom was telling her the truth. Faith that Tommy was his. Faith that Tom's need to keep silent about Tommy's mother was worth his secrecy.

What if she were wrong?

"Why the frown?" Tom asked as he stepped into the bedroom with Tommy in his arms.

Anne looked up from her thoughts. Tom's thick, straight hair was totally mussed, mostly from her eager hands. A golden stubble lined his chin. He was wearing nothing but light-blue briefs on his lean body. She didn't think she'd ever get over the pleasure of seeing the muscles bunch beneath his naked bronze skin.

Tom read the changing expression on Anne's face and smiled. She had gone from looking worried to watching him with that unconscious intensity that had driven him wild the first moment he saw it.

He was beside her in the bed in a flash, setting the baby in her lap and reaching for her.

"We have to get up, Tom," Anne protested, then sighed as he kissed that lovely, long, sensitive neck of hers.

"I thought you might want to try Tommy on your breast again," Tom coaxed as he delicately brushed his fingers across her already peaking nipples poking above the sheets.

"You think that's going to work, do you?"

There was a dare in her eyes and defiance in her tone, but the quickening of her breath belied both.

"Shall we see?" he asked, gently taking her mouth with his and drawing the sheets away. She sighed with pleasure as she pulled him to her.

"WE LOST A WHOLE DAY," Anne lamented as she and Tom entered the offices of the Bureau of Health Statistics in Dorchester the next morning.

The light danced in Tom's eyes. "Anne, the last thing I would call a day spent in bed with you is *lost.*"

Anne glanced down at Tommy to hide the color rising to her cheeks. The baby was looking around, bright eyed and very alert. His color was back to normal, as was his temperature.

"The rest was probably good for Tommy," she acquiesced. "He seems so much better today."

"That's because the love you give him is even more important than breast milk."

Anne couldn't help but smile. Tom always seemed to know the right thing to say to her. And do to her. What she had learned about lovemaking over the last twenty-four hours could fill more volumes than all the law books in her office library.

Until she met Tom, she hadn't known what sensuality really meant. Or pleasure. If it had been up to him, they would probably be spending today in bed, as well. It hadn't been easy convincing him otherwise. Or herself.

Still, the very practical side of her had to admit that she could now suckle Tommy on either breast without the slightest discomfort. As long as Tom kissed or touched her first. And she loved the way Tommy fell into such a peaceful sleep after being at her breast.

Thoughts of Tommy brought Anne's focus back to the task at hand. They had to learn about this baby that Shrubber claimed was Tommy. And why Shrubber would make such a claim when Tom said otherwise.

Anne studied their surroundings. She could see that the county office had limited personnel, all clearly swamped with paperwork.

"I could introduce myself as a judge and see if that will speed things up," Anne said as she contemplated the long waiting line in front of them. "Thing is, I'm out of my jurisdiction here and I can't pretend that this is an official inquiry."

"Why don't you sit over there," Tom said, pointing to some chairs. "I'll see what I can do."

Anne understood he had worn his clerical garb and white collar today in the hope of facilitating their investigation.

She nodded and sat down with Tommy on her lap. He was such a bundle of energy this morning. He'd already pulled the top button off her blouse. She had only just saved him from swallowing it. She had few blouses left now without one or two buttons missing. She should have brought along a sewing kit.

But he was so cute she couldn't mind. He reached up, pulled her bangs and giggled. It was so wonderful to see him well and happy. Every time she thought about how close Shrubber had come to taking away this sweet child, it gave her a small chill. Tommy belonged with Tom. She was sure of it.

And with his mother?

She sighed. The reality of Tommy's mother was a wedge between Anne and the baby. And Tom. She was certain Tom did not love the mother of his child. He'd told her that he had never proposed to a woman before her—or wanted to. Anne believed him. But what was his relationship with the mother of his child? And why was it such a big secret?

Anne was used to facing problems squarely and dealing with them. But this woman's presence in their lives was like an ominous shadow. And only Tom was capable of bringing her into the light. Would he?

Tom's clerical collar, patience and courtesy won over the harried clerk who finally waited on him. Despite the fact that he couldn't provide the place or precise date of birth, she continued to search her database until the right record had been retrieved.

When Tom brought a certified copy of the birth certificate over to Anne, he sat beside her and they went over it together.

Anne quickly skimmed through the facts. "Birth date January 5. Four-fifteen in the morning. Delivered by a Dr. Martin Faust. The baby was born in a South Boston hospital?"

"Something about that disturbs you, Anne?"

"Andy told us the Kendralls live on Beacon Hill. Why would Heather Kendrall have gone all the way to South Boston to deliver her baby?"

"I see what you're saying. You don't think it's possible she could have been away from home, gone into labor and been rushed to the nearest hospital?"

"Maybe," Anne said, but she wasn't convinced. "Let's go to that South Boston hospital where she delivered. Any thoughts as to how we can get confidential information out of hospital personnel?"

"Not off the top of my head," Tom admitted. "But something tells me you do."

"I have an idea that might work," she said.

Tom watched the light dancing in her eyes. It was invigorating working with someone whose mind was so quick. And whose heart was so warm. He had fallen in love with Anne in ways that weren't remotely romantic, and yet were so much richer and real.

How much he wanted to tell her what was in his heart. But he knew it was still too soon to say the words. All he could do was continue to show her.

THE HOSPITAL TURNED OUT to be small and private. Anne hopped out of the car, eager to get started. Tom stayed behind to change the baby, and arranged to meet her later in the lobby. She had told Tom what she was going to do and he'd kissed her cheek, telling her she was brilliant.

Anne had never felt so accepted or appreciated for who she was.

Tom didn't try to control her as the other men in her life had. He controlled himself. His deep confidence had him applauding her accomplishments, not placing himself in petty competition with them.

He was the first man she'd ever met who didn't have to prove anything to anyone. He not only knew exactly who he was, he was totally comfortable with who he was.

She had been drawn to those qualities in him from the first, and with every passing second, she grew to appreciate them even more.

Anne entered the hospital and proceeded to the gift shop, where she bought a spring bouquet of irises, lilies, tulips and daisies. She then took the elevator to the maternal-newborn suite.

It was quiet on the floor. No expecting parents were in the waiting room. Anne approached the nurse who manned the central station, a stout woman somewhere in her forties, with rimless glasses and a busy air. The name tag on her lapel said Google.

Anne sent her a smile. "Hi. I've come to thank a nurse who took care of a new mother who delivered here recently. Can you help me?"

"What's the nurse's name?" Google asked in a clipped, quick tone.

"That's the problem," Anne said. "I don't know."

"Well, then, I don't see how I can help you."

"I thought maybe you could check the records to see who assisted the doctor," Anne said. "It would be in there, wouldn't it?"

Google didn't really want to do that. It was written all over her face. But Anne was smiling and holding up the bouquet of flowers, and it was clear that the nurse felt the pressure to at least try to be helpful.

"All right," she said, moving over to the computer. "What's the name of your friend?"

"Heather Kendrall."

Google typed in the name, then waited until the computer retrieved the information. "Kendrall delivered on the morning of January 5," she said in a tone that had definitely turned sour. "And you're just now deciding to thank the nurse?"

Anne smiled brilliantly. "Oh, wonderful. You found the record. What's her name?"

Google wore a lemon-sucking look on her face. "Ronley."

"And where may I find Nurse Ronley?" Anne asked.

"She's not here."

"May I reach her at her home?"

"I can't give out that information."

"Can you at least tell me when she'll next be on duty?"

"She's Faust's private nurse. She works on his schedule."

"Is Dr. Faust here?" Anne asked.

"Nope." Google was clearly getting tired of answering questions.

"Do you expect him anytime soon?" Anne persisted.

"He's only here when his patients check in to deliver. Babies don't get born on schedules."

Anne hid her irritation at the nurse's condescending tone as she thanked her. So much for her sleuthing skills. She was thoroughly disappointed as she walked toward the elevators to return to the lobby.

''Excuse me?'' a female voice called from behind her.

Anne stopped and turned to see a young nurse's aide approaching. She was in her late teens, with short, curly brown hair and a sweet smile. The name tag on her lapel said Lambert.

''Hi, I'm Bev,'' the nurse's aide said. ''I couldn't help overhearing your conversation with Google-puss...uh, I mean—''

''Google-puss fits her perfectly,'' Anne assured her.

Bev giggled. ''Anyway, I just wanted you to know that I was there, too, on the night your friend came in, and she was real nice to me. She even gave me this locket.''

The young woman held up a gold-plated locket hanging from a gold chain around her neck. The locket was engraved with the letter *L*.

Anne smiled. Maybe luck was with her, after all. ''Bev, these flowers are for you,'' she said, handing them to the nurse's aide. ''Can I buy you a cup of coffee or a soft drink or something?''

Bev took the flowers from her hand, looking thoroughly pleased. ''Yeah, well sure. I was just going on my break. Thanks.''

Five minutes later they were in the cafeteria, Anne with a tall glass of water—per her lactation instructions—and Bev with a giant Diet Coke and a plate of French fries.

''I'm sure her doctor picked this hospital,'' Bev said in answer to a question Anne had just asked. ''Faust always brings his patients here to deliver.''

''So Heather wasn't rushed here or anything?'' Anne asked.

''Hardly. She had already been in labor for nearly six hours when I came on shift at eleven that night,'' Bev said between bites. ''But she was real good about the pain, joking around and stuff. Some of the women. Whew! Do they scream.''

''What else do you remember about that night, Bev?'' Anne asked.

''I wasn't in the delivery room, but I got to see Heather and her baby when they rolled her back to her room. She looked so happy with her little boy in her arms. First thing she said to me was that he had his daddy's hair and eyes.''

"His daddy's hair," Anne repeated, remembering what Andy had said about Rolan Kendrall's toupee.

"Well, yeah, she had all that long, curly red hair and the baby had that straight patch of blond."

She had red hair? But Anne could have sworn Andy had said Heather Kendrall was a blond beauty.

"And her little boy had just the bluest eyes you ever did see," Bev said. "I know they say that all newborns have blue eyes. But it's not true. I've seen lots of 'em born with brown and even black."

"Did Heather's husband ever visit her in the hospital?" Anne asked.

"I don't know. Only man I ever saw her with was the male nurse who works for Dr. Faust."

"What's his name?" Anne asked.

"A huge guy with black hair and a really squeaky voice. He's not the kind you ask."

Bender? Anne's heart started to race right along with her speculations.

"Heather and me, we talked about rock groups and just all kinds of cool stuff," Bev related. "You would never know she was so old… I mean, so much older. Only that big male nurse kept telling me to get lost every time I tried to come by to say hello."

"Bev, the locket that Heather gave you. Did she get it in the gift shop?"

"No, she was wearing it when she came in."

Anne had begun to suspect as much.

"She gave it to me on the afternoon after she delivered, while I helped her walk up and down the hall," Bev continued. "She was asking me about the nurse's entrance and exit to the parking lot. Of course, I didn't know why at the time."

"You didn't know why she gave you the locket?" Anne asked, confused.

"Oh, I know she gave me the locket because she liked me and knew the *L* was the first letter of my last name. It was her wanting to know about the back way out of the hospital that I didn't get at first.''

''How do you mean?''

''She didn't tell you?''

''Tell me what, Bev?''

''She lit out the back exit that night with her baby when the nurse brought him for a feeding,'' Bev said. ''Didn't even bother waiting for her doctor to check her out. Just took off. That male nurse and her doctor were really ticked, I can tell you.''

ANNE HURRIED THROUGH the hospital lobby, looking for Tom and the baby. She had so much to share with him. But she couldn't see him or Tommy anywhere. Finally, she approached the gray-haired receptionist at the admissions desk.

''Excuse me, I was supposed to meet a priest—''

''Are you Anne?'' the receptionist interrupted.

''Yes,'' she said, surprised to be addressed by her name.

''Father Christen was called to the bedside of a dying man in intensive care. He asked if you'd meet him there. It's just around the corner to your right. Go straight down the hall. You'll see the signs for the family waiting room.''

Anne thanked the receptionist and headed down the hall. When she reached the waiting room, she found a couple in their sixties sitting together, softly crying.

On the woman's lap was Tommy. He, too, was crying, but not so softly. Anne went directly up to the woman.

''I'm Anne,'' she said, reaching for Tommy.

''Oh,'' the woman said, immediately relinquishing the baby.

Anne held Tommy close to her. He clutched her as though he had feared she had abandoned him. She knew Tom wouldn't have let the baby out of his arms if it hadn't been necessary, but she still hated the thought of Tommy being in a stranger's hands, even for a few minutes.

Tommy obviously wasn't too thrilled about it, either. Anne cuddled him, stroked his head and talked soothingly to him until he quieted. Then she took the vacant chair beside the weeping woman.

"Where's Father Christen?" Anne asked softly.

"He's in with our son," the man said.

So, it was this couple's son who was dying. Anne wished she knew what she could say to these distraught parents, but she had no words.

"We never knew!" the woman sobbed, her distress so intense that it welled and overflowed, like the tears streaming out of her eyes. "How could we have guessed what he had done?"

Anne understood that the woman wasn't really talking to her. The man wrapped his arm around his wife, holding him to her as tears flooded his face, as well. "Sweetheart, we got him the priest. It's all we could do. The rest is up to him."

A moment later Tom emerged from the intensive care unit with a chunky, gray-haired male surgeon. Both the surgeon and Tom approached the waiting couple.

"I'm sorry, Mr. and Mrs. Tomei," the surgeon said, grim faced. "We did what we could."

The couple looked at Tom. He sent them a reassuring smile. "He died in peace."

Anne knew then that Tom must have been summoned to their dying son's bedside to hear his confession and to give him absolution for whatever it was they had just learned he had done.

She'd never realized what a gift that could be until she saw the relief that cut into their sorrow.

Then the full impact of what she had just witnessed struck her with startling clarity.

And suddenly Anne had the answer to what had puzzled her for so long.

CHAPTER TEN

AS TOM WATCHED Mr. and Mrs. Tomei disappear into the intensive care unit with the doctor, he was glad that he had been here today for them, as well as their son. They had received a shock and had a tough decision before them. But after having first talked with them and then their son, Tom was confident that they would make the right choice.

He turned to Anne, intending to ask her what she had found out, only to be surprised into silence by the intense expression on her face as she stared at him.

"The damn answer was right there in front of me the whole time," she said.

Tom was stunned. Both by Anne's sudden cursing and the irritated edge to her tone.

She held Tommy out to him. Tom gently took the baby from her arms, wondering what had happened.

"I've just been too blind to see it," Anne said in that same irritated tone.

"What's wrong?" Tom asked as calmly as he could.

"You gave me the big clue, didn't you?" she said as she started to pace, her movements just as agitated as her words.

"Anne—" Tom began.

"'I'm not just a man,' you said," Anne interrupted. "'I'm a priest. I stand by my vows.' You even said that meant that you couldn't always tell me what I wanted to know."

Suddenly, Tom realized that Anne's anger wasn't directed at him. It was directed at herself. He carefully controlled the growing excitement inside him.

Anne stopped her pacing and came to stand directly in front

of him. Her eyes rose to his. "Lindy didn't just come by last Friday to have Tommy baptized. She also came by so you could hear her confession."

Tom's sigh of relief was soft and private, registering deep within his heart.

"Well, Tom?"

He was careful to keep his face and tone noncommittal. "Anne, if you're asking me whether I heard the confession of someone, you must understand I can't tell you. Even the fact that I might have heard a confession is a confidential matter between a priest and a parishioner."

Her eyes sparked with insight.

"Just what I thought," she said. "Everything you've refused to tell me—still refuse to tell me—is what you learned in Lindy's confession. Even the identity of Tommy's mother. The only fact that Lindy shared outside of her confession is that Tommy is yours."

Tom loved this bright, beautiful woman so much at this moment that it was taking every ounce of his control not to show it. But he couldn't show it because it could be interpreted for what it was—his total relief that she had finally understood.

Anne moved closer to him until they were breast-to-breast, and looked him right in the eye. "I've never liked the strong, silent type," she said in a voice too calm, too sensible.

When she paused, Tom felt the breath stall in his lungs.

"But I think I'm definitely going to make an exception in your case," she finished with a smile, and he recognized the similarity of the phrase he'd said to her three days before.

She leaned up then, grabbed the lapels of his black clerical jacket and kissed him hard on the mouth just as he had kissed her. And Tom fell in love with her all over again.

Anne leaned back and slipped her arm in the crook of his. "Come on, Father Christen," she said as she dragged him toward the exit. "While I'm on a roll, I have another mystery or two to solve today."

TOM AND ANNE SAT in adjoining cubicles in a nearby library less than twenty minutes later, going through the microfiche records of old newspapers.

"Your friend Andy did say that Heather Kendrall was a local beauty queen ten years ago?" Anne asked from the cubicle next to Tom's.

"That's what he said," Tom replied, shifting little Tommy in his arms.

Anne wished Andy had been a bit more specific. The local newspapers were pretty thick, and the local beauty queens were numerous. Having so many pages whiz by on the screen was beginning to give her a headache.

She had told Tom all about her conversation with the nurse's aide, Bev Lambert, on the way to the library. From the grim expression on Tom's face, Anne could tell that he hadn't been aware of the details surrounding Lindy's delivery and subsequent flight from the hospital.

Getting to the truth of all this was going to take some doing, with Tom not able to help out in the crucial areas—and Anne not exactly sure what those areas were.

But she didn't care. She was riding high on the relief of having finally figured out what had kept Tom silent for so long. She felt as though nothing could stop them now from uncovering the secret behind little Tommy's birth and Lindy's death.

Anne was bleary eyed by the time she finally found what she was looking for in the microfiche records. "Here she is," she called, excited to be at the end of her search.

Tom scooted his chair over to her. "Heather Svenson, Miss Firecracker," he read beneath the newspaper shot of the big beauty queen with the brilliant smile and shoulder-length blond hair pictured on the screen.

"That woman is a natural blonde," Anne said with conviction.

"And you obviously think that's important because...?" Tom asked.

"I don't know of any natural blondes who would dye their hair red," Anne said. "Did you find a picture of Rolan Kendrall in the society pages?"

Tom handed her a copy of the newspaper microfiche he had printed out. "This is the happy couple last year at a fund-raiser," he said.

Anne looked at the smiling photo of Heather Svenson Kendrall and her husband, Rolan. Heather now had short blond hair. In contrast to her very light coloring, he had black hair and eyes.

"The facts are impossible to ignore, Tom," Anne said as she looked at the picture of the Kendralls. "Bev told me that the baby's mother was wearing a locket inscribed with the initial *L*. That's *L* as in Lindy, not Heather. Bev also described her as having long, curly red hair. Heather Kendrall didn't give birth to that baby whose certificate bears her name. Lindy did."

"Yet the Kendralls clearly planned to claim the baby as theirs," Tom said as he stroked Tommy's cheek.

"And the presence of Bender in that hospital room proves that Attorney George Shrubber is up to his snout in that attempt to take Lindy's baby from her," Anne said.

Tom nodded. "The only reason they didn't succeed is because Lindy sneaked him out of the hospital with her."

"Can you tell me when you first heard of Shrubber, Bender and the Kendralls?" Anne asked.

"When Shrubber and Bender came to the Church of the Good Shepherd a few days ago," Tom answered.

"I pretty much figured that must be it," Anne said. "If Lindy had mentioned them in her confession, you never would have been so open about trying to find out about them."

"Speaking of Shrubber," Tom said, "I'd like to swing by his house and have a look."

"Couldn't hurt," Anne agreed as she grabbed her shoulder bag and rose. "There are a few things that are really bothering me," she confided as they headed out of the library. "One, what happened to Lindy's baby and how did she get hold of Tommy? And, two, why did Lindy agree to be admitted to the hospital and give birth under Heather Kendrall's name?"

"That second one is bothering me, as well," Tom said.

Anne hadn't expected he would comment on the first. She

imagined she could look forward to a lot of one-way conversations on that topic.

"I'd best warn you now, Tom Christen. Whether it turns out to be embarrassing to you or not because of all the women you were with a year ago, I'm going to find out which one is Tommy's mother and get to the bottom of these secrets."

Tom seemed amused by her threat. She supposed it was just the nature of the male beast to be anything but embarrassed by the number of women who had succumbed to his charms. And she had to admit, Tom was damnably charming.

Damn him.

THE FIRST ADDRESS Pat Hosmer had given Anne and Tom for Shrubber turned out to be a Georgian house on Brattle Street in Cambridge. It was red brick, with stately columns alongside the door and antique panes above it.

Anne consulted the assessor's sheet she held. "Two bedroom, two bath. Appraised at two million. Shrubber bought it just under two years ago, and get this. He paid cash."

"The private adoption business must be lucrative," Tom said as he stopped the Porsche a few doors down and parked it at the curb.

Anne gazed up and down the street of the well-kept, exclusive neighborhood. "I wish we could—"

"Get down, Anne," Tom interrupted, his deep voice a command as he slid down in his seat and pulled Anne with him.

"Tom, what—"

"It's Bender," Tom whispered, keeping an eye on the image in his side view mirror. "Stay down."

She actually didn't have a choice. Tom's strong arm was firmly anchored on her chest, and she sensed a deep, almost dangerous current flowing through him. When mere seconds later he withdrew his arm and sat up, he was so calm and seemed so relaxed that Anne wondered if she had imagined it.

"It's all right now," he said. "Bender's gone inside."

When she straightened, Anne looked toward the Georgian

house. Her eyes fixed on the green four-by-four that was now parked out front. Excitement pumped through her.

"Tom—"

"Yes, I know, a green van," he interrupted. He tore off a slip of paper from a pad he'd been scribbling on. "This is the license number. I'm assuming the next thing you'll want to do is to call your friend at the D.A.'s office?"

Anne had already pulled out her cell phone. After exchanging a few words with Pat and waiting for the records to be accessed, she got the information she needed, thanked her friend and flipped the cell phone closed.

"It's registered to a Claude Butz," Anne said. "Pat checked the name in her computer. Butz is a shady private investigator who lost his license four years ago when he shot a guy. His lawyer got the charge reduced to simple assault in the plea bargaining. And guess who that lawyer was."

"Shrubber," Tom said.

She nodded. "Butz served eighteen months in prison. Last information from his parole officer is that he's working as a bouncer at nightclubs. And, Tom, get this. Pat says the physical description on her record for Butz matches that of the guy Shrubber introduced to us as Chet Bender."

"So Shrubber lied," Tom said. "Bender really is Butz."

"His background and green van aren't enough to implicate Butz in Lindy's accident, but they're important pieces of evidence to add to the case against him and Shrubber."

"I thought it might be the prosecutor's wheels I've seen turning around in that beautiful head of yours," Tom said.

"You haven't seen anything yet," Anne promised, still riding high on her recent discoveries.

Tom glanced at the list of addresses Pat Hosmer had given Anne. "I didn't notice before, but this second address for Shrubber is in South Boston and not far from the hospital where Lindy delivered. We should head there next."

Tommy started to fuss in his car seat and Tom checked his watch.

"The little guy's hungry again and probably needs changing. We'd best make a stop at home first."

"Traveling with him would be so much easier if I were breast-feeding," Anne lamented.

"As soon as we get home, I'll see what I can do to hurry that process along," Tom said as he pulled the car away from the curb.

"We don't have any time to waste," Anne said, trying her best to sound practical, despite the juicy little thrills already shooting through her in anticipation of what Tom intended.

"Don't worry, Anne," Tom assured her with that irresistible air of a man who knew exactly what he was doing. "I'm not planning on wasting any time."

"ANNE VANDREE DIDN'T GIVE birth to any baby," Claude Butz said as he stood in front of Shrubber's ornate desk inside the Georgian house on Brattle Street.

Shrubber leaned forward in his heavy baroque chair, juggling a brass paperweight in the shape of a football. "This better not be another one of your screwups, Butz."

"Believe me, Mr. Shrubber," Butz said. "I checked every birth record in the Berkshires. The judge lied. That's Lindy Olson's baby she and the priest have."

"Damn," Shrubber said. "Why are they claiming it's theirs? What are they up to?"

"Does it matter?" Butz asked with a shrug. "Important thing is that you can demand they return the baby. After all, you have the birth records showing the kid is the Kendralls'."

"Don't be a fool," Shrubber said irritably as he swung out of his chair. "I can't afford to make this a legal matter. If I go to court to press the point over this kid against a priest and a judge, our whole operation could come under scrutiny."

"You going to give the Kendralls another kid?"

"Thanks to you they don't want another kid," Shrubber said, spitting out the words. "I told you never to let one of our clients hold a baby until it was out of the hospital and officially in their hands."

"Heather Kendrall didn't go through me, Mr. Shrubber," Butz said. "She bribed one of the nurses in the maternity ward."

"I don't care who she bribed. You were at the hospital to keep a lid on things."

"But I had my hands full watching the girl."

"Fat lot of good that did," Shrubber said, slamming the brass paperweight onto his desk. "You still let her and the baby slip through your fingers. Now the Kendralls are threatening to go public if they don't get that damn kid."

"What are we going to do?" Butz asked.

"*We* aren't going to do anything. *You're* going to get that baby back."

"You mean just take him?" Butz asked. "But what about the priest and the judge?"

"What about them?" Shrubber challenged. "They know the kid's not theirs. And it's obvious Lindy didn't tell them anything important. Otherwise the cops would be all over us."

"Even if I can snatch the kid when they're not looking, they're bound to figure out who did it and come after me," Butz said.

"They don't know your real name. I can afford to send you out of the country for a while until things cool down."

"What if they come after you?"

"I'll have an airtight alibi, and I won't have the kid by then, anyway," Shrubber said. "The Kendralls will be at their home in Spain—out of the country and out of reach. All they'll have to say, if asked, is that their baby has been with them since his birth."

"They'll do that?" Butz asked.

"They want that kid so badly they'll say anything I tell them to. They'll have his birth record. And they'll have him."

"Yeah, I guess you're right," Butz agreed.

"No guessing about it. Possession is nine-tenths of the law. That priest and judge won't be able to prove a thing."

"There's just one problem, Mr. Shrubber," Butz said.

"What is it now?"

"The priest and judge left the Berkshires with the baby, and I don't know where they went."

"Well, find them, damn it!" Shrubber said as he picked up the paperweight and threw it across the room. "And you better make it fast. Or I swear you'll be back to bouncing drunks."

IT WAS THE MIDDLE of the afternoon when Tom and Anne arrived in the South Boston neighborhood where George Shrubber's second home was located. Tom parked across the street in the residential section as he and Anne studied the property together.

It was an older, two-story structure. The high, thick wall of shrubbery that surrounded it hid all but the uppermost portion of the second story.

"How is the property described on the assessor's sheet?" Tom asked.

Anne referred to the record her friend Pat had provided.

"Multilevel Victorian home built in 1900. It has seven bedrooms, three full baths, one half bath, and is approximately forty-three hundred square feet," she related. "And it, too, is paid for as of last April."

"When did Shrubber buy it?" Tom asked.

"Two and a half years ago."

"About six months before the home in Cambridge," Tom said.

"It's appraised at around a million dollars," Anne said. "We know Shrubber didn't get his wife's money when they divorced. According to Pat, he only became a private adoption attorney three years ago. How did he come by so much money so fast?"

"And why would a divorced man with no kids want to acquire a house this large?" Tom added.

He spied an older woman coming out of a house a few doors down from the Shrubber property, a Labrador retriever on the end of the leash in her hand.

"Let's see what the neighbor knows," Tom said, unfastening his seat belt.

"You're just going to walk up to a strange woman and ask her about Shrubber and his house?" Anne asked.

"No, we're going to," Tom said as he took off his clerical collar. "See that For Sale sign over there?"

Anne twisted in her seat to follow Tom's pointing finger. She saw the sign in front of one of the houses farther down the street and nodded.

"Looks just like the kind of starter home a new family like ours might be looking for, doesn't it?" Tom asked.

"You mean the kind of starter home we're going to pretend to be looking for," Anne said, catching on.

"All we have to say is that we saw the sign, then ask her if she can tell us about the neighborhood," Tom said.

Anne shook her head as she unfastened her seat belt. "I should have known you wouldn't lie. Still, you display an amazing aptitude for subterfuge, Tom Christen."

"One of those good points of mine I forgot to mention earlier," Tom said, grinning as he reached back to unstrap the baby from his car seat.

"IT'S A NICE, FRIENDLY neighborhood, like I told you," Violet Fransen assured Tom and Anne over tea and cookies in her cozy kitchen.

It hadn't taken much to maneuver the loquacious Vi with the silver hair and a face as lined as a roadmap to not only talk about her neighbors, but invite Anne and Tom back to the comfort of her home while she did it. For the past forty minutes they had listened patiently to the intimate details of nearly every family on the block.

Now, finally, Vi had gotten to the Shrubber house. "But I just don't like what's happening in that big old house on the corner."

"Oh?" Anne prompted.

"The previous owners were such a nice young family," Vi said as she poured more tea into all their cups. "Like you and your hubby, they had a cute new baby. They also had a toddler and a sweet six-year-old girl with a Great Dane puppy. Only they had to move up to New Hampshire when he got a job transfer. And now...''

Anne knew Vi wanted to talk about it. Was just waiting for the slightest encouragement. She was happy to give it. ''Who owns the place now?''

Vi leaned across the table as though about to share a secret. ''I don't know, but the young women who go to live there are all pregnant! I've seen them through the hedge when me and Licorice, here, go for our daily walk. The hedge is one of his favorite spots. Isn't it, Licorice?'' She patted the gentle Labrador's head as he sat next to her chair.

''How many young women?'' Tom asked.

''Anywhere from eight to twelve,'' Vi said. ''Some aren't even showing when they arrive, but in a few months, well, it's obvious. Of course, the faces change as their time comes and they go off to deliver. But new ones keep arriving to replace the ones who leave. And always so young. I've even seen some of them on the yard swing playing with dolls. Can you imagine? Babies having babies.''

Vi shook her head.

''Doesn't sound good,'' Anne agreed. ''Have you ever talked to any of the young women?''

''Once,'' Vi said. ''Last fall a pretty brunette—had to be seven, eight months along—was strolling down the street right outside my house and stopped to pet Licorice. We were having a nice chat about the weather when suddenly this chunky nurse comes barreling out of the gates of that old Victorian house and descends on us like a bad wind. 'Get back inside,' she yells at the girl. 'You know you're not supposed to be out here.' Why, she talked to her just like a warden would a prisoner.''

''The girl returned to the house?'' Tom asked.

''Like a little whipped puppy,'' Vi said. ''And that nurse locked the gate behind her. Yep, just like a jailer.''

''What do you think it all means, Vi?'' Anne heard Tom ask with wonderful innocence as he bounced Tommy on his knee.

''Well, Mr. Christen, they've got to be girls who've gotten themselves in trouble and whose families have sent them away to have their babies,'' the older woman said. ''It's what families used to do in my day.'' She paused, then turned to Anne. ''Although you'd think in this day and age, things would have become more tolerant. Those poor girls are living away from their families, kept out of school. It's not right they should be so confined.''

Anne nodded, and not just because she knew Vi was looking for agreement. ''Surely their parents visit them?''

Vi shook her head. ''No, I've never seen anything but delivery trucks with groceries go inside. Oh, and the gardener, although I haven't see him in a couple of months.''

''Some reason why he doesn't come by anymore?'' Anne asked.

''Just stopped showing up,'' Vi said. ''Which is a shame. He's a nice young man. I used to chat with him when he trimmed the hedges around the place. Of course, he was a little shy at first on account of his scar.''

''Is the scar on his face?'' Tom asked.

''Bad one on his right cheek,'' Vi said, pointing to the spot on her own. ''Accident when he was a kid, I think he said. But just as friendly as can be when you got to know him. I used to hear him talking to one of the girls behind the hedge, joking with her.''

''What's his name?'' Anne asked. ''In case Tom and I need his services,'' she quickly added.

''Benny.''

''And his last name?''

Vi shook her head. ''Sorry. Never asked. I do my own gardening. But I think the name on the company van he drove was Sunny Gardens or something like that. Oh, I nearly forgot the doctor.''

''Doctor?'' Tom repeated.

''He's in and out of the place all the time,'' Vi said.

''Well, at least the young women are getting medical care,'' Tom replied conversationally.

''I suppose, but between you and me, I don't like the look of him,'' Vi said. ''Tall, hard faced, parks that big, black Mercedes of his out in front and barrels through the gates carrying his small black doctor's bag. I tried to say hello once and he just ignored me.''

''How rude,'' Anne agreed with a shake of her head.

Tom and Anne chitchatted with Vi some more before thanking her for the tea and cookies and leaving. When Tom pulled the car away from the curb, he put into words what was on both their minds.

''Now we know why Shrubber bought this South Boston property. He's using it to house pregnant teenagers until they give birth. This is where he's getting the babies for his private adoptions.''

''I don't like the way he's keeping them locked up,'' Anne said.

''Neither do I.''

''Tom, do you think he's doing the same thing to them he did to Lindy?''

''You mean not letting them give birth under their own name,'' Tom guessed.

''It's totally illegal, of course,'' Anne said, ''but it would be a slick way to circumvent the need for a formal adoption.''

''First he instructs his client to pretend to be pregnant, and then when the baby's ready to be born to the teenager, he has her deliver using the client's name,'' Tom said. ''The birth record shows the client is the parent.''

''And no one is the wiser except the girl and her parents,'' Anne agreed. ''Although they can't be very caring parents to allow their daughters to be locked up like that during their pregnancy and not even visit them.''

''Unless, like Lindy, their parents aren't in the picture,'' Tom proposed.

Anne shot up in her seat. ''Are you saying you think all the girls could be runaways?''

''It would sure make it easier on Shrubber if they were,'' Tom said grimly. ''No parents to deal with. Far less chance the underage mother would change her mind and decide to keep her baby.''

"And he sends the burly Butz along to the hospital just to make sure they don't." Anne shook her head. "Tom, if those girls are runaways, that gardener, Benny, might be able to verify it. Vi said he talked to at least one of the girls."

Tom nodded. "We'll pull over at the next phone booth and check the yellow pages for Sunny Gardens and see what we find."

TOM DIDN'T FIND a Sunny Gardens listed in the yellow pages. But he did find a Summer Gardens and a Garden of Sunny Delights. Tom called one using the pay phone, while Anne used her cell phone to contact the other.

"No luck with Summer Gardens," Tom said when he returned to the car. "What about the Garden of Sunny Delights?"

"I'm not sure," Anne said. "The person who answered the phone didn't speak English very well. When I asked for Benny, he said, 'No, so sorry,' and hung up on me."

Tom checked the address. "It's only a few blocks away. Let's drive over."

When they arrived at the Garden of Sunny Delights nursery, they found it to be a small but beautifully maintained sea of green nestled within a block of brick-and-mortar buildings. In the lush greenhouse, spring flowers were in fragrant bloom.

Anne was fingering the velvet petals of some peach-colored tulips when a smiling Chinese-American man came out of the back and approached. "May I help you?" he asked.

"We're looking for Benny," Tom said.

The proprietor lost his smile. "No work here no more." He turned and started to walk away. Tom called out to him in Chinese. The man turned around, a look of pleasant surprise lighting his features.

But it was Anne who was the most surprised as Tom proceeded to carry on what sounded like a very fluent conversation in the other man's native language.

When they were finished, he exchanged bows with the proprietor and took Anne's arm to leave.

"Where did you learn to speak Chinese?" she asked.

''A friend taught me,'' Tom said easily. ''It seems Benny was dismissed from the employment at the Garden of Sunny Delights when a customer complained that he was getting too familiar with his daughters. Want to guess who that customer was?''

''Shrubber,'' Anne said.

Tom nodded.

''Shrubber has no daughters,'' Anne said. ''He just wanted to get rid of Benny. Why?''

''Let's go ask Benny,'' Tom said. ''The very accommodating gentleman gave me his address. It's just a couple of miles from here.''

''Shouldn't we call first?'' Anne asked.

''He doesn't have a telephone.''

THE RESIDENTIAL SECTION where Benny lived was full of older, small family homes not particularly well kept. Young kids played kick ball on the street. On the far corner, several teenage males bunched together, smoking cigarettes and laughing as they listened to loud rock music.

Tom pulled to the curb in the middle of the block, in front of a graying clapboard house that had once been white. A junked car rusted where the lawn used to be.

''This is it,'' Tom said.

He put his clerical collar back on before he got out of the car and circled to the passenger side to open the door for Anne. Then he lifted Tommy out of his car seat and handed him to her.

''Stay close beside me,'' he said softly.

''You don't expect trouble?'' Anne asked.

''Not really,'' he said as he closed the car door. ''Just a precaution.''

When Tom didn't go up to the front door, but led Anne down the narrow dirt driveway toward the back, she became confused.

Tom read the expression on her face. ''Benny's parents live in the main house. Benny's in a converted garage at the back.''

It wasn't large, but the converted garage didn't look quite as dilapidated as Anne had anticipated. There were curtains at its two small windows. And around its periphery was a recently fertilized garden with healthy-looking shrubs and even some early spring flowers.

Anne could hear the sounds of a loud TV sports show playing inside as Tom knocked on the door.

"Whadya want?" a gruff, irritated male voice called over the noise.

"Benny, I'd like to talk to you," Tom called back.

"Yeah, and who are you?" Benny demanded.

"Father Tom Christen."

The TV sports show was abruptly muted. A moment later the door swung wide.

A young man no more than twenty stood facing them. He was well over six feet tall, dark, hairy and husky, wearing a stained T-shirt, dirty jeans and smelling of beer. Even several days' stubble could not hide the thick, ugly scar that puckered the flesh on his right cheek.

But it was his eyes that caught Anne's immediate attention. They were coal-black, furious, frightening. And staring directly at Tom.

"You no-good bastard!" Benny yelled.

Then the angry young man threw a punch right at Tom's face.

CHAPTER ELEVEN

TOM SAW THE PUNCH coming and pulled Anne with him as he smoothly stepped aside. Benny's fist connected with nothing but air. Tom swiftly grabbed Benny's arm, twisted it behind his back, spun him around and pitched him headfirst onto cushions that lined the floor a few feet into the room.

Benny crumpled on top of them with a groan.

Two other guys in the room immediately charged Tom. They were around the same age as Benny, the first one dark and wiry, the second one red-haired and bulkier than Benny.

Tom used the force of their combined momentum to hurl them out the door and face-first into the freshly fertilized flower bed. The wiry one smashed his shoulder against a wooden stake and let out a yelp before he took off running. The redheaded one landed hard and rolled over, spitting manure out of his mouth. He shot Tom a scared look before he scurried to his feet and sprinted off down the drive after his companion.

Calmly turning to Anne, Tom asked, ''Would you care to wait in the car?''

Anne's eyes shone with surprise and admiration. ''And miss more of this? Not on your life,'' she said, stepping into the room.

Tom hid his smile as he followed her inside and closed the door behind them, locking it securely. He surveyed the interior of the converted garage. It was just one big room, the only other door leading to a bathroom at the end. An area had been sectioned off to serve as a kitchen, and contained a microwave, refrigerator and hot plate. Another area contained a bed and nightstand.

Empty pizza cartons and beer cans littered the coffee table

and floor. The cushions of the only couch in the room had been tossed on the floor in front of the TV. Those were the cushions Benny was sprawled over.

When Tom leaned down to switch off the muted TV, he saw the newspaper next to the cushions. Its headline read Boston Runaway Found Dead in the Berkshires, and Lindy's picture was beneath it.

He gestured to Anne to take one of the two straight-back kitchen chairs. She nodded as she sat, settling Tommy on her lap.

Tom remained standing over Benny, waiting for him to get up. It was another minute before the young man rolled over and made it to his knees. He raised his head and stared up at Tom.

"Where's Spike and Hank?" Benny demanded.

"If you mean your friends, they seem to have remembered a previous engagement," Tom said. "I don't imagine they'll be back anytime soon. You want to tell me why you think you have a right to take a swing at me?"

"She's dead because of you," Benny said, spitting out the words.

Tom didn't have to ask whom he meant. "Why don't you tell me how you knew Lindy."

"Go to hell."

Benny tried to get up and wobbled. Tom took his arm to steady him and brought him the rest of the way to his feet.

"You're not the only one who cared about her," Tom said quietly.

Benny stood staring at him for a long moment as though trying to make up his mind whether to believe him. Finally, Benny shrugged and gestured in Anne's direction. "Who's she?"

"My wife," Tom said.

Surprise hopped into Benny's eyes as he turned to stare at the rings on Anne's left finger. "Lindy never told me you were married."

"What did she tell you, Benny?"

The youth snorted and shook his head. "Never enough." He

plopped down on the cushions he'd just gotten up from and let out a long breath.

"I'd like to hear about it," Tom said.

Benny grabbed a can of beer that sat on the floor next to him. He chugged what was left in it, then crushed the can with his bare hands and tossed it back on the concrete floor. "Why not?" he said, as though to himself. "What does it matter anymore?"

Tom slipped onto the chair across from Anne, no longer concerned that Benny might try to slug him. Whatever fight was in the young man had gone.

"You met Lindy while you were tending the grounds at the Shrubber place," Tom guessed.

"Yeah," Benny said. "The other girls would take one look at this sorry face of mine and cringe. But not Lindy. 'Course, she was careful when she talked to me. Always waited until that battle-ax of a nurse had gone inside."

"The one who acts like a warden," Tom said, remembering Vi Fransen's words.

"Old fat-face Ronley," Benny said, nodding. "She told all the girls to stay away from me. But Lindy ignored her. Even asked me if she could help. I was trying to right this sapling that had blown down in a storm. Lindy held it for me while I drove a new brace into the ground."

"When was this, Benny?" Tom asked.

"Must've been six months ago now. Lindy was pretty pregnant by then. But on her it looked good 'cause she was happy about it. Not like some of the others, who were only doing it for the money."

"Money?" Anne repeated.

Benny looked over at her. "You don't know?"

"Why don't you tell us about it, Benny?" Tom suggested.

"Them runaways," Benny said, still looking at Anne. "They get pregnant for the money Butz promises them for their babies."

"They're not already pregnant?" Anne asked.

"Nope. Least ways not most of 'em. Couple hit town that way. But Butz prefers the young ones who aren't already knocked up. He normally can't interest the prostitutes. They don't need the money.''

''So Butz is out looking for runaways,'' Tom asked.

''All the time,'' Benny said. ''It's the runaways that need the money.''

''But you said Lindy didn't do it for money,'' Anne prompted.

''No, she had other reasons.'' Benny paused to glare at Tom. ''When Butz approached her, she told him she'd get pregnant, no problem, as long as she could pick the father.''

''Who normally fathers the children of the runaways?'' Anne asked.

''Lindy never said.''

''Was Lindy living on the streets when Butz approached her with his proposition?'' Tom asked.

''You know she was,'' Benny said sulkily. ''It was right after you shut her out.''

''How exactly did I shut her out?''

''She was in love with you, man.'' Anger laced Benny's words. ''Would've done anything for you. And you turned your back on her.''

''I couldn't love Lindy the way she wanted me to, Benny,'' Tom said calmly. ''But that doesn't mean I didn't try to do my best for her.''

Benny looked down at the picture of Lindy in the newspaper. ''It wasn't enough, preacher.''

''You're right, Benny,'' Tom agreed softly. ''It wasn't enough.''

Benny's head came up at Tom's words and he looked into his face. What Benny read there took the last vestiges of anger out of his eyes.

''How much money is Shrubber paying the girls?'' Anne asked after a moment.

Benny looked over at her when he answered. ''Lindy said two thousand cash apiece. 'Course, they get nine months of free room and board and all the doctoring stuff to go with it. As soon as they're knocked up, Shrubber insists on 'em being confined to that old house of his with that witch of a nurse. She lives with 'em twenty-four hours a day.''

''Why is that?'' Tom asked.

''Shrubber has 'em tested first, makes sure they're clean of drugs and disease. That's why Butz tries to get the young ones who've just hit town and haven't gotten into the drug scene. Shrubber tells 'em part of the deal is that they have to stay clean until they deliver.''

''So the nurse is there to keep them away from drugs,'' Anne said.

''And sex. Lindy always had to sneak away from the nurse to talk to me. They make sure the girls don't get around any guys so they don't catch nothin'. Not that she and I did anything but talk.''

''Do the girls know where their babies are going?'' Anne asked.

''Infertile couples,'' Benny said. ''Each girl is given a name she's supposed to use when it comes time for her to deliver. It's just in case some nosy hospital staff ask. But the doc always takes that Ronley nurse along to the delivery room to avoid as much contact with regular hospital staff as he can.''

''What happens to the girls after they deliver?'' Tom asked.

''Shrubber takes their babies, pays 'em their money and has Butz dump 'em back on the streets.''

''But Lindy sneaked out of the hospital with her baby before they could take him,'' Anne said.

''Yeah. Planned it that way from the first. Lindy wasn't like them other girls, all broke and scared and willing to do almost anything for some cash. She had money she never told Butz or Shrubber about.'' Benny flashed Tom a look. ''Told me she earned it working for you.''

''She did,'' Tom said. ''So how did she arrange to get away from the hospital?''

''She wanted to buy the old Beetle that my uncle gave me for my birthday,'' Benny said. ''Offered me a hundred more than it was worth. All I had to do was park it down the street from the hospital when she went to deliver.''

''Is that what you did?'' Tom asked.

''No way,'' Benny said. ''She'd only driven a couple of times, and never a stick shift. I wasn't going to let her get behind the wheel, especially after just having a baby.''

''You were a good friend,'' Anne said.

Benny looked over at her and shrugged.

''So you waited for her in the VW,'' Tom guessed.

''Nearly ten hours,'' Benny admitted. ''It was January and the snow was a foot high. I nearly froze my butt off. Then suddenly there she was, coming down the street toward me, wearing only a hospital gown and slippers and carrying the baby. I got her into the car as fast as I could and we lit out of there.''

''Where did you go?'' Tom asked.

''Here,'' Benny said. ''Had no place else. After she rested up a couple of days, she asked me to drive her over to see you at the parish. She wanted to show you the baby. I think she thought that when you saw him you'd...well, you'd marry her and everything would be all right. Only when we got there, the rector said Lindy's call to the bishop had ended up driving you out of the parish. And he wouldn't tell Lindy where you had gone.''

''How did Lindy react to the news?'' Anne inquired quietly.

''It bummed her out at first,'' Benny said. ''Then, after a few days, she seemed to be okay again. Asked me to teach her to drive. Said she wanted to take me to work and pick me up afterward. Said that would give her a chance to do the grocery shopping for us and not leave everything to me. I was happy to teach her. I thought that meant... I hoped she might be thinking of staying around awhile.''

''You were in love with her, Benny?'' Anne's voice was very gentle as she asked the question.

The bleak look on Benny's face was answer enough. ''I bought curtains for the windows, even got her a box of chocolates. But when I tried to kiss her, she pushed me away. Stupid to think a pretty girl like Lindy could ever love a face like this.''

Benny paused and looked down at his hands. ''She didn't pick me up after work the next day. I wasn't surprised when I got home and found she and the car were gone.''

"Did you try to find her?" Tom asked.

"No point," Benny said as he raised his eyes to him. "I knew she'd be searching for you. It was always you."

"You never heard from her again?" Anne asked.

"No, but Butz paid me a call a couple of days later."

"He came here?" Tom asked.

"Yeah," Benny said. "Busted in my door. Demanded to know where Lindy and the baby were. Someone at the house must've seen me talking to Lindy and blabbed. But I knew Butz couldn't have really known anything, otherwise he would have come by a lot sooner. Anyway, he knocked me around a bit trying to get me to talk. When I kept telling him he was crazy and I didn't know anything about Lindy or a baby, he finally gave up and left."

"Yet Shrubber still got you fired," Tom said.

"The bastard told my boss I was coming on to his daughters. What a crock, pretending those runaways were his daughters."

Benny looked at Anne and the baby. "That's Lindy's baby, isn't it?" he said.

Tom saw the frown on Anne's face.

"What makes you think so?" she asked.

"Got the same coloring and all. 'Course, he's bigger now. And he's awake and looking around. All he did when he was here was eat, sleep, pee or poop. But what the hell. I didn't complain. He was her kid. And he made her happy. That's all I ever wanted to do. Just make her happy."

And Tom believed it because he saw the misery in Benny's eyes.

"TOM, I HAVE TO TALK to you," Anne said as they sat across from each other that night at his Boston home. They had fed the baby and just finished a dinner of beef stew and biscuits from the supplies that Connie and the women of the parish had provided.

Tom knew that Anne was troubled. She had barely said two words since they'd left Benny's house three hours before. And she was looking at Tommy sleeping in her lap with a frown on her face. She never frowned when she looked at Tommy.

"What is it, Anne?" he asked, bracing himself.

"I want to tell Pat—no, I *have* to tell Pat about what Shrubber and Butz are up to with those runaway girls."

"When do you plan to do this?" he asked.

"I have to do it soon," Anne said. "The thing is, I don't have the answers to some questions she's bound to ask."

"Such as?"

"I know you told me you didn't impregnate Lindy," Anne continued, her eyes still on Tommy as she gently stroked his cheek, the frown digging a dent between her eyebrows. "And I believe you. But from everything we've learned so far, it just seems..."

"It seems what, Anne?" Tom prompted.

"The nurse's aide at the hospital said that Lindy had a blond-haired, blue-eyed baby that Lindy claimed looked just like his father. Rolan Kendrall sure couldn't have been the dad, since he has black hair and eyes. And Lindy obviously told Benny it was you. Benny also recognized Tommy as being the baby Lindy brought home from the hospital."

Tom waited for what he knew Anne was going to ask.

Finally, her eyes rose from the baby's face to his. "Where is Lindy's child and how did she get Tommy?"

"Anne, I cannot talk about this."

She sighed. "I was afraid that was what you were going to say."

"You know I will tell you whatever I can."

"Yes. But I can't go to the D.A.'s office with what I have now. There are too many unanswered questions. We could prove Tommy is yours with a DNA test. But if I go for one, Pat is going to ask who his mother is. When I don't have an answer to give her, she is going to be between that proverbial rock and a hard place. She's my friend, Tom. But she's also an officer of the court. A child's missing mother is not something she can overlook. Even my order giving you temporary custody could be rescinded."

"Why?" Tom asked.

"Since I've become your wife, I can no longer be considered a disinterested party."

"I see."

She was quiet a moment more before she said, "There's something else."

"What's that, Anne?"

"You subdued Benny and his friends so easily this afternoon. And there were three of them."

"And that's begun to bother you," Tom guessed.

"No. What's bothering me is that I now realize you didn't need me to burst in and tell Shrubber and Butz that Tommy was ours in order to prevent them from taking him. You could have stopped them yourself, couldn't you?"

He smiled. "That doesn't mean I don't love and admire what you did for me that day, Anne."

"What I did that day led to us both being trapped into this fake marriage," she said with an unhappy sigh.

Tom felt the sting of her words. She still thought their marriage a fake? He had hoped with everything they had shared over the past few days that she had begun to realize how very real it was.

"You have some special kind of training in fighting, don't you?" Anne asked.

"A little."

"A little," she repeated. "Is that like a *little* pregnant?"

Tom chuckled.

"Just what I thought." A rueful smile drew back Anne's lips. "I doubt it was part of the curriculum covered at the seminary."

"Not exactly," Tom agreed.

"I asked you once before what led you to become a priest. You didn't want to tell me then. Will you tell me now?"

Maybe it was time he did. At least this was something he could share with her, even if he preferred not to.

Tom picked up the bottle of burgundy she had opened earlier to go with their dinner, and offered Anne some. When she shook her head, he filled his glass.

''I told you how my parents, grandfather, aunt and uncle died when I was five,'' he began.

''And your grandmother took care of you,'' Anne said, remembering Tom's words.

''My grandmother wasn't physically strong. The death of her husband and three children hit her hard. I was her only grandchild. I believe she did her best for me in the time we were together. But the grief that never lifted from her heart finally took her two years later.''

''When you were seven,'' Anne said, feeling incredibly sad for his losses.

''My grandmother made sure that the family's estate was placed in trust for me. But by law I couldn't get access to it until I was eighteen. Since I had no living relatives, I became a ward of the state and ended up in a foster home.''

''In New York City?''

Tom nodded. ''On the surface the foster home looked fine. The father had a good-paying job. The mother was a homemaker with two boys of her own.''

But as Anne soon learned, there was a lot wrong beneath the surface of this ideal foster family. The father gambled away most of his paycheck every week. The mother had taken Tom in only to get enough money to pay for food for herself and her sons. They were three and four years older, and took turns beating him up. Their mother never stopped them. Tom's bedroom was a closet, his bed the floor.

''And I once wondered why you had something against the foster care system,'' Anne said with a sad shake of her head.

''The neighborhood wasn't the best. There were bullies who preyed on kids with lunch money on their way to school. I learned not to carry any.''

''You didn't get any lunch?'' she asked.

''Anne, I'm only bringing up this part to explain about Li Yu-Tang.''

''Who is Li Yu-Tang?''

He was a new boy to the neighborhood, Tom related. Of Chinese ancestry. A lot smaller than the other eleven-year-olds in their class. Which made him immediate prey for the bullies. Tom was walking to school the morning after the new boy arrived when he saw three bullies getting ready to jump him. Tom couldn't let them beat up the little kid. He charged them, threw his lunch at the biggest of the bullies and yelled for Yu-Tang to run. He didn't.

"What happened?" Anne asked, wondering if she really wanted to know.

"While I was barely holding my own with the big guy," Tom said, "Yu-Tang flattened the other two. Then he came over and finished the guy I was fighting."

"He knew martial arts," Anne said with a relieved smile.

"His two uncles were Kung-Fu masters," Tom confirmed. "And Yu-Tang was well on his way to being one. We were best friends from that day on. After he finished teaching me what he knew, I no longer worried about carrying lunch money to school."

"What of the older boys in that foster home?"

"Let's just say they began to respect my closet space."

"I'm glad you learned to defend yourself so well," Anne said.

Tom was happy to hear it. Especially with what he had to tell her next.

Yu-Tang's reputation for being an unbeatable fighter spread over the next year. His fighting skills kept trouble away a lot of the time, but they also drew trouble. A sixteen-year-old named Gordo, who had been trained in karate and kick boxing and was twice Yu-Tang's size, challenged him to a fight. But Yu-Tang never fought unless attacked. Gordo was so bent on proving he was a better fighter that he jumped Yu-Tang. Yu-Tang knocked Gordo out in less than a minute.

"Gordo came to boiling mad," Tom said. "He swore he'd get revenge. The next day he got hold of his father's gun, lay in wait for Yu-Tang and shot him dead."

"Dear God," Anne gave a long, sad sigh.

Tom drank the wine in his glass, then waited until the warmth reached his stomach. He needed that warmth at the moment as painful memories returned. And the remembered hatred that had encased his twelve-year-old heart.

"Yu-Tang was my best friend, Anne. In truth, the only friend I'd known up to that point. I went after Gordo. When I found him, I used everything that Yu-Tang had taught me. I intended to kill him. But I was stopped."

"What stopped you?" Anne asked.

"We were in an alley behind an Episcopal church. Father Edward Thurman was the rector there. He heard the commotion and came out to see what was going on. Father Ed was pushing sixty but he still had the guts to pull me off Gordo. When the police came, I told them Gordo had killed Yu-Tang and why. When Gordo got out of the hospital a month later—"

"Wait a minute," Anne said. "You beat him up so badly he was in the hospital for a month?"

"If Father Ed had pulled me off him five seconds later, he would have been in the morgue," Tom said quietly.

Anne let out a long, shaky breath.

"Gordo was tried as an adult for the murder of Yu-Tang," Tom continued. "He's still serving his sentence. I was charged, as well."

"With assault?" Anne asked.

Tom nodded. "I served six months in a juvenile detention center."

It would have been a lot longer, Tom admitted to Anne, if Father Thurman hadn't interceded. He'd told the judge that Tom could have easily beaten him, too, but he hadn't. After he'd served his time, the foster family refused to take Tom back. He was glad. Still, no other family was willing to take him. Not a kid who had just served six months for assault.

"Where did you go?" Anne asked.

"Out on the streets just as soon as I could escape the state-run boardinghouse."

"You were on the streets at twelve years old?"

"Trust me, Anne. I met better people there than I did in that state-run facility."

"But how did you live?"

"I got by. Then one day while I was digging French fries out of a dumpster, I met up with Father Edward Thurman again."

"The priest who pulled you off Gordo."

Tom nodded. Father Ed had bought him a hamburger and some milk and sat with him while he ate. Tom had found him easy to talk to. He'd told Father Ed about his parents, his grandmother, his foster home. The priest took Tom home with him. His wife, Beatrice, was blind, but her nose was working well. The moment she got a whiff of Tom, she sent him off to the bathroom to shower.

"How long had you been on the streets?" Anne asked.

"Several months."

Beatrice gave Tom an old bathrobe of Ed's to wear while she washed his clothes. Over dinner that night, he learned she and Ed had married late. Too late to have children. Too late to adopt. Too late to be considered for foster care. But they took care of him from then on.

They educated him at their home. Ed also taught Tom carpentry, Ed's hobby. He was a devout man, Tom said, who firmly believed in church teachings. Yet he never once pushed his faith on Tom.

"All he ever told me was to remember that my right to choose was the most powerful right I possessed," Tom said. "And with every choice I made, I created who I was."

"He sounds like a very special man."

"He was the best," Tom said with feeling.

When he was eighteen Tom gained access to his family's estate and tried to pay Ed and Beatrice back for all they had done for him. They had so very little. Yet they wouldn't accept a dime from him. They told him the way to repay them was to use the money to get a good education. Thanks to their tutoring, he easily passed a high school equivalency test and enrolled in college. He majored in engineering, and when he graduated, took a job in commercial construction.

"Because of the interest Ed had given you in carpentry," Anne said.

Tom nodded. "Everything that was important to me, I learned

from Ed and Beatrice. They taught me how to love by the way they loved me and each other. They were my real family. Then five years ago they were shot to death by a drug-crazed mugger outside a restaurant where I had taken them for their anniversary dinner.''

''Oh, Tom, no.'' Anne's voice was filled with sadness.

Tom stared at his empty glass. He wanted more wine to ease the awful dryness in his throat that these memories were bringing. But he didn't refill his glass. He hadn't drunk more than two glasses of wine at one sitting in five years, and he wasn't going to start tonight.

When a man told the woman he loved the worst about himself, he had to do it sober.

''It was raining, so I left them standing under the awning in front while I went to get the car. Suddenly, I heard an angry man's voice demanding their money. I whirled around to see a guy with a gun pointed at them. I ran toward them, but I wasn't in time. He shot Ed first, then Beatrice.''

Tom paused for a moment as the soul-searing images returned. Still, there was more to tell. Long ago he had learned that the only way to say something terrible, something unspeakable, was calmly and quietly.

That was how he said it now. ''I knocked the gun from the mugger's hand. It only took a couple of well-placed blows to kill him.''

He stared at his empty wineglass, aware of Anne's eyes on him. But she said nothing. Just waited for him to continue.

''When I bent down to Beatrice, she was gone. When I turned to Ed, I found he was still alive. He looked into my eyes and knew at once that I had killed their attacker. 'I had already forgiven him, Tom,' he told me. 'We're here on this earth to learn to love, not hate.' Then he died in my arms.''

Tom closed his eyes for a moment as the memories became too vivid. When he opened them again, Anne's grave face was before him.

''Until that moment, I hadn't understood what Ed had been trying to tell me all those years. You see, I could have easily just knocked out their attacker. I had chosen to kill him. And because the mugger had a long record, I was hailed as a hero. I was no hero. Ed was the hero. He had chosen love. His had been the right choice. Love gave meaning to his life…and even to his death.''

Anne's eyes held that lovely look of wonder that had first spoken to Tom's heart.

''So you became a priest like Ed,'' Anne said. ''Choosing love. Willing to go out on a limb for homeless kids and those most in need of comfort. It all makes perfect sense.''

Tom smiled at Anne's gentle expression and the soft silver light in her eyes. She knew the worst about him now and had responded with compassion and understanding.

He reached across the table and took her hand in his. ''Anne, do you have any idea how much I love you?''

Just for an instant, the light in her eyes was so bright it blinded him. But then it went out as though a switch had been thrown.

''Tom, it's not necessary to say that.''

''I didn't say it because I thought it was necessary. I said it because it's true. I love you, Anne.''

He felt her start to withdraw.

''I know your previous relationships have hurt you,'' he said quickly, holding on tightly, not letting go of her hand, trying to get through the barriers she was fast erecting. ''Please, don't let them be the yardstick you use to judge what we have together.''

''I don't do that, Tom. What we have together is sweeter and truer than anything I ever had with Bill or any other man. I've known an intimacy and honesty with you that I didn't believe possible between a man and a woman.''

Warm relief flowed through Tom's heart. Until he heard her next words.

''But I'm not a dewy-eyed fool,'' she said as she pulled her hand away. ''I know that this is temporary. And I know it can't be anything else.''

''Why do you say that?''

''Because men aren't monogamous by nature. Sooner or later

you'll be looking elsewhere. I'm not finding fault. I'm just letting you know that I know."

"You're measuring me by the two men who have disappointed you."

"No, I'm measuring you by every man I've ever met. Including my father."

"Your father, Anne?"

"Last year I came home for a surprise visit and walked in on him and a woman neighbor. After he scurried her out the back door, we had a long talk. Seems he's been having affairs for years. When I asked him how he could do this to my mother, you know what he said?"

Tom waited quietly for her to tell him.

"He said it had nothing to do with my mother. It was just the nature of a man to need the sexual excitement that came with variety. A natural biological imperative for the male of the species to spread his sperm. Totally beyond his control."

Tom's gut twisted at the disgust on Anne's face as she said those words.

"I asked him why he'd even bothered to get married if he felt that way," Anne murmured. "He told me that marriage didn't have anything to do with a man's biological nature. He even claimed he still loved my mother."

"Your father doesn't understand real love," Tom said quietly. "Does your mother know about his affairs?"

"He told me she accepted them," Anne said. "I didn't believe it until I asked her. The sadness in her eyes tore at my soul. She won't divorce him. She still loves him. And that foolish, stupid love traps her in all that misery."

Tom tried to reach for Anne's hand again, to ease the sadness in her eyes. But she held herself away.

"My father also told me that the only reason men let women think they're going to be faithful to them is because they know women can't handle the truth. He told me I should have figured out that truth since my partners' sexual promiscuity had been behind the breakup of my relationships, as well as my sister's marriage."

"And you believed him."

"He was right. I should have figured it out. But I hadn't. Not until then."

"Your father doesn't speak for all men," Tom said. "And he certainly doesn't speak for me."

"Tom, you're one of the best men I've ever met. No, make that the best. The last thing you ever have to do is defend yourself to me. But you are an incredible lover. And you didn't learn that out of any book."

"Anne, don't—"

"A year ago you were with Tommy's mother. Now you're with me. Who you'll be with next year, I don't know. I'll enjoy the time we have together for what it is. But I'm not going to end up like my mother. So, please, don't talk to me of love."

And with that she got up from the table and walked out of the room.

Tom sat alone staring at the half-full bottle of wine for a long time. It would be so easy to drink it and let it dull the pain of disappointment inside him. And he wanted to dull that pain. But it wouldn't do anything to change Anne's mind.

He had thought all he had to do was give her time. But now…now he wasn't sure there would ever be enough time.

She loved him. He knew it in his soul. But she would never be able to see it, much less admit it, not with the thick weeds of doubt that were so deeply rooted in her heart.

Tom corked the wine bottle, turned off the kitchen light and went upstairs. He stood outside Anne's bedroom door for a long while, looking at the column of light spilling underneath it.

He wanted to go in, take her in his arms and make love to her with all his heart. He had exchanged solemn vows with her, promised to forsake all others, promised to love her through the end of their days. He had meant every word. But she obviously hadn't believed them. Her flat refusal of his love made that very clear.

Tonight, he hadn't just bared his heart to her, he had bared his soul. How else could he show her? What else could he say?

Nothing. There wasn't anything left he could do or say.

He turned away from her door and let himself into the second bedroom.

Anne heard the door close across the hall and knew that Tom would not be coming to her tonight. And she knew why. She had hurt him. And the pain of that knowledge ached.

Tom was not the kind of man who lied. He believed what he'd told her tonight. Even if she couldn't.

She had not been able to stop the happiness that had filled her when he told her he loved her. Even with everything she knew, with all she'd been through, having Tom say those words to her had nearly made her forget every one of her hard-earned lessons.

Tom made her want to believe again. So badly, she wanted to believe again. But her self-preservation wouldn't let her. She had to hold on to it. Because when Tom's feelings changed and he was gone, it would be all she had left.

Gone. When Tom was gone... The ache in Anne's heart grew worse. How much time would they have together before it was over?

Not enough to let this rift remain between them. Not enough to waste a moment away from him.

She hadn't tried Tommy on her breast tonight. Needing to do that would be the perfect excuse for going to Tom.

She gently gathered the baby into her arms, slipped out of bed and walked across the hall to Tom's door. She stood there for a long moment before getting up the courage to knock.

When she finally did, Tom opened the door almost immediately. He wore pajama bottoms, nothing more.

"Tommy needs you to..." Anne stopped, staring at the expanse of Tom's smooth, bare chest, not able to look in his eyes, suddenly embarrassed to say what the baby needed. What she needed.

He cupped her chin with his hand and raised it until she met his eyes, his look open and gentle. "Your room all right?"

The awful ache in Anne's heart dissipated. Tom was making it easy on her. No game playing. No trying to hurt her back for the pain she had given him. Just simple understanding. And kindness. And love.

She blinked back the tears that stung her eyes. ''Any room, Tom.''

He scooped Anne and the baby into his arms in one effortless move, holding them tightly against his chest as if they weighed no more than a feather.

His eyes searched hers. ''Did you really come for the baby's sake?''

She wrapped an arm around his neck. ''No.''

Tom brushed a kiss against her hair—a kiss that was as soft as a sigh. ''I love you, Anne.''

''I know, Tom. Just please don't say it anymore.''

''But you believe me?''

''You told me you've never lied to me. And you never will. I believe that.''

''Keep believing it, Anne,'' Tom said as he carried both her and the baby back into the bedroom. ''Just keep believing it.''

CHAPTER TWELVE

ANNE COULDN'T REMEMBER a more beautiful Saturday morning. The sun was shining. Birds were singing. The spring breeze flowing through the open kitchen window was lush and warm.

Tom sat across the breakfast table from her, bouncing the baby in his lap. He was rumpled and unshaven and so unfairly sexy. Tommy bounced and cooed and smiled at him adorably. And Tom cooed and smiled right back. There was such love on Tom's face for his son that it made Anne's heart swell.

If only she had met Tom instead of Bill those many years ago! How different things might have been. If only.

No, she was not going to play that game. It was pointless. The past and its mistakes were best forgotten. All she could do was remember the lessons she'd learned from those mistakes, and make smarter choices in the present.

Rising from the breakfast table, she gathered the dishes and stacked them in the dishwasher.

"Tom, we're going to need to go grocery shopping," she called over her shoulder as she set the dishwasher cycle.

"Hmm."

Anne wondered why Tom's answer seemed so preoccupied. She turned to see him staring at something in the morning newspaper laid out on the table in front of him.

She walked over, rested her hands on his shoulders and read the headline—*Tomei Murder Case to be Reopened.*

The Tomei name sounded familiar to Anne.

"Tom, wasn't Tomei the last name of the couple whose son died in the emergency room at the hospital yesterday?"

Tom nodded.

Anne's eyes scanned down to the article.

The district attorney's office has learned from Mr. and Mrs. James Tomei that their son, James Tomei, Jr., confessed to killing his wife just before he died from injuries sustained in a self-inflicted gunshot wound Friday night. Tomei, Jr., allegedly told his parents that he strangled his wife, Elizabeth, two years ago after learning of her affair with their neighbor, Donald Abbott. He then framed Abbott for the crime. Abbott was tried and convicted for the murder last year and is currently serving a life sentence.

Anne sat down in the chair next to Tom and studied his calm face. "You heard Tomei's confession. If his parents hadn't come forward, would you have been able to let an innocent man serve a life sentence for a crime he didn't commit?"

"Anne, I can talk to you about the general guidelines concerning confessions, but I can't discuss any specific confession."

"Sorry, I forgot. Okay. In general terms, let's say you hear a person confess to a crime for which someone else has been convicted. Can't you say anything?"

"A priest cannot under any circumstances divulge what he has heard in a confession."

"Even if the person confesses to having done something evil, like this man Tomei, and later dies?"

"Under any circumstances, Anne, means under any circumstances. That's why some Episcopal clergy don't accept confessions anymore."

"But you do. Why?"

"Do you know what the original derivation of the word *evil* was?"

She shook her head.

"It meant to have lost one's way. We all lose our way at some time in this life. To recognize you've done wrong, to be truly sorry for it and to ask for and receive forgiveness is to have found your way again. Confession and absolution are powerful healers.''

Anne remembered the look of relief on the face of both Mr. and Mrs. Tomei when Tom had told them their son had died in peace. She realized that Tom had done that for their son, as well. What he could do for someone as a priest was beyond anything she'd been able to do as a judge.

No, she wouldn't do what he did for a living for anything, but she admired him greatly for choosing that path. And for so many other things. She had told him he was the best man she had ever met. With every moment that statement grew deeper with meaning.

Tommy had grabbed Tom's ear and was pulling it with his determined little hand. Tom captured the baby's other hand and munched on the tiny knuckles while Tommy giggled delightedly.

It was just impossible to resist this man.

She stood up. ''I'm going to go take a shower. Would you care to join me?''

Tom looked up at her and smiled. ''Is this a trick question?'' he asked as he reached over and expertly undid the sash on her silk dressing gown.

''WE KNOW SHRUBBER IS using these underage, runaway girls as breeders to produce babies for his wealthy clients,'' Anne said as she pushed the grocery cart down the supermarket aisle. ''But we haven't even discussed Dr. Faust's role in this.''

Tom picked up a bag of potato chips and flipped them over his shoulder into the cart. Anne picked up the bag and put it back on the shelf. Tom smiled. They were like an old married couple already. And he loved it.

His heart felt so much lighter this morning. She had come to him last night because she couldn't stay away. No matter what her experiences had been, no matter how afraid she was of love, she couldn't stay away from him.

''Tom? Did you hear me?''

''Even if this Dr. Faust were ignorant of the girls' real

names,'' Tom said, ''he knows the ages of the parents on the birth record he signs. A doctor would have to be able to tell the difference between the body of an expecting mother who was only fifteen years old and one who was almost thirty.''

''So, you were listening.''

''To you, Anne, always,'' Tom said as he slam-dunked two bags of cookies into the basket.

Anne immediately dug them out and shoved them back on the shelf. ''How can you consume such junk food and not have an ounce of fat on you?''

''Healthy genes. I suppose your favorite section of a grocery store is the fruit and vegetable aisle?''

''Yes, as a matter of fact it is,'' Anne said. ''Don't tell me you don't like them.''

''My love, I like anything I don't have to prepare.''

An amused smile drew back her lips.

When they had bought their groceries and were on the way to the car, Tom took the opportunity to wrap his arm across her shoulders. It felt so good to be able to touch her at will, to feel her response as she leaned into him.

''It's a shame it's the weekend already,'' she said. ''Everything is closed and I really wanted to find out about that doctor.''

''If that's your wish, I have a friend who should be able to help,'' Tom said. ''I'll call him when we get home. Right after our celebration.''

''Celebration?'' Anne repeated.

Tom took a perfect peach tulip from behind his back and presented it to Anne. ''Happy anniversary.''

''What anniversary?'' Anne asked as she took the flower, inordinately pleased that he had both noticed and remembered her preference for tulips.

''You've already forgotten we met a week ago today?'' Tom asked, shaking his head. ''Whoever said women were the romantic sex?''

''A week,'' Anne exclaimed as she leaned into the car to put the baby in the car seat. ''I can't believe it's only been a week.''

Tom checked his watch. "And now it's a week and ten seconds."

"You can't possibly have remembered the exact second," Anne protested.

"Can't I?" Tom asked, smiling as he held the car door open for her.

"IT WAS NICE OF YOUR friends to invite us over for dinner," Anne said as Tom drove them to their house that evening. "Have you known them long?"

"Jeff and Theresa Ballard are parishioners in the Boston parish I told you about."

"The parish where you ran the homeless shelter."

"Yes. Jeff employed a couple of the kids for me. He's the kind of guy who would give you the shirt off his back. He's also on the medical review board of ethical practices. He pretty much knows every doctor in the Commonwealth of Massachusetts."

The Ballards' home turned out to be in Brookline, a suburb of Boston. It was a well-kept, two-story colonial with a lovely flower-filled front yard that made Anne envious.

Jeff greeted them at the door with a ready smile. He was stocky, in his early forties, nearly bald, with an open face and lively dark eyes. His wife, Theresa, was taller and slim, with medium-brown hair and eyes, and an infectious laugh.

Anne liked the couple on sight.

When Tom introduced Anne to them as his wife, an uneasy sensation coursed through her. She considered the ceremony they had gone through as merely a temporary means to an end. But Tom's declaration of their relationship to his friends and the returning warmth of their congratulations made her realize that Tom considered it more.

She knew she was a fool not to have thought of this before. Tom was a priest. He believed he loved her. He had married her. And it wasn't as though she hadn't been willing to consummate that marriage. Many times over again.

He considers this a real marriage.

That realization detonated in her mind, a time bomb of new complications.

Jeff and Theresa went out of their way to make Anne feel welcome. There was nothing formal or pretentious about them. They opened their comfortable home to her with friendly hospitality and made her feel like one of the family.

Anne helped Theresa in the kitchen while Tom took care of Tommy and Jeff tried to keep up with his and Theresa's triplets, three brown-haired little boys who had just turned fourteen months old. The rambunctious toddlers weren't still a moment, tearing around the living room and hollering happily.

"Your children are charming," Anne told Theresa as she tossed a salad.

Theresa flashed her a proud mother's smile. "Don't be too eager for Tommy to start walking," she warned as she elbowed the refrigerator door closed after grabbing some milk. "Once they do, life as you know it is over."

Anne laughed. But beneath her laughter she was sobered by the assumption implicit in Theresa's words—that she would be around to see Tommy walk.

"You must have been thrilled when you learned you were going to have triplets," Anne said.

"Oh, yes. Of course, with embryo transplant, it's not nearly so rare an occurrence."

Embryo transplant? The phrase brought back memories for Anne. She had contemplated that possibility once—when she made herself face the options open to her and Bill if one of them proved to be infertile. Before he had proved to be unfaithful.

Dinner was relaxed and quite informal. Everyone helped themselves to the green salad Anne had prepared, and Theresa's freshly baked lasagna, along with an assortment of mixed vegetables, hot rolls and fresh fruit.

The triplets ended up wearing most of the lasagna sauce, as did the carpet beneath their chairs. Both Theresa and Jeff took it in stride. They clearly adored their children and considered them more important than the messes they made.

When everyone had finished eating, Jeff turned to Tom. "So who is this doctor you wanted to know about?"

Tom swallowed some coffee before answering. "Martin Faust."

Jeff nodded. "I know of him."

"He's an obstetrician, right?" Tom asked.

"He's board certified as such," Jeff said, clearly choosing his words carefully.

"What is it that bothers you about him, Jeff?" Tom asked, recognizing the restraint in his friend.

"I know you and Anne won't let this go out of this room," Jeff said. "But there have been several complaints filed against him by his patients, saying he's taken advantage of them when they're in the stirrups."

Tom got the message. "And he's still being allowed to practice?"

"He wouldn't if it were up to me," Jeff stated. "But he's careful. Never any witnesses. Never any physical evidence. Always an innocent-sounding explanation. And the truth is that some of the doctors on our review boards bend over backward to protect their own."

"What about legal measures?" Anne asked.

"It would help if there were a legal verdict against him," Jeff asserted. "But, like I said, he's careful, which makes it difficult to prove. And the process of going to court is expensive and embarrassing for the women."

"Still, you'd think that word would get around," Tom said.

"His patient numbers dwindled considerably a few years ago when the complaints started to hit," Jeff agreed. "But he's still out there practicing. And a guy who's gotten away with this kind of thing isn't likely to stop. If there's something you can tell me that will change that, I hope you will."

"You can count on it, Jeff," Tom assured his friend.

While Jeff and Tom saw to kitchen cleanup, Anne held Tommy on her lap and watched Theresa trying to convince her boys it was time to sit quietly on the living room couch. It wasn't working.

She finally gave up and let them play in a child-size medieval castle set up in the corner of the large family room.

"I don't know what we would have done if Tom hadn't built that castle for them," she said. "It's the only thing that keeps them occupied for any length of time."

Anne looked closely at the beautifully carved wood and intricate designs on the buildings. She could see the same attention to detail as Tom's work on the mall models at the rectory.

When Anne turned back to Theresa, she found the woman smiling at her. "It's good to see Tom so happy. I'm glad he found you, Anne."

Anne smiled back, oddly pleased. It had been such a pleasant evening with his friends. And it felt so nice being part of a couple, knowing that she wouldn't be going home alone to an empty house. There was Tom and Tommy now.

It's not real, she forcibly reminded herself. *It's not going to last. There is no happily ever after.*

"I can't get over how much your baby looks like Tom," Theresa said. "You'll think me silly, I suppose, but I'm thankful the others didn't."

"Others?" Anne repeated, confused.

Theresa swept a hand toward her triplets, babbling happily away. "Jason, Jeremy and Jeff, Jr. look a lot more like me, don't you think?"

"Well, yes, I—"

"I know my Jeff wouldn't have said anything," Theresa continued with a slight shrug of her shoulders. "After all, he was the one who suggested Tom be our donor. But their having inherited my coloring helped, I think, to..."

Anne didn't hear what Theresa thought. She couldn't. The blood was pounding too loudly in her ears. Tom had donated sperm to these friends!

Something was shifting in her mind, a piece falling into place, filling in the missing part of the puzzle that had previously not made any sense.

"Anne, are you all right?" Theresa asked.

Anne realized that she was staring at the triplets. She jerked her head toward Theresa, not thinking about what must be showing on her face.

"Oh, my God, you didn't know," Theresa said, acute dismay turning her natural pink complexion chalk-white. "Oh, Anne, I'm so sorry. I thought Tom would have told you. I never imagined—"

"Theresa, it's all right," Anne said in as soothing a voice as her current excitement would let her. "I'm glad you told me. I think it's wonderful what Tom did for you and Jeff. And I very much doubt he'll mind when he realizes you told me."

"But he should have been the one—" Theresa began.

"Not necessarily," Anne interrupted, pretty sure this was something Tom could never have told her because it was something that related to what Lindy had told him in her confession.

"I feel terrible," Theresa said.

"You shouldn't. You've just been a big help."

"Help?"

"Theresa, when you gave birth fourteen months ago, did you or Jeff telephone Tom at the parish?"

"Well, yes. Naturally, we were eager to share the news and arrange for the boys' baptism."

"Did you say anything over the phone at that time to indicate that Tom was the biological father of your children?"

"I think Jeff might have thanked Tom again for making it possible. Why do you ask?"

"I was just wondering if you might have been overheard," Anne said.

"I doubt it. It was just me and Jeff in the hospital room with the babies when we called."

"I didn't mean from your end," Anne said, her mind popping with possibilities. "Theresa, who was your fertility doctor?"

Theresa looked confused at Anne's question but answered easily enough. "Dorothy Bennett."

"May I speak to Dr. Bennett about your embryo transplant procedure?"

Theresa still looked puzzled, but nodded. "Anne, what's going on?"

"I'm trying to track down the missing pieces of a very important puzzle. Will you trust me enough to just leave it at that until after I've spoken with Dr. Bennett?"

Theresa studied Anne's face for a moment. "Sure. If you can't trust a judge and a priest, who can you trust?"

Anne flashed her a smile. "I'll need a note from you telling Dr. Bennett that it's all right to talk to me."

Theresa nodded as she got up and went over to a small desk in the corner of the family room. She quickly scribbled out the note and handed it to Anne.

"Dr. Bennett's address and telephone number are at the top. But I should warn you, she's booked for a month in advance."

"Oh," Anne said, her voice full of disappointment. Now that she felt she was so close to the answer, her impatience for that confirmation was almost overwhelming.

"Jeff and I have an appointment with her at ten on Monday. You could take it if you want."

"That would be great," Anne said. "You sure you don't mind?"

"Not at all," Theresa said. "We can reschedule."

Tom and Jeff came out of the kitchen then.

"What are we going to reschedule?" Jeff asked.

"Anne's going to take our appointment with Dr. Bennett on Monday."

Anne watched Tom. Not a flicker, not a twinge, not a nerve moved in his face.

They said good-night to his friends, thanking them for the evening. Tom gathered Tommy's things and he and Anne headed out to the car.

"Everything all right, Anne?"

She looked over at the calm expression on his handsome face and wondered how anyone could keep the kind of secrets he did. When she had called him the strong, silent type, even she had not appreciated how strong and silent.

"Couldn't be better," Anne said.

And at that moment, she realized she had spoken the literal truth. For what she had just learned changed so much.

TOM MADE LOVE TO ANNE that night under the moonlight falling through the window glass. He began slow and easy to give her time to suckle the baby at her breasts. But by the time Tommy had fallen asleep, the passion they had for each other had already escalated to the point that only a fevered joining could satisfy.

It had not been enough. Tom had so much more to tell her. So he had simply begun again.

When Tom began to make love to Anne the second time that night, she felt a difference in him. He touched her as though she were made of very fine, very fragile fibers, as though she might break at any moment. Without a word, he let her know so many things that were important to him. How beautiful she was. How precious she was to him. How proud and grateful he was that she was his.

His. She felt it. In every possessive sweep of his hand. In every soft caress. With every warm breath of his kiss. She had never known such eloquence. As their bodies joined and they became one, her heart expanded in her chest.

The baby woke them a few hours later. Tom got up and prepared his bottle. He brought it back to the bed so Anne could hold the baby to the warmth of her bare skin as she fed him. Tom wrapped his arms around her and nestled her and the baby against him.

The moonlight bathed her soft naked body. The sweet heat and fragrance of her skin filled his senses to overflowing. It was an exquisite moment, as so many with her were. Gratitude swept through him with such power that it left him shaken.

"You know how no matter where you are physically, a part of you is somewhere else?" Anne asked, gently stroking the baby's hair.

"You mean when your mind is on something you need to do, or evaluating something you've done?" Tom asked.

"Yes, exactly," she said. "And yet at this precise moment with you and Tommy, I feel totally present. All of me. Nothing is missing. It's so…perfect."

Tom couldn't have expressed it better. He rested his cheek

against hers. She might not be able to say the exact words, but whether she realized it or not, she did tell him she loved him in so many other ways.

A few minutes later, Tommy stopped feeding. Tom burped him over the towel on his shoulder. Then he laid the little boy in his crib and returned to Anne's side, drawing her close against him. He closed his eyes as he ran his hand over the curve of her delicate shoulder, down the sleek length of her arm, across the flat surface of her tummy, absorbing her warmth and textures with his fingertips.

"What you told me is true," Anne said into the silence of the night. "Tommy is yours and yet you didn't impregnate Lindy."

"Did you only just become sure of that, Anne?"

"No, I knew you wouldn't lie to me. What I didn't know until now, though, is how it could be possible. Lindy learned you had donated sperm to Jeff and Theresa when she listened in on your calls at the parish. She stole some of your sperm. That's what she meant when she told Butz she was going to pick out the father of her child. Dr. Faust inseminated her with your sperm and that's how she gave birth to Tommy."

Tom was absolutely quiet.

"Oh, I know you can't comment on this, Tom. It was what Lindy confessed to you when she came by the church that Friday afternoon. I understand completely about your adherence to confidentiality. But I don't need you to say anything. All I need is to talk to Dr. Bennett. She'll confirm it for us when she discovers your sperm is missing. Then we can go through with the DNA test because we'll have the proof of how Tommy came to be your child. That fake birth certificate the Kendralls have won't mean a thing."

Still Tom said nothing.

"As soon as we see Dr. Bennett, I'll call Pat and have her go after Shrubber and Butz. Of course, I want Fred to get the credit for tying Butz into Lindy's death. If it hadn't been for her help, we wouldn't have known about the car crash. You don't mind, do you?"

"No, Anne, I don't mind."

A long, peaceful moment passed in which Anne thought about many things.

"Tom?"

"Yes?"

"Who will conduct services in Cooper's Corner tomorrow?"

"I asked the priest in the neighboring parish to cover for me."

"For how long?"

"For as long as I need to be away."

"So you don't have to be back soon?"

"You have something in mind?"

"It's such beautiful weather here," she said. "And I have another full week off."

"After church tomorrow, we'll take Tommy for a picnic in the park," Tom said. "Then we can come back here and make love all afternoon."

Anne smiled. Sounded wonderful to her. "I think it's possible that I'll be producing the breast milk Tommy needs soon. I don't suppose there's any need for us to hurry into a divorce?"

Tom wrapped his arms around her so tightly that not even the moonlight could come between them. "No need at all," he assured her.

Yes, she could play a role in Tommy's life, Anne thought. Be there for him, watch him grow up. It would be just as if he were her own child.

Her own child. The warmth of those words brought a wonderful gladness to Anne's soul. She didn't have to hold back her heart anymore. Tommy didn't have another mother. She didn't have to give him up.

She could be his real mother.

And a real wife to Tom? He said he loved her. And if there were ever a man who could mean those words, it was Tom.

There was just one thing left that she needed to know.

"Tom?"

"Yes?"

"When we first made love, you told me it had been a long time for you," she said. "Would you tell me now how long?"

"Since I entered the seminary five years ago."

She turned in his arms to look at him. "You're so damn close to being a saint. Celibate for five whole years! And here I imagined dozens of women left swooning in your wake."

Tom smiled, amused at her description. "You said it had been a long time for you, as well."

"Since I discovered my husband was unfaithful four years ago," Anne admitted.

"Ah, so that was a halo I saw around your head the first time you attended the Church of the Good Shepherd."

"Very funny, Thomas Christen."

He laughed, and the warmth of the sound nestled secure inside her soul.

Maybe this marriage could last awhile, she thought. A good long while.

"All along I thought you'd fallen down in your vows," she said as she snuggled her body against his and wrapped her arms around his neck. "But the truth is, you've been standing by them."

Tom leaned down to brush his lips against hers. "All of them, Anne. Always. Please remember that."

"It's kind of a shock discovering you're not such a sexy sinner."

He chuckled as he ran his hand down the exquisite curve of her spine. "If you're disappointed, I can always tell you about all the women that came before the seminary...."

"Do it and die," she threatened as she molded her mouth to his.

DR. BENNETT WAS a stout, middle-aged woman with graying brown hair and a face that had a lived-in look, as if its owner wouldn't be surprised by much. She recognized Tom immediately and greeted him by name.

"Theresa and Jeff Ballard graciously gave us their appointment," Anne explained. "I'm Judge Vandree."

"Are you interested in some fertility counseling, Judge Vandree?" the doctor asked as she gestured them to seats in front of her desk.

"No. I'm here to find out some of the specifics concerning Theresa Ballard's fertility treatments." Anne handed Dr. Bennett the note Theresa had written. "As you know, Father Christen was her sperm donor."

Dr. Bennett read the note, then looked at Tom. "So you obviously don't mind if I discuss this with Judge Vandree?"

"Please feel free," he said.

The doctor turned back to Anne. "How may I help?"

"Dr. Bennett," Anne said, "I have reason to believe that some of the sperm donated by Father Christen reached unauthorized hands."

"That's not possible," Dr. Bennett said. There was nothing defensive in her tone, just polite denial.

"How can you be so sure?"

"My security is foolproof."

"Perhaps you'd like to explain it to me," Anne said.

"If you'll come with me, I'll show you. But you'll have to leave the baby with a staff member."

"He doesn't take well to strangers," Anne said.

"I'll stay here with him," Tom offered.

Anne nodded as she followed Dr. Bennett into the back of the fertility lab. They stepped into an enclosed booth, where Dr. Bennett donned a dark blue smock over her street clothes and beckoned for Anne to do the same. Next she affixed caps over their hair and white surgical masks over their faces.

"We're not really sterile, so don't touch anything," Dr. Bennett cautioned. "This is just to keep the ambient bacteria to a minimum."

Anne nodded as she followed Dr. Bennett deeper into the lab.

The in vitro fertilization laboratory proved to be an expanse of stainless steel cabinets and scientific apparatus. Dr. Bennett pointed out equipment with names like Isolette, incubators, laminar flow hoods and stereo microscopes.

"The woman is first stimulated for eight to ten days with injected medications to insure multiple egg development," Dr. Bennett explained. "We need a minimum number of four to five eggs. When the woman's follicles are mature, a transvaginal ultrasound-guided egg aspiration procedure is performed to extract the eggs from the follicles.''

''In other words, you remove the eggs from the woman's body,'' Anne said.

''It only takes about five minutes here in the lab,'' Dr. Bennett told her. ''The sperm donor is brought in at the same time. The eggs are immediately fertilized with the fresh, donated sperm and the embryos are cultured here for two to six days. This is my embryologist, Cecily. She's screening a cultured embryo now. Would you like to take a look?''

The masked and fully draped Cecily stepped aside so Anne could gaze into the microscope.

''It's a day-five embryo at the blastocyst stage,'' Cecily said helpfully.

It looked just like a big circle with bumps to Anne. She drew back from the microscope. ''What happens next?''

''The embryos are transferred into the woman's uterus, where they will hopefully implant and develop into a live birth. We have an excellent implantation rate. Theresa Ballard giving birth to triplets is not unusual.''

''And what of the leftover sperm?'' Anne asked.

''There is no leftover sperm, Judge Vandree,'' Dr. Bennett said. ''Whatever sperm is not required to fertilize an egg on the day it's retrieved is immediately disposed of. We only deal in fresh sperm, never frozen.''

No frozen sperm? Then how did Lindy get a hold of Tom's? Anne was confused. She had been so sure she had the answer. What was she missing?

''Dr. Bennett, are you sure—''

''We do not store sperm here, Judge Vandree. Only embryos.''

Embryos?

Anne's pulse quickened as a new thought presented itself. ''How many viable embryos were produced for Theresa Ballard?''

''I'll have to check,'' Dr. Bennett said as she walked over to the computer terminal sitting on the stainless steel counter. It took her a moment to bring up Theresa Ballard's file.

''A total of four embryos were produced in the fertility process. The embryo transfer procedure was used on three.''

''What happened to the other embryo?'' Anne asked.

''It was cryopreserved at the request of the Ballards and placed in a storage receptacle. It may be used if they decide they want to get pregnant again.''

''Where is the storage receptacle?''

''It's in the next room in one of several special tanks. The embryos are stored in a special straw and then immersed in liquid nitrogen at minus one hundred ninety-six degrees Celsius.''

''Dr. Bennett, I need to verify that that fertilized embryo is where it's supposed to be.''

''Is all this really necessary?'' the doctor asked.

''Yes,'' Anne answered.

The doctor studied Anne's determined look for a moment before she referred back to the record on her screen and jotted down a notation. Then she cleared the screen, got up and entered the next room, which contained rows and rows of tanks with a biohazard sticker on the top and a large 34HC imprinted on the base.

The doctor referred to the notation she had copied from Theresa Ballard's computer record. After donning special gloves, she walked over to a tank, and opened the top. Visible vapors rose from it, curling into the air.

Dr. Bennett studied the identification strips of the special straws inside, looking for the code that would match the one on the computer for Theresa's embryo. Several minutes went by.

''It's gone,'' she said as she turned toward Anne, unwelcome surprise flickering in her eyes.

Anne felt a sharp splinter of ice pierce her heart.

Dr. Bennett stared at her. ''You knew. How?''

''You had a forced entry into the lab approximately a year ago, didn't you?'' Anne guessed.

"Well, yes. But it was just vandalism. A broken window in the back. Nothing was taken."

"You checked on all your embryos at the time to make sure?"

"Well, no," Dr. Bennett admitted. "We have hundreds of embryos stored here."

Anne had feared as much, but until the doctor's confirmation, she had still hoped. Now there was no hope.

"But if you're implying that someone broke in to purposely steal this one, it can't be true," Dr. Bennett told Anne. "Our computer records can only be accessed with the right password. It wold take a computer expert to find Theresa Ballard's file and discover where her embryo was."

"She was a computer expert," Anne said.

"Who are you talking about?"

"It doesn't matter. Dr. Bennett, I need you to perform a genetic test on the baby Father Christen is holding in your office to verify that he's a match to Tom Christen and Theresa Ballard. And I need it now."

"You think that child is a live birth from the missing embryo?"

"No, Doctor," Anne said sadly. "I know it."

CHAPTER THIRTEEN

"YOU KNEW THE TRUTH the whole time," Anne said in a tone full of disillusionment.

Tom could feel her eyes on him as he drove them home from seeing Dr. Bennett. The moment he'd learned Anne had found out about his having donated sperm to Jeff and Theresa, Tom knew that this conversation was inevitable. And he had dreaded it.

"Yet you let me think Tommy was really yours," Anne said, anger licking beneath her words.

"I am his biological father, Anne."

"But not his legal father. Jeff Ballard is his legal father. And Theresa Ballard is his legal mother."

Anne looked away from Tom to stare out the windshield, blinking back the tears that stung her eyes, trying to do private battle with her distress. Trying, but not succeeding.

The scenes from their picture-perfect Sunday together kept playing in her mind. Tom making her breakfast and serving it to her in bed. Their family picnic in the park with little Tommy. Their long, lazy afternoon of lovemaking. The pride and happiness she had felt holding *her* baby to her breast as he drifted off to sleep.

The sweet memories stabbed at her soul.

"How ridiculous I must have looked going through all that effort to try to generate milk for Tommy," Anne said. "And how pathetic you must have thought me as I went on the other night about being able to breast-feed him soon."

"Everything you've done has been out of love," Tom said gently. "There is nothing ridiculous or pathetic about love."

"On the contrary," Anne said, her voice now harsh with desolation. "It's all ridiculous and pathetic."

Tom's sigh was deep and private. All along he'd known that Anne's growing attachment to Tommy was going to lead to problems. Because they were going to have to give him up.

Still, he had not been able to warn her. In any way.

And even if he had been able to warn her, how could he have told her not to let the little boy steal her heart when he hadn't been able to keep the baby from stealing his?

Anne's own pain made her blind to his. She had no idea what it meant for him to give up Tommy.

Tom had never had a problem accepting the triplets born to Jeff and Theresa as the children of his friends. He was their godfather, nothing more.

But Tommy was different. Had been since the first time Tom held him and tried to ease the little boy's sorrow. He had felt the bond between them, just as real as though the infant had always been a part of his heart.

Tommy was his—and yet not his.

"You knew when you told me Tommy was your baby that I would misunderstand," Anne said after a moment. "Why did you do it?"

"I never wanted to tell you Tommy was mine. But if I hadn't that day you came by the church, you would have put him in the hands of Child Care Services."

"So what you're saying is that it's all my fault for getting involved."

"That's not what I'm saying. The truth is, if you hadn't become involved, hadn't discovered how Tommy was conceived, Jeff and Theresa Ballard might never learn they have another son."

"Because you wouldn't have been able to tell them," Anne said, and her words suddenly took on the force of an accusation. "Is that why you kept me around? So I'd follow the clues and come out with the information outside of the confessional?"

Stunned, Tom turned to look at her. "You can't believe that, Anne."

"I don't know what to believe anymore," she said, and the very real doubt on her face and in her voice drove a stake into his heart.

Tom took a deep, steadying breath. "I know this has been a shock. Please, give yourself time. We can handle it together."

"I don't want to handle anything. I just want to go home."

"We'll be there in a minute."

"I don't mean your home."

"It's not my home. It's ours."

"I know what's mine and what isn't," Anne said, speaking quickly, forcibly through the pain. "I'll call Pat and tell her about Shrubber and Butz and Faust. She can get the report directly from Dr. Bennett on Tommy's paternity. Then I'm leaving for the Berkshires. You needn't worry about driving me. Fred will come and get me."

"Anne, don't," Tom said. "We have to work through this."

"There's nothing to work through. We only got together because of the baby. We only got married to make sure you remained a priest. None of that is necessary now. I'll tell the bishop the truth."

Tom pulled the car into a parking spot just down from the house, shut off the engine and turned to Anne.

"The truth is that Tommy has had nothing to do with my wanting to be with you, Anne. And I didn't marry you to remain a priest. I married you because I love you."

Anne's sigh was so sad it was almost a sob. "I don't believe in love. And I don't want to be the wife of a priest. You keep the most dreadful secrets. And this secret you kept from me, Tom…this secret is breaking my heart."

She did sob then, and Tom's heart wrenched with pain for her. But when he reached to hold her, she pulled away and got out of the car.

He watched her as she stood on the sidewalk, rubbing the tears from her cheeks as fast as they fell, struggling to regain control. She was so strong that he had forgotten how tender her heart was. Until this moment, he hadn't realized how deeply she loved Tommy or how much losing him would hurt her.

Tom knew he had been the one to bring her this pain. Somehow he was going to have to find the words to ease that pain and make this right between them. But at the moment he had no idea what those words were.

He slowly got out of the car and slipped Tommy out of his car seat. As he carried him toward the front door to the house, he realized it was probably for the last time. He treasured the feel of the little boy in his arms, gathering the memory into his heart.

And prayed he wouldn't be losing Anne, as well.

All the way he heard Anne's footsteps following behind him. Way behind him. She was keeping her distance both emotionally and physically. And with every passing second, he could feel the gulf widening between them.

I don't want to be the wife of a priest.

The remembered words rubbed raw against his soul. He could and would give up anything for her—except who he was.

Tom put the key into the lock and opened the door to their home. They had to work through this. He could not lose her now.

He would not lose her now.

But as Tom turned toward Anne, his heart gave a sharp jolt.

Claude Butz stood at the bottom step of the brownstone. The big man had hold of Anne's shoulder and held a gun to her head. Tom's pulse pounded as every muscle in his body ached for action.

"Step inside nice and slow, preacher," Butz said.

Tom knew he didn't have any choice. He had to bide his time, wait for an opening despite the desperate need churning in his gut to get that gun away from Anne's head. Slowly he backed into the house, shifting Tommy to the crook of his arm, keeping his eyes on Butz, looking for the slightest opening.

But Butz was cautious. He advanced slowly into the house himself, his hand gripping Anne's shoulder as he pushed her before him, keeping the gun to her head. Once inside, he kicked the door closed behind him.

"Do what I tell you and nobody's going to get hurt," Butz

said. "Very slowly I want you to walk toward the judge here and hand her the kid. Then she and I will be leaving."

Anne's face was deathly white. Tom knew that he would die before he let this man take her anywhere. Or Tommy.

"No," Tom said.

Tommy started to whimper. Tom wrapped his other arm around him protectively.

"I'm only interested in the brat," Butz said. "I'll let her go as soon as I'm safely away. She's just my insurance you don't go calling the cops."

"No," Tom repeated over Tommy's escalating cry.

"All right then, how about I shoot you in both legs?"

"You won't shoot," Tom said. "You won't risk injuring the child. He's worth too much to you and Shrubber."

Butz cocked the revolver. He turned its barrel until it was aimed at Tom's legs.

"At this range, I don't even need to be that good of a shot," Butz said with a nasty lift of his lips. "And I'm betting the judge here can move fast enough to catch the kid before you fall on your face. Let's see, shall I am for the kneecaps or the thighs?"

"Tom, please do what he says," Anne said, her voice calm, despite the flash of fear in her eyes.

"Better listen to her, preacher," Butz said. "This gun's got a hair trigger on it and I don't feel real patient today."

Tom was satisfied now that the gun was pointed away from Anne. "All right," he conceded as he bounced the crying baby in his arms.

Butz smirked, his fleshy face full of triumph. It was the way Tom wanted the man. Overconfident.

Still, Tom had no doubt that Butz was ready to shoot, and would at the slightest provocation. Which meant that he was going to have to keep Anne and the baby safely out of the range of fire.

Tom started forward.

"Slowly, preacher," Butz warned. "Don't make me nervous."

Step by step Tom advanced toward Anne, forcing himself not to look at her pale face but at the man who clutched her delicate shoulder so cruelly with his thick, sausage fingers. When Tom finally stood before her, he carefully unfurled Tommy from the crook of his arm into her waiting embrace.

"Now step back," Butz commanded.

The instant Tom felt Anne take the baby's weight, he leaped forward, kicking the revolver from Butz's hand.

The gun discharged with a deafening noise as it flew into the air. Tom heard the expended bullet rip into the wall behind him. He grasped Butz with both hands and flipped the heavy man onto the floor. Butz landed with a crack of spine and a howl of pain.

Tom pressed his thumbs against the carotid arteries in Butz's fat neck, squeezing them closed with enough pressure to render Butz unconscious. The heavy man went out without a peep.

Tom turned to Anne. "Are you all right?"

Her face was white with residual shock, but her lovely gray eyes were steady and calm. She held the now quiet Tommy tightly to her. "We're fine. I'm going to call the police."

"Better have them send an ambulance, too," Tom said.

As she hurried off to the phone, Tom rolled Butz onto his stomach, whipped his belt off and secured his arms tightly behind his back. Then he picked up Butz's gun, put it into his pocket and drew a thick braid from the living room drapes to hog-tie the man's legs to his arms.

Tom worked quickly, not knowing how much time he had. Anne returned when he had secured the last knot.

"The police and ambulance are on their way," she said. "Although I debated whether to even ask them to send an ambulance for this clown."

When he heard the anger in her voice, Tom felt happy. It told him she had come through the scare fine. His fear for her had been so intense that he still felt its residue raining inside him. He wanted to wrap her in his arms and hold her close and never let her go. But Butz was moving beneath him on the floor, regaining consciousness.

Tom rested a knee against one of Butz's kidneys, just as a precaution in case the big man decided to try to move. Butz strained against his restraints.

"You're not going anywhere," Tom assured him. The big man gave up.

"Was this stupidity your idea or Shrubber's?" Anne asked with undisguised contempt.

"I'm not saying anything until I talk to my lawyer," Butz said as Tom kept the man's cheek firmly pressed against the hardwood floor.

"He'll be in jail with you," Tom told him.

"You're the ones who'll be in jail. That kid isn't yours."

"Bluffing is useless, Butz," Anne said. "We know all about your part in procuring underage runaways as baby breeders for Shrubber's wealthy clients. And when those girls in South Boston are picked up in a few minutes, you're getting the book thrown at you."

Butz's one visible eye went wide with surprise at Anne's words. Clearly the man was taken aback by their knowledge.

"Of course you don't have to say anything," Tom said. "But I bet Shrubber does."

"You're right, Tom," Anne said. "He'll probably claim he knew nothing about the girls being underage. After all, you were the one who found them, Butz. And went with them to the hospital. And took their babies from them. And got them pregnant in the first place."

"I never impregnated them," Butz quickly swore in his high, squeaky voice. "That was Shrubber and Faust. They took turns with the girls until they got them pregnant."

Tom had to hold in his revulsion. "Except for Lindy," he said.

"She was trouble from the first," Butz agreed. "Wouldn't let Faust or Shrubber touch her. Insisted Faust inseminate her with an embryo in this straw thing she brought to his office. Said they'd be glad because it was going to be a cute baby. That damn kid's been nothing but trouble."

"Why didn't Shrubber just give the Kendralls another baby?" Anne asked.

"They only wanted Lindy's kid. They'd already paid Shrubber half a mil for it."

"Half a million dollars?" Anne repeated.

"That's what Shrubber gets for the kids. I should've known Lindy wasn't going to give up hers, insisting on picking out the father and all. But she played it so cool. And I figured I'd be there to watch her."

"But she still got away," Tom said.

"It took me three months to find her."

"And when you did, you ran her off the road and killed her," Tom said.

"No, I didn't run her off the road."

"You were seen, Butz," Anne said.

"Okay, maybe I chased her a bit. But when she rounded that curve, she had to be going sixty. She just lost control and went sailing into that ravine. It was an accident. I swear."

The doorbell rang at the same time a pounding sounded on the door.

"That'll be the police," Tom said as he got off Butz.

Tom expected Anne to hurry to the door. But she didn't. She stood stock-still, staring at how clumsily he got to his feet. Then her eyes went wide.

"Tom, you've been shot!"

Tom took Butz's gun out of his pocket and calmly handed it to her.

"Keep it aimed at him," he said as he glanced at the bright red blood seeping from his throbbing side.

Then the white, dizzying waves that had grown so thick over the last minute finally claimed him and he collapsed over Butz into a deep, silent blackness.

CHAPTER FOURTEEN

"TOM, IT'S GOOD to see you awake," the bishop said as he stood next to the hospital bed.

Tom blinked up at him, trying to bring his face into focus. "You here to administer last rites, Harry?"

"Nope, did that yesterday when they brought you in," the bishop said cheerfully.

"I seem to have lost a lot of yesterday," Tom admitted as he pushed himself into a sitting position, fighting the pain radiating from the tight bandage around his middle, and the fuzziness of his thoughts.

"Not surprising," the bishop said as he made himself comfortable on the chair beside Tom's bed. "You were under anesthesia for most of it. That bullet you took came close to boring a hole through a bunch of vital organs. It was a miracle it didn't."

Butz. The bullet. Anne.

"Where's Anne?" Tom asked as the memories flooded back.

"The D.A. dragged her away a couple of hours ago," the bishop said. "And I do mean dragged her away. She's been here night and day making sure the hospital staff has been taking proper care of you. They're all intimidated by her. She's really something to watch in action."

Tom smiled. "Yes, she is."

"As I was saying," the bishop continued, "you lost a lot of blood, but the doctors tell me you're going to be fine. Just need some time to rest and mend."

"Where did the D.A. take Anne?"

"They needed her at the arraignment for Butz, Shrubber and

Faust. Which reminds me. Why didn't you tell me what you two were into last Wednesday?''

''We weren't even quite sure what it was at the time,'' Tom admitted.

''Anne explained about the real circumstances surrounding the birth of the baby,'' the bishop said. ''Forgive me for having misjudged you.''

''You were only doing what you had to do with the facts you had. Where is Tommy?''

''After Dr. Bennett's genetic confirmation came in yesterday, Anne asked me to speak with Jeff and Theresa Ballard. I dropped by their place last night.''

''Must have shocked them,'' Tom said.

Harry nodded. ''Thoroughly. But when it wore off they were quite pleased. It seems they were thinking of using their last embryo to round out their family. It was what they were going to discuss with Dr. Bennett at the appointment they gave up for you yesterday. They came and got Tommy here at the hospital early this morning.''

''How did Anne take it?'' Tom asked.

''Very bravely, considering how much she loves the child.'' The bishop looked at Tom's face and shook his head. ''No, she didn't have to tell me she loves the little boy, any more than you have to tell me you love him. It was written all over both your faces the first time I saw you with him. Which is why it was so easy to believe that you and Anne were Tommy's parents.''

Tom stared at the white wall of the hospital room, but in his mind's eye he was seeing Anne's face as she stood on the street, the tears spilling down her cheeks.

''Tom, I do need you to tell me something before the nurse comes in to kick me out so you can rest.''

''Whatever I can.''

''Did you marry Anne in order to remain a priest?''

''No, Harry,'' Tom said quietly. ''I married Anne because I love her with all my heart.''

''I thought as much, but I had to ask,'' the bishop said. ''Ever since Anne told me the truth and I realized you two had only known each other five days, I've felt very guilty for having pushed you into getting married so quickly.''

''Anne didn't lie to you when she told you that day that I had already asked her to marry me,'' Tom said.

''But she only accepted when I asked you to resign, is that it?''

Tom nodded.

''Now I understand why she was so glassy-eyed through the entire wedding ceremony,'' Harry said with a troubled look. ''And why she delayed so long in responding to my questions. Tom, I believe she was in shock. I doubt she was even aware of what she said.''

Tom didn't like thinking that the bishop might be right.

''She's a wonderful woman, Tom. And she made an enormous sacrifice for you that day. She obviously cares for you.''

''She loves me, Harry.''

''She certainly acts that way,'' Harry said as he got to his feet. ''I know these things can happen quickly sometimes. Still, you've known each other for such a short while.''

Tom heard everything the bishop was saying. And what he was implying.

''You're a good priest, Tom. And a good man. I know you won't try to hold Anne to vows she wasn't really conscious she was making.''

Harry left then so that Tom could rest. But Tom didn't rest. He lay in the hospital bed for a long time thinking about the bishop's words and wrestling with the new pain they brought.

''YOU'RE LOOKING BETTER,'' Anne said as she entered Tom's hospital room that afternoon, carrying an enormous basket of fresh fruit and a casserole dish.

''Better than what?'' Tom asked as he grinned, so happy to see her that he forgot all about the pain in his side.

''Better than being covered in blood,'' she said matter-of-factly as she leaned over the hospital bed and planted a light kiss on the day-old whiskers on his cheek.

She smelled of fresh air and flowers, and her soft lips were a touch of heaven.

After setting the fruit and casserole on the side table, Anne sat on the edge of the bed near his uninjured side. "I know you're probably tired of people asking, but how are you feeling?" Her eyes were soft and searching.

"Fine, now that you're here."

Anne seemed self-conscious and looked away, gesturing to the casserole dish. "The casserole is from Burt and Lori Tubbs, the basket of fruit from Cooper's Corner's vestry."

"How did they get here?" Tom asked.

"Fred brought them with her a little while ago when she arrived to take Butz into custody and transport him back to the Berkshires for arraignment there."

"Lindy?" Tom asked.

Anne nodded. "Scott Hunter found green paint on the side of Lindy's car. He also located the garage where Butz took his car to be repaired after Lindy's crash. That's where it was that day he and Shrubber arrived at the Church of the Good Shepherd to try to take Tommy away from you."

"He rammed her VW with his van," Tom said.

"Of course, Butz is still claiming it was an accident and he only meant to scare her. But Hunter has a good case against him and I feel confident he'll make it stick. Which still doesn't make me feel any better about the deal the Suffolk County D.A. cut with Butz."

"What kind of deal was that?" Tom asked.

"Butz has agreed to testify against Shrubber and Faust and hand over the names of all their wealthy clients in exchange for the D.A. reducing the charges against him for shooting you."

"I don't mind, Anne."

"I mind," she said, fire flashing in her eyes. "I want to see him hang. He almost killed you, Tom!"

There was a fierceness in her voice that Tom adored. "Not to worry, I'm fine. Be out of here in no time."

She shook her head and sighed. "And you're not even mad at him. You are a damn saint."

Tom gently imprisoned her hands within his. ''If he had hurt you,'' he said in a deadly soft voice, ''I'm afraid you would have seen just how far from a saint I really am.''

She looked at him with such a complex mixture of admiration, understanding and tenderness that his soul ached.

''Hunter released Lindy's body for burial,'' Anne said after a moment. ''Her mother refused to claim her. I told him I would.''

''Thank you, Anne,'' Tom said. ''We'll have services for her as soon as we get back to Cooper's Corner.''

She looked down at their entwined hands and a small frown creased her eyebrows. He wanted to gather her into his arms and kiss away that frown. But he didn't. And it wasn't because of his injury. It was because he couldn't forget Harry's words.

I doubt she was even aware of what she said.

''The bishop tells me you had a long talk,'' Tom said in the calmest voice he could manage. ''He says he knows now why you were so glassy-eyed during our marriage ceremony. He also believes that you didn't hear anything that was said that day.''

''I was married before. I know how the ceremony goes.''

''But you don't remember ours, do you?''

She raised her eyes to his. ''It doesn't matter, Tom.''

''It matters to me. I made vows to you that day, Anne. Solemn vows. You need to hear them.''

''There's no reason. I don't intend to hold you to them.''

''Anne, when I make vows, I hold to them. It doesn't matter what others intend.''

She frowned down at the rings on her finger. ''Don't, Tom.''

She didn't want to hear what he had to say. Was it because the baby was still between them?

He stroked the soft palm of her hand. ''A prayer in our ceremony asked that the husband and wife have the grace to recognize and acknowledge their fault when they hurt each other, and to seek forgiveness. Forgive me for Tommy.''

''There's nothing to forgive,'' she said, still looking down at the rings. ''You kept quiet about the specifics of his conception because you had no choice. You can't be less than who you are—for any reason, for anyone.''

Her words, delivered with such simple eloquence and honesty, filled him with profound relief.

"I know you love Tommy, too," she continued as she lifted her head and looked at him. "It has to be just as hard for you to give him up."

There was understanding in her eyes, and the steely strength that was such a big part of her. And a heart-wrenching sadness.

"Giving him up was the right thing to do," she added. "The only thing to do. And Jeff and Theresa will be wonderful parents to him. It's just—" She stopped suddenly and her eyes shimmered with imprisoned tears. "Tom, he cried when Theresa took him this morning."

Tom squeezed her hands gently as her sorrow touched his soul. "We'll get through this, Anne. Together, we can get through anything."

"No, Tom, not together," she said. She pulled her hands away and took off the rings he had given her. She held them out to him. "You weren't meant for a life without children."

Her words were so earnest, so heartfelt they made his heart sigh. He no longer cared whether she'd been conscious of the vows she'd made to him. It didn't matter. She understood them. She was showing them to him.

He took her hands in his and held on. "Anne, you don't want to leave me."

She tried to pull away. "It's the right thing to do."

"You think the right thing to do is to break my heart?" he asked, pulling her back.

"You have to find your soul mate," she said, with such determined courage.

"You are my soul mate, Anne. You only see the love in what I do. And I only see the love in what you're trying to do for me now. But I can't let you go. Not ever. I can live without children. I can't live without you."

He replaced the rings on her finger. "I love you, Anne."

She let out a sigh of surrender as he carefully enfolded her into his arms. Gently, he kissed her forehead, her cheeks and then her mouth, so warm and loving and giving.

It was a long moment later when she drew back to look into his eyes. ''When you collapsed yesterday and I saw all that blood…oh, Tom, I've never been so scared in my life. It was only then that I realized how empty my life would be without you.''

He eased her back to him, holding her close. ''You're not going to be without me. I'm going to be around a long, long time. We're going to grow old together. Very, very old.''

A knock came at the door and the bishop peered into the room. When he saw Tom and Anne in each other's arms, he looked embarrassed for having intruded. ''Excuse me, but you have some visitors, Tom. Mind if I bring them in?''

Tom was tempted to tell the bishop he did mind, but he could see from the look on Harry's face that he considered these visitors important.

''Okay,'' Tom said.

''I'll give you some privacy,'' Anne said, getting up to leave.

Tom caught her hand. ''Stay. I don't care who it is. I've been without you too long. I don't intend to be without you another second.''

She moved back to his side with a smile and interlaced her fingers with his.

They heard it then. The unmistakable sound of Tommy's inconsolable crying.

The door to the hospital room swung open and Theresa and Jeff Ballard came in, Tommy howling his little head off in Theresa's arms.

Anne didn't pause a second but went directly to the unhappy child. ''May I?'' she asked.

Theresa nodded as she relinquished the baby to Anne's open arms. Anne held Tommy close to her chest, rocking him as she crooned to him softly. He clutched her as if she were his lifeline, and rested his head against her with a shaky little sigh, his cries ceasing.

Theresa and Jeff looked at Anne and then each other before turning to Tom.

The couple approached his bed. "You don't look half-bad for someone who was shot," Jeff said good-naturedly.

His wife smiled at Tom. "You made the *Boston Herald.*"

Jeff handed Tom the newspaper he'd been carrying. Tom glanced at the headline: Doctor and Lawyer Arrested in Baby Breeding Ring.

"It mentions both you and Anne as being instrumental in getting the goods on those two," Jeff said. "When I asked you to let me know if you could pin something on Faust, I wasn't expecting anything this dramatic."

"Neither was I," Tom admitted as he handed the paper back to Jeff.

"As soon as the legal verdict comes down, I'll be able to get the slime's license revoked," Jeff said. "I just hope it'll be soon."

"You needn't worry about his practicing medicine until then," Anne said, stepping to the other side of Tom's bed. "The prosecutor on the case convinced the judge that both Faust and Shrubber are flight risks. She traced the money trail from Shrubber's clients and was able to show that it had been deposited in an offshore account. They're both being held without bail until their trial. As is Nurse Ronley."

"That's a relief, Anne," Jeff said. He turned back to Tom. "Theresa and I didn't come down just to show you the newspaper. We came to give you a get-well gift."

"Thanks, but it's not necessary, Jeff," Tom protested.

"Don't be so hasty," Jeff replied. "I think you're going to want this gift."

He paused to exchange smiles with his wife. "Theresa and I saw how much you and Anne love Tommy the other night at dinner. And how happy he was when either of you held him. Tommy has been heartbroken since the moment Anne gave him up to us this morning. He knows who his mother is, Tom. And she's holding him right now. He also knows who his father is. And that's you."

"You gave us three wonderful children, Tom," Theresa said.

"We want to give Tommy to you and Anne. We know in our hearts that he belongs with you two. You're his real parents."

Tom looked over at the beautiful little boy in Anne's arms. Then he looked up at the shining joy on Anne's face.

He turned back to his friends.

"You're right, Jeff," Tom said. "This is a gift I do want."

TOM RETURNED to the rectory after his Friday class with Cooper's Corner's adolescent boys. He couldn't believe it had been just four weeks ago tonight that he'd answered the parish buzzer to find Tommy on the doorstep.

Tommy, his son. How wonderful it was to be able to think of him that way! To know he was his and Anne's forever.

When he walked into the study, he found them on the couch, softly lit by lamplight. Anne was breast-feeding Tommy and singing quietly to him. It was a scene filled with such profound beauty that it made Tom's heart ache.

When Anne looked up and saw him, her smile was a sudden glow.

Tom was filled with that same sense of wonder he'd had the first moment he saw her. And he knew that he would always feel that way looking at his wife—his soul mate.

"How was class?" she asked.

"Challenging as always," Tom said as he came over to the couch and leaned down to brush a kiss against her lips. "But these boys are going to be very good men."

"They certainly will be if you have a hand in molding them," Anne said, and the simple pride in her voice did wonderfully complex things to his heart.

"When did you get home?" Tom asked as he snuggled next to her side. She smelled enticingly of baby oil. He'd never realized how sexy a smell it could be.

"Half an hour ago. I had an extra errand to run."

Tom wrapped his arm around Anne, luxuriating in the feel of her warmth and the simple magic of the moment.

"Hungry?" she asked.

''No, I'm perfect. You're perfect. Tommy's perfect. Life is perfect. I have absolutely no desire for anything else.''

''Not even a little brother or sister for Tommy?'' Anne asked after a moment.

Was that still troubling her? Tom kissed the copper silk of her hair. ''You and Tommy are all I want, Anne. All I'll ever need.''

She sighed. ''Oh, Tom, I'm so sorry to hear that.''

Tom blinked, certain he couldn't have heard right. He turned her in his arms to look at her face. ''Anne, is something wrong?''

''I've been regular since I was twelve, so when I missed my period a couple of weeks ago, I began to wonder. Still, I didn't want to tell you until I was sure.''

''You're pregnant?'' Tom asked in a strangled whisper.

Anne smiled, obviously delighted with his shock. ''I stopped by the doctor's today. That's why I was late getting back. We're going to have a baby, Tom.''

As Tom gazed spellbound at the glowing smile on Anne's face, he was filled with a joy so potent that he suddenly knew why the angels sang.

He held her to him gently, possessively, kissing the sudden, happy tears on her cheeks, knowing they were mixing with his own.

''It happened that first night we were together, Tom. I know it. After all those years with Bill, all it took was one night with you. This baby wanted you to be his father. No one else would do.''

The sweet bliss on her face blazed through his soul. ''Anne, I love you so much.''

''And I love you, Tom. With you life is full of such lovely miracles. You've even got me believing in happily ever after.''

''To have and to hold from this day forward,'' Tom softly quoted. ''For better for worse, for richer for poorer, in sickness and in health, to love and to cherish, until we are parted by death. And not a moment sooner, Anne. This is my solemn vow.''

EPILOGUE

MAUREEN COOPER turned her SUV onto Highway 7 as she headed out on her weekly shopping trip into Williamstown for supplies. She was getting a late start. They were full up at Twin Oaks and it had been a busy day.

She was still smiling from her recent telephone conversation with Anne. It was such great news to learn she and Tom were going to have a baby!

Maureen would never forget the moment she'd found out she was pregnant with the twins. There just wasn't anything that could compare to that kind of excitement and joy.

How eager she had been to share it with Chance.

She took a deep breath and let it out slowly, trying not to think of her daughters' daddy. Chance Maguire had been out of her life for a long time now. And she knew it was best that way.

Chance's life revolved around the plush, concrete palaces of world commerce—multimillion-dollar mergers and major deals, an elite society of movers and shakers and business breakers.

She, on the other hand, had come to love her life in rugged, rural Cooper's Corner—the deep woods and bouncy brooks, meadows frantic with wildflowers, the charm of the quaint shops and the plain and simple decency of its people.

Yes, she and Chance lived in very different worlds, and she wouldn't trade hers for his. Not for anything.

Maureen peered through her windshield as the wipers worked to beat away the heavy rain. She saw the turnoff to the maple syrup farm up ahead. She normally bought her syrup on the way home from Williamstown, but because of her late start today, it would be well into the night before she came back this way.

She didn't like dropping in on the family so late. Not that they would ever complain. But she was not the kind of person to take advantage of friends.

Making her decision quickly, she signaled, slowed down and took the exit. She would buy the syrup now and do the rest of her shopping afterward. A few turns later and she was climbing the narrow country road that would take her to the small farm, tucked away in the hills.

The hard rain pounded the windshield and turned the unpaved road into mud. Maureen drove slowly around the twisting turns. She was glad she had decided to do this now. It would have been much more difficult navigating this winding road at night instead of in the evening twilight.

A favorite song played on her car stereo and Maureen's fingers tapped to its beat as she sang along.

She was so focused on the road and the music that at first she didn't notice the big delivery truck coming up fast behind her. By the time she did, it was already filling her rearview mirror.

Irritation flickered through her. The driver was going way too fast on this winding road, made all the more treacherous because of the heavy rain.

Normally Maureen avoided such fools by pulling over and letting them pass. But there was no room on this narrow, one-lane road—just the thick curtain of trees to her right and the sheer drop to her left.

She tapped her brakes to alert the driver behind her as she started to slow for the next turn. But when she checked her rearview mirror, she discovered the vehicle hadn't slowed.

The truck hit her hard. Maureen was thrown against her shoulder belt as she headed into the turn. The trees, the road, the mud, the truck, the beat of the song, the beat of her windshield wipers all seemed to blur together.

With a firm grip on the wheel, she took the turn tight, fighting the speed as she struggled to keep the car on the slippery road. She skidded along the edge, mud spitting out under her tires as she rounded the curve.

She made it. But the relief that washed through her was soon replaced with anger. She was going to strangle that truck driver! She glanced in her rearview mirror to see him coming out of the turn. But instead of slowing and pulling over as she expected, the truck started to accelerate. Right at her.

Icy reality stabbed her thoughts. Nevil! The truck driver was Owen Nevil!

Maureen stomped on the gas, frantic now to keep ahead of the truck boring down on her.

The next turn was coming up fast. If she didn't slow down, she'd never make it. But if she did slow down, that bastard was going to hit her again and force her vehicle into the thick trees to her right or off the two-hundred-foot drop to her left.

Either way, she wouldn't survive.

And then Maureen saw it. Coming up on her right. A recently logged clear-cut. It was her chance. Her only chance.

Nevil must have seen it, too. The truck behind her made a sudden roar as it accelerated. He was going to try to hit her before she could make the clearing. Push her past it. Push her into the next turn. Push her over the edge.

Maureen held tightly to the steering wheel, bracing herself as the truck loomed large in her rearview mirror. It was going to be close. Very, very close.

She yanked the wheel, turning into the clear-cut at the same instant that the truck struck her left rear fender. The force flipped her SUV, spinning it into the air.

The earth and sky traded places, and Maureen was caught in an eerie sense of slow motion as the car flew above the ground. Then the front smacked into a thick tree stump with a noisy whack, jolting the bones in her body and spinning the SUV like a top.

The next thing she knew, the air bag deployed around her like a gigantic mushroom and the car landed with a thud on the soft mud.

The concussion knocked the breath out of her. She fought to fill her lungs, her pulses pounding, her shoulders and neck aching. She was suspended in the seat and shoulder belts and realized the vehicle had landed upside down.

Cautiously Maureen moved her arms and legs. Nothing was broken. She exhaled in relief. She'd made it.

She tossed aside the now deflated air bag and reached over to turn off the ignition. Then she released herself from the seat belt and shoulder restraint and fell to the roof of the truck. Flipping onto her back, she peered out at the fading light glinting through the fractured glass of the windows.

And discovered to her shock that the SUV's cab was sinking fast into the mud!

Maureen pushed hard on the driver's door, desperately trying to open it and get out. But the door was bent and jammed shut. And every second she strained her shoulder against it, the SUV sank farther into the mud.

Panic threatened to engulf her as she forced herself to take a deep breath. The only other way out was through the windshield. And she didn't have much time. She turned and kicked with both feet, as hard as she could. The shattered glass broke away in a spidery heap.

Maureen grabbed her shoulder bag with one hand and the bent metal of the cab's roof with the other. She pulled herself through the narrow opening onto the gooey earth, then rolled quickly away, gaining freedom just before the cab section sunk below the mud line, trapping her there forever.

Her heart was hammering her ribs and her body was bruised and aching. But there was no time to rest. Maureen dug into her shoulder bag, grabbed her loaded .38, rolled onto her stomach and aimed her weapon back at the road.

Nevil gunned the delivery truck's engine. Maureen aimed and fired. But she was too far away and the truck moved too fast. The bullet missed. Before she could get off another shot, the truck was down the road, out of sight.

The rain pounded down on Maureen as she lay panting in the mud. She listened to the fading sounds of the truck's engine until it was gone.

She had known Nevil wouldn't stay around to face her. The sneaky bastard's specialty was murders made to look like accidents. And he had just failed in his latest attempt on her.

Once again, she had survived. But Maureen didn't feel much like celebrating. She knew Nevil would be back.

And she also knew that the next time she might not be so lucky.

Welcome to Twin Oaks—the new B and B in Cooper's Corner, Massachusetts.
Bed and breakfast will never be the same!
COOPER'S CORNER

continues with

JUST ONE LOOK
by Joanna Wayne

Cooper's Corner postmistress Alison Fairchild had the most fabulous little upturned nose ever—thanks to recent plastic surgery. After a lifetime of teasing and insecurity, she looked stunning as she made her entrance at the rehearsal for her friend's wedding. All eyes were on her—except for the gorgeous stranger in the dark glasses.

Here's a preview!

CHAPTER ONE

ALISON ROLLED THE FLAT of her right palm along the edge of the steering wheel while holding it steady with the left. "Have you ever heard the saying that today is the first day of the rest of your life?"

"Sure. It's pretty corny, but I guess it could work for some people."

"No. In my case, it's true. I'm starting over, going for the gusto, so to speak."

"What was wrong with your life before today?" Ethan asked.

"I was—I don't know why I'm telling you this. It's nothing you'd be interested in."

"But I am interested. Besides, sometimes it's easier to talk to a stranger, especially one you won't be seeing after this weekend."

"That's true. And you're..."

"You can finish the sentence, Alison. You don't have to be afraid to acknowledge the fact that I'm visually impaired, or visually challenged, if you go with the popular theory that no one's really impaired and everyone faces challenges."

"I was just thinking how people always say that when one sense is lacking, the others make up for it. If that's true, you've probably already sensed that I'm trying out a new personality tonight."

"Oh, I get it. You're one of those women with multiple personalities that I read about in psych class."

"I certainly am not."

"Then I guess you'd better explain."

She slowed to a stop in front of the B and B. "The old me was—boring. All work and no play."

"All rules and no risks?"

"That's probably even more accurate. Now I want to experience life. That means I have to change a lot of things about me. I know you can't see it, but the dress I'm wearing is totally out of character for me."

She killed the engine and planned to do the same with this conversation.

Ethan leaned closer. "I know this may sound strange to you, but do you mind if I touch your face?"

Her grip tightened on the wheel, but she turned toward him. "Why would you do that?"

"Touch is how I see my world."

"Of course." She released the wheel and reached across the space that separated them. Her hand trembled as she took his right hand and placed it on her left cheek.

He roamed the flesh with his fingertips, skimming her eyes, her cheeks, everywhere except her nose, before stopping at her lips. She was trembling, aroused. If she didn't stop him, he was going to kiss her. Or she was going to kiss him. She brushed his hand away. "I need to go now, Ethan. I really need to get home."

"Then I'll see you tomorrow at the wedding."

"Right. The wedding."

"Thanks for the ride," he said as he picked up his cane.

She watched him walk to the door, his cane pecking along the edge of the walk, while her senses whirled like crazy. The touch of his fingers against her face had been incredible, like a kiss, only much more sensual.

Of all the things she'd expected tonight, reeling from a blind man's touch had not been on the list. The one man who couldn't possibly have been impressed by her new nose, her sexy dress or her flawlessly applied makeup, and he was the one she was sitting here drooling over like a schoolgirl.

A love 'em and leave 'em kind of guy.

Wendy's words of caution flashed into her mind, and Alison

had no trouble believing them. The guy might be visually impaired, but he was a smooth operator. He'd managed to catch her off guard and had kept her reacting to him all night. Here today, gone tomorrow—well, day after tomorrow. If she wasn't careful, she'd blow the weekend she'd been waiting for all her life on a man who used his impairment like an aphrodisiac.

Tonight, she'd played into his hands, literally and figuratively, but tomorrow night would be a different story entirely. She'd be pleasant, but aloof. She wouldn't give him a chance to use that touching routine on her again.

Still, a warm, gooey sensation that felt a lot like melted marshmallows on chocolate bubbled in her stomach as she drove home.